KEEP
DANCING

Reviews for Leslie Wells' previous novel,

Come Dancing— an Amazon Romantic Comedy Bestseller:

"Once you start, you are completely unable to put it down."
—Devilishly Delicious Book Reviews

"It read like a very, very good romantic comedy movie."
—Michelle & Leslie's Book Picks

"You know what? Sometimes a book like this comes along and takes me out of the niche reading that I tend to find myself in . . . So very sex+the city."
—Must Read Books or Die

"Displayed against the glittery excess of the 80's, Wells pens a sexy, sweet, and somewhat complicated romance . . . Wells builds an emotionally poignant love story, abounding with romance and humor."
—Smexy Book Reviews

"Like a well-oiled machine or a well-tuned guitar, Julia and friends work their way into your heart. . . Just try to resist Jack and his imperfect life!"
—Satisfaction for Insatiable Readers

KEEP DANCING

A NOVEL

Leslie Wells

For Peter, with all my love

CONTENTS

Chapter 1

HIGH FIDELITY

)=⊂={

"What page are you up to?" asked an accented male voice. I could hardly hear over the record's thumping bass in the background.

"I'm almost ready to leave. I just have to type up one more report." Pressing the phone to my ear, I gazed at the manuscripts cluttering my desk.

"You'd better hurry up. Little Jack's growing cobwebs."

"I doubt that." I smiled at the image.

His voice deepened. "Baby, when you get home, I'm gonna boil your cabbage."

"Are you trying to turn me on with your dirty blues talk?"

"I sure am. Hurry it up."

On the way out, I stopped by Meredith's office. "Have a great break!" I said. She took off her half-rims and rose from her desk.

"Are you and your rocker boyfriend going somewhere fabulous for Christmas?" she asked. The managing editor was one of only two friends who knew I was with Jack.

"I think we're staying put. They're getting ready for their big tour, so he's been rehearsing nonstop." I dug my gloves out of my pocket and put them on.

Meredith smiled. "Well, be sure to spend some quality time together." She came over and gave me a hug. "I hope you aren't taking a lot of work home. It'll all be sitting here when you get back. And unfortunately, your Neanderthal of a boss will still be lurking in his cave." Harvey, the publisher, was known for putting the moves on young female employees, but for the past few months he'd been letting me alone.

"I'm only bringing one manuscript with me. Have a great holiday!" I said.

"You too," she called out as I continued down the hall.

Half an hour later, I picked my way across the slushy sidewalks, past Canal Jeans, Zoot, and other vintage shops, and continued down lower Broadway. The smell of burnt chestnuts from the street vendor hung heavily in the bitterly cold late December air. I shifted the shoulder strap on my backpack and tried to beat the traffic light.

It had been so hard to concentrate at work today. I'd blown it in the production meeting, daydreaming about my upcoming time off with Jack when I should have been listening to my boss. As Harvey droned on about the print run for a new self-help book—*Cherishing Your Inner Child*—I'd had a vision of Jack, his choppy dark hair falling into his eyes, silky lashes brushing his cheeks, lowering his body slowly, teasingly . . . Every free moment when I wasn't answering the phone or typing letters, I was fantasizing about what new thing he would do to me tonight.

In a fever of anticipation, I hurried around the corner and slogged over to the entrance of his building. Before I could even reach for the handle, the doorman opened it for me.

"How's it going?" I asked Tom as he walked me to the elevator.

"I can't believe we'll be ringing in 1982 in a week." Tom pressed the button. "We're supposed to get a lot more snow this weekend. I hope that won't put a crimp in your plans."

I pictured us snuggled together under the covers, lost in our own world, not bothering to leave the loft because we could devise our own entertainment. "Oh no, I don't mind at all," I said airily as I stepped inside.

Whooshing up to the penthouse, I reflected on my surroundings. After living with Jack for over a month, I was getting used to the cushy digs. I still paid the rent on my narrow Broome Street loft in SoHo, and I stopped by every week to make sure a pipe hadn't burst, or that it hadn't been broken into. But I could feel myself getting soft. I'd quickly become used to a doorman building where I didn't have to worry about getting mugged coming in at night. An elevator instead of the three flights to my walk-up. Noiseless heating vents instead of radiators that were either cold to the touch or clanked loudly at five a.m., like someone was taking a hammer to the pipes. Ordering takeout from any restaurant that struck our fancy. Not to mention, getting to hear chords being woven into songs that would eventually climb the Top 40 charts. I still felt like pinching myself every time he picked up his Gibson. Jack seemed to have endless variations in his repertoire—and not just in the musical sense.

Every night, he made mind-blowing love to me. On top of that—so to speak—I was still in a state of disbelief that I was living in sin with the sexiest British guitarist on the planet.

The elevator slid open and I pushed through the front door. Jack didn't lock his apartment, which made me uneasy at times. Ever since I'd moved in with him, I'd tried to convince him to use keys, but he said he'd only leave them all over the city. At least he had doormen to buzz him whenever a visitor showed up.

The front table was covered with piles of Jack's mail, neatly sorted by his manager, Mary Jo. I'd go through the stacks of invitations later; Jack usually tossed them out, but they fascinated me. Sometimes there was a museum's first night, gallery opening, film premiere, or party that I'd want to go to. So far he'd humored me, although it wasn't really his thing. I guessed for someone like him, who'd seen and done it all, those events were pretty boring. But not for me; I was still fairly new to Manhattan, and a novice at such glam affairs.

I removed my knitted hat in front of the large wall mirror. Someone—it didn't seem like the kind of thing Jack would do—had inserted tickets from Four to the Floor's past concerts all the way around the edges of the frame. Every time I saw the reminders of Jack's wild life, I wondered who he'd been with at all those shows in all those cities.

Resisting the impulse to rip them off the mirror, I tried to tame my staticky hair. My loosely layered style was in imitation of my female rock idol, Chrissie Hynde of the Pretenders. Before I met Jack, I couldn't afford a salon, so I'd propped the album cover on the bathroom sink and cut my hair with kitchen scissors. Now my chestnut layers had grown to the middle of my back, and needed a trim. Frowning, I met my gaze in the mirror. People tended to comment on the blue of my eyes, but I still saw myself in the glasses that had been the bane of my teenage existence. Only when I left for college did I scrape together my after-school job money and buy contacts. Much of the time, I still felt like that four-eyed girl hiding behind her thick lenses.

As I pulled off my snow-sluiced boots, I heard the shower running. Jack's guitars were propped up on the couch and on various chairs; he must have been working on a new song. Even though The Floor had just released a new album and were going on tour in February, Jack never seemed to stop creating new material. If I hurried, I'd have time to get him back for what he did to me last night.

I went through the loft to the kitchen and ran the water until it was icy cold. Filling a large cup, I walked past the fireplace and a second sitting area filled with guitar stands, amps, keyboard, and drum set. *The shower's still running; better hurry.* I entered his spacious bedroom and stepped over some clothes that he'd dropped: jeans and one of his "Just Say No" tee-shirts. His fans definitely had a sense of humor; they'd been sending them by the truckload ever since the campaign began a few months ago.

Stealthily I turned the knob to the bathroom and listened. *Shower still going full-on—good.* I cracked the door and peeked in. His back was to me, wet hair streaming down to just below his shoulders. God, Jack was sexy with his long thick mane, muscled shoulders tapering to his lean waist;

the lovely curve of his rear. He was humming something, looking down as he soaped his chest. *Now!* I darted to the shower door, reached up over the top, and dumped the ice-cold water down his back.

"Aaagh!" Jack whipped around, wet hair flying, his lightning bolt necklace askew. He glared at me for a moment through the steamy shower glass. I was practically doubled over, laughing at his pained expression.

"Bloody hell!" he exclaimed, hands on his hips. I backed away as he quickly slid the door open. "I'm gonna get you for that!"

"No, you're not!" Spinning around, I ran through the bedroom, almost tripping over his jeans. I raced toward the front of the loft, figuring he wouldn't follow me since he was dripping wet. But his feet pounded behind me, slapping on the wooden parquet floor. Just as I reached the couch, an arm snaked around my waist. I pushed at his wrist, trying to peel him off, but his other hand clutched me through my blouse. His damp body pressed into my back, his mouth at my ear.

"You're quick. But I'm quicker," he murmured.

I reached around behind me and grabbed him in the one place I knew would have an effect.

"Now you've got my attention." He made the mistake of relaxing his grip on my waist. I let go of him and scooted around the corner of the couch.

"So you're playing dirty," he said. He brushed a damp lock of hair out of his eyes.

"And you were playing fair last night?" I taunted him. "Hiding my manuscript while I was changing clothes. Then you wouldn't give it back until I gave you not one, but two—"

"As I recall, you seemed to enjoy yourself. *Oh, Jack . . . do that again . . .*" he mimicked in his falsetto Julia voice.

"Only because I was under duress."

We faced each other across the couch; me in my rumpled work clothes, Jack breathing hard, naked and dripping wet. Fine dark hair sprinkled his chest and came together in a suggestive line below his navel, now mostly obscured. His smile gleamed dangerously.

"Think you can get away from me?" Jack cocked an eyebrow. He made a feint, but I went in the other direction—only to get snagged on a guitar strap. I tripped and scrabbled forward on my hands and knees. *God, which way did he go?*

An iron grip fastened on my ankle. "Let me loose!" I yelped as he dragged me backwards. I tried to hold onto the couch leg, but he jerked me away. "You're giving me rug burn!" I cried, flipping around to my back and looking up at him. Jack pulled me toward him again, making my skirt ride up under me.

"Now you'll pay for interrupting my nice warm shower," he said in a menacing tone. Still holding my ankle with one hand, he reached down and yanked my underwear to my knees.

"You barbarian!" I tried to kick free, but his grip was too strong.

"That's right, I'm a Saxon. And now I'm gonna ransack *you*." He knelt and put his mouth on my neck, which he knew rendered me helpless. I ran my hands over the curve of his lower back and felt his muscles tighten.

"Mmm . . . don't try any more tricks." Deftly he unbuttoned my blouse one-handed and undid my bra clasp. His lips on me were heaven; involuntarily I arched my back.

"So why did you dump cold water on me?" he asked as he kissed his way to my waist. "Shriveled me balls down to raisins."

I laughed. "I told you. I was getting back at you for last night."

"Last time I go down on you then." His tongue slithered up my inner thigh. "Well, maybe once more before I cut you off completely." He tried to push my skirt up further but it stopped, wedged under me.

"I told you I had to finish reading that manuscript. There was an auction this morning."

"Did you get the book?" His tongue moved in lazy circles. *Oh god . . .*

"Another house . . . bid more," I gasped.

"Too bad."

Chapter 2

LONDON CALLING

)⸻⟩⟨⸻(

Three days later, I was buckling myself into a seat in first class. I had been shocked on Christmas Eve when Jack surprised me with tickets to England, hidden inside an innocuous-seeming pair of red mittens. Now that we were actually on our way to visit his mother, who lived an hour outside of London, my jittery fingers could hardly work the seatbelt's clasp. At twenty-four, having never left the States, I was excited about seeing a new country. And despite Jack's reassurances, I was also white-knuckled with anxiety over whether his Mum would like me.

"I'm gonna hit the loo before we take off," Jack said, standing up. He was still wearing his sunglasses, not because the jet's interior was bright, but to avoid being buttonholed by passengers seeking autographs. Ducking his head, he moved quickly down the aisle. I saw several people staring after him and knew he'd been nailed. Even with the shades on, his below-the-shoulder hair, tight jeans encasing his thighs, and indigo velvet jacket with trailing lacy cuffs signaled "rock star failing to be incognito". He also never wore underwear, which I guessed was a rock'n'roll fashion statement—but sometimes I wished he did.

I looked out the window as the plane roared down the runway and lifted into the air, making my stomach flip. I'd hardly had time to think after the flurry of gift-opening and the lovemaking that followed—featuring the assortment of lingerie he'd given me. Now that I had a quiet moment to myself, I pondered what it meant that Jack was taking me to meet his mother. After all, we'd only gotten back together six weeks ago, after our catastrophic breakup earlier in the fall.

Every single day that went by, I was counting my lucky stars that we had made it through so many rough patches. We had first met in June, when he noticed me dancing at the Palladium with my best friend, Vicky. Dancing was my release from sitting in my office for hours on end, typing Harvey's letters and answering his phone. I loved going with girlfriends to the many downtown clubs we frequented—the Roxy, Danceteria, the Mudd Club, Hurrah—and sweating out all my frustrations on the floor.

The night I met Jack, he had noticed me from the VIP room's upstairs window and sent his band mate Sammy down to summon us. Sammy and Vicky had hit it off right from the start, and Jack had tried to pick me up. While dazzled by his attention, I declined to bring him home with me that night—much to his astonishment. As he later admitted, it intrigued him that I didn't come running at the snap of his fingers.

For that whole first month, we'd listened to music at his loft or partied with his famous pals, but nothing happened physically. I had been badly burned in a previous relationship, and wasn't in the mood to be used and then discarded by some arrogant rock star. So Jack and I got to know each other gradually and bonded over our love of the blues. By the time we jumped into his big, messy bed, the electric current between us had reached the voltage of a lightning strike.

In spite of our intense attraction, we'd had a rough ride at first. Jack was allergic to being tied down, and I was determined to keep my guard up. But after traveling with him to L.A. in August to see The Floor in concert, it seemed our feelings were mutual. Then a former girlfriend showed her fangs and caused a huge misunderstanding. We had gotten back together in mid-November; a reunion that, oddly enough, my mother had helped to bring about. Afterwards, to my amazement, Jack asked me to move in with him. I packed my duffel bag and vacated my tiny walk-up on Broome Street without a backward glance.

And so far, so good. Jack made it home every night, even if it was in the wee hours of the morning after hitting the bars with his band mates. When we were out in public together, he made it clear that he was with me. Which wasn't all that often, to be honest, because everywhere he went turned into a hassle; people wanting autographs, photographers harassing him. He seemed to brush it off, but I hadn't gotten used to it in the least. If we went to a restaurant, his manager Mary Jo set it up ahead of time so we could get in and out quickly. If we went to a club, we were rushed up to the VIP room where his friends would be waiting. I wasn't complaining—admittedly the star treatment was a thrill—but it was just . . . different. A very different kind of life from what I'd been used to, coming from my small town in Pennsylvania and scraping by in Manhattan on my puny publishing salary.

Hearing Jack's Cockney accent, I glanced up the aisle. Sure enough, he'd been spotted on his way back to our seats. His shades slipped halfway down his nose, he was signing autographs for a thrilled bunch of passengers as the flight attendant tried to get them all to sit down. I smiled to myself and tucked my cozy suede coat around me more snugly.

Jack had given me a bunch of new clothes for Christmas, including a fancy pair of boots and this gorgeous winter coat. Going forward, I wouldn't have to rely on the second-hand thrift-store gear that had been the staple of my wardrobe up until now. For my part, I'd given Jack several books, a supply of guitar strings and picks, and—knowing he'd been fascinated by insects since he was a boy—a praying mantis farm. I'd hoped my less-than-extravagant presents would seem imaginative rather than paltry, so I was pleased when Jack proclaimed the mantises the best Christmas gift he'd ever received.

And out of everything he'd given me, what I valued most of all wasn't the fancy outfits, the silky lingerie, or the delicate sapphire necklace and earrings—in fact, I'd been embarrassed by the lavish shower of presents. The most meaningful and thoughtful gift had been a signed first edition of Virginia Woolf's *To the Lighthouse*, one of my all-time favorites. Jack let it slip that he'd had a bookseller combing the antique shops for weeks in order to locate it. That vintage book, and the tickets to London, were the things I cherished most.

The other huge surprise was that after five days in England, we were flying to a private Caribbean island. As a Christmas gift to my mother, Jack was flying Dot there to meet us. I just hoped his own Mum's reaction to me wouldn't be as frigid as the famously cold British weather.

As Jack finally signed the last slip of paper and made his way back, I noted the gazes of the women, from the curvaceous flight attendants to middle-aged mommies and ponytailed teenagers. Sure, he was a celebrity, but he was also strikingly attractive, his long dark eyelashes lending an almost feminine beauty to his masculine features. Even if he hadn't been the lead guitarist of the world-renowned band, Four to the Floor, I knew their eyes would be glued to his handsome face and lithe body.

When we had gotten back together, I had told Jack that I loved him, and he'd said that he loved me, too. Yet whenever I saw him enveloped in a palpitating wall of adoration, I felt unsure about our chances of lasting for very long.

As Jack slid past me into his window seat, I had time for one last private thought. *Yes, the past month and a half has been fantastic,* I reflected as he settled in beside me. I knew I was living a fantasy that his hordes of female admirers only dreamed of—but that idea was disconcerting rather than pleasing. In the back of my mind, a chorus kept repeating like a song that gets stuck in your head: *What are you going to do when it's over?*

"You're home!" Margaret Kipling threw open the front doors of the palatial manse set back in a tree-lined property. I recognized her from a picture Jack had shown me; she had dark hair with a few streaks of white, and his emphatic eyebrows. Slim and tall, she wore a rather formal print dress and pearls. Jack went up the granite steps and gave her a hug. I hung back near the limo for a moment; now that I was here, I was even more anxious than I'd been on the plane. It didn't help that Jack had once described his mother as a "ball-buster". And I definitely wished I had on something other than the jeans that had seemed right for the long flight.

"Maggie, meet Julia," Jack said, gesturing between us. I approached, not sure whether she was the hugging type. Her outstretched hand gave me the answer. I shook it, noting her firm grip.

"I can't believe it's been eight months since you've been home. Nice that you could come too, Julia," she added in a not-overly-excited voice. Up close, I could see where he'd gotten his deep brown eyes; hers were just as soulful, if they lacked Jack's warmth. She had fine wrinkles at the corners, but none of the smile lines that were etched into the sides of Jack's mouth.

"Thank you for having me." I met her scrutinizing gaze.

"Let's go in. I'm freezing me arse off," Jack said, hustling me inside. The foyer had a huge antique mirror opposite a mounted elk's head with branching antlers. "I see you've taken up hunting." Jack nodded at the elk.

"Dilly's had another go at decorating," Maggie replied. "She says the old is new again."

"The old is looking rather flea-bitten." Jack fingered a branch of the elk, which up close did seem a little shopworn. A young woman in an apron rushed over to take our coats. "And who is this?" he asked, smiling at the terrified girl.

"This is Tracy from the village," Maggie said. "She comes to us Tuesdays and Fridays. Let's go in the parlor; we're just having tea."

"How are you, Tracy From the Village?" Jack asked.

"Just fine, sir," she squeaked before scurrying down the hall.

Jack made an after-you motion and I walked behind his mother, attempting to ignore his hand tickling my butt. I tried to slap it away surreptitiously, but got caught in the act as Maggie turned to us.

"I take it you drink tea? Tracy can make some instant coffee if you'd like," she said to me.

"Oh no, tea would be nice." I didn't want to stand out as the crass java-loving American.

"D'you have that nice squidgy cake you had last time?" Jack asked.

"Of course," Maggie said. "And smoked salmon and cucumber sandwiches, lemon curd, and your favorite cream puffs."

"Good. The food on the plane was total crap."

The house was grand in size; not quite a mansion, but definitely imposing. Before I could take much of it in, we were led into a parlor done up in a dizzying degree of chintz. A miniature Yorkie wearing a red and green sweater was quivering on the sofa next to a sleeping cat. A petite young woman with a stylish blonde shag rose from one of the chairs, a little girl clutching her skirt: Jack's half-sister Sharon and her four-year-old daughter Emma.

"Uncle Jack!" Two brown-and-white missiles shot from a corner of the room. Jack caught the brunt of the six-year-old boy as a bulldog wheezed and snuffled beside him.

"Oliver," Jack said after they hugged. He took his nephew by the shoulders and examined him. "I haven't seen you in yonks. You've grown several inches." Jack had once told me the newspapers thought Ollie was his "love child", and I could see why. He was the spitting image of Jack: dark hair standing up in back of his head, sparkling brown eyes, and mischievously arched eyebrows. The bulldog waggled its rump and mouthed Jack's pants leg. "Hello Randy, howsa boy?" He patted its neck, and a long strand of saliva spooled from its mouth.

"Jack, you're making Randall drool," Maggie said. She lifted the tiny Yorkie onto her lap.

"You're glad to see me, aren't you, boy?" Jack said, rubbing the bulldog's blocky head. "This is Julia," he announced to the others. The dog looked up at me, and another string of drool escaped its lips.

"She has the same effect on me." Jack put his arm around Sharon, who went up on tiptoe to give him a kiss on the cheek. Emma hid behind her mom's skirt, and I understood the impulse. I was a little overwhelmed by the familial chaos;

my own family consisted of only my mother and me.

"Nice new 'do," Jack said as he fluffed Sharon's hair. "But who's this big girl? What have you done with Emma?" he teased.

The child stepped forward. "*I'm* Emma!" she announced.

"Oh no, you're far too big to be Emma," Jack said as Oliver tugged on his sleeve.

"Uncle Jack! Are you going to take me driving this time?"

"Oliver. Let Jack relax a bit before you start whinging. Hello Julia, I'm Sharon. We're so glad you could come." His sister shook my hand and gave me a subtle once-over. I felt rumpled and smeary after the flight; I'd only had time for a quick lip gloss fix in the airport bathroom. Which Jack had mauled off in the limo during the hour's drive to Hounslow.

"Have a seat." Sharon indicated a large armchair next to hers. "Jack, you're such a liar."

Jack was standing over a low table, piling a plate high with little sandwiches, scones with jam and cream, and cakes from a tiered stand. "What do you mean?"

"You said Julia was six-foot and blonde, with lots of piercings."

"That was the other Julia I was seeing." Jack added one more cream puff to the pile and sat in a chair next to his mother. "Why do you insist on these tiny plates?" he complained. Oliver stood by his side, breathlessly narrating his recent soccer match.

"—and then I almost got the ball, but this stonking big duffer kicked me in the shin—"

"You're small, like I was at your age. But you'll grow like a weed when you're about fourteen," Jack said to him. "Where's the old sod?" he asked Sharon. I knew he didn't care for her husband.

"Duncan's off to a barrister's conference in Horncastle." Sharon frowned as she poured for me.

"Good riddance." Jack blew on his tea.

"Now, Jack," Maggie admonished. "How do you like the way Dilly did the parlor? Emma, leave the cat alone," she said to her granddaughter, who was pulling its tail.

"I've never been too fond of chintz," Jack said, cramming half a tart into his mouth. "Mmm, scrummy." He fed the other half to Randall, who waddled over to me, masticating.

"You know tarts give him wind," Maggie said.

"Here, pussy," Emma was saying. Oliver made a grab for the cat, which hid under my chair.

"Do you have a pussy?" Oliver looked up at me.

"She has a very nice one. What?" Jack said innocently when I gave him a look.

"You're gonna take me driving, aren't you Uncle Jack?" Oliver insisted.

"Jack tells me you're just out of university. What did you read?" Maggie asked, stroking the trembling Yorkie in her lap.

I placed my teacup in its saucer and tried to surreptitiously nudge Randall away as he sniffed my leg. "Oh, a little of everything. Virginia Woolf, Faulkner . . ." Randall gave my ankle a tentative lick.

"She means what did you major in." Jack took a slurp of tea. "That's what Julia and I have in common; our deep abiding interest in English literature." He grinned and licked a smear of lemon curd off the corner of his mouth. "And now she's a book editor, always swotting away at the manuscripts. What's this?" He scooped up the Yorkie with one hand and held it high so we could see the lettering on its sweater: *I AM the grandchild!*

"That was an early Christmas gift from me," Sharon said as Jack dumped the dog back onto Maggie's lap.

"Does your company publish Barbara Cartland? She's very popular over here," Maggie asked.

"No, we don't have that many big fiction authors. My boss would like to acquire some more." I was distracted by the bulldog's lavish ankle-licking. Suddenly it reared up, front paws grasping my knee.

"Randy, get down! You see where he gets his name," Jack said as the bulldog began enthusiastically humping my leg. "Just shove him away. Now, who's ready for presents?"

"Me! Me!" Oliver screamed. Sharon grabbed Randy's collar and dragged him off my leg, making him choke up the tart in the process.

"No, me!" Emma cried, jumping up.

"I may have one or two things for you both," Jack said, getting up from his seat. "Let me just crack a window first."

"I told you those tarts gave him wind," Maggie said.

An hour later, wrapping paper was strewn from one end of the room to the other. Oliver and Jack were on the floor putting together a complicated racecar track, and Emma had opened her 48-piece china tea set to feed her six new dolls. Sharon had begun by weakly protesting all the gifts, but in the end she gave up as Jack brought out one box after another from the limo's "boot," as he called it. Maggie modeled the elegant floor-length coat he'd had shipped to her, and Sharon thanked Jack for its double, which she'd left back home in Surrey.

The women unwrapped sweaters and scarves from Jack and exclaimed politely over my gifts of candles and potpourri. Sharon gave me a lovely bottle of perfume. I pushed Randy off my leg for the third time and took the package Maggie handed me. Inside the box was a large leering nutcracker with a wild tuft of red hair.

"Thank you! This will be so ... useful," I said, opening and shutting its jaws.

"I recognize that; it's what Dilly gave you last Christmas," Sharon said accusingly.

"It is no such thing," Maggie said haughtily. "Anyway, I have three of them already."

Sharon rolled her eyes at me. "Mum can't help herself; she always passes along the gifts. At least it wasn't a water pick."

"Nonsense. It only looks like the one Dilly gave me. Anyway, Julia, I'm sure you want to wash up and unpack. I'll show you to your room. Tracy will have brought up your bags."

"I'll show her the way." Jack jumped up and grabbed my hand. "What time's supper? We're going to relax for a bit."

Maggie narrowed her eyes. "I'm sure Julia would like to rest after such a long flight. I've put her in Caroline's old room," she said pointedly. "And your room is made up for you."

"We'll just have a quick kip," Jack said. He pulled me into the hallway toward the big staircase.

"Did you just tell her we're going to have sex?" I whispered as I followed him up the carpeted steps.

"Well, we are, aren't we? Don't you fancy a bit of a hump?" Jack grinned. "Nah, a kip is a nap. You didn't know that from your extensive reading?"

"I'm not familiar with some of these expressions," I muttered as we reached the second floor. "Caroline was the girlfriend in your mid-twenties, right?" I felt a surprisingly sharp stab of jealousy. He'd showed me her picture once when he'd gotten out an old box of photos; she was thin, blonde, and rich. "How long did you say you went out with her?"

"I dunno, several years. It was never 'her' room; she only stayed here a couple of Christmases. Mum was just impressed because her Dad was an Earl or something."

Jack led me down a long hallway with hunter-green walls, hung with dark paintings. I made a mental note to check them out later. He stopped at the third door and pushed it open. "Ah, she's put you in Old Squeaky," he said as we entered the room. My bag was on the floor next to a large chest of drawers with an age-spotted mirror, a fireplace, two armchairs, and a settee.

"This is really nice," I said, glancing around.

"Take a good look, because you aren't staying here," Jack said.

"But your mother!" I was horrified at the thought of antagonizing Maggie.

"I'll handle her. This is bullshit; she knows we're living

together." Jack took off his boots and leaped onto the bed.

"What are you doing?" Jack began jumping, the bed emanating loud creaks and squeaks. He leaped higher, his hair flying. The bed juddered like it was about to break in two. "Stop—you're wrecking it!" I cried.

"Now for the encore." Jack knelt facing the headboard and began slamming it rhythmically against the wall. He banged it one last time and gave a loud, drawn-out groan.

My cheeks were burning. "How am I going to face them now?"

"Serves her right. C'mon, my room's the best one in the house."

"I hope you had a good kip," Maggie said, eyeing me when we came downstairs a few hours later. To my horror, a hot blush crept up my face.

"Oh, it was fantastic," Jack said with a wolfish grin. "One of the best ever."

Dinner, which they called "supper," was poached eggs, mashed potatoes with sausages, and toast. Apparently it was the custom to eat a large meal in the middle of the day—their dinner—and then have a big formal tea at four, followed by a light meal around eight p.m. I was starving, since I'd been too nervous to eat any of the previous spread. While I devoured my eggs, Oliver ran in circles around the table. Every time he passed Emma, he yanked her hair, making her shriek.

"Ollie, sit next to me," Jack finally said. "Reminds me

of m'self when I was that age," he added fondly. I noticed Sharon's exhausted expression and wondered how she managed. From what I'd gathered, her husband wasn't around much. Emma was just as rambunctious, complaining all the while that she hated bangers and mash.

"It's your uncle's favorite supper," Maggie said reprovingly. When she turned to pass the butter, Emma stuck out her tongue.

"Ahh, I've missed home cooking," Jack said as he served himself seconds. "Too bad I only know how to make breakfast."

"You don't cook, Julia?" Maggie gave me a pointed look.

"I never really learned," I said, chagrinned at having to explain. If Jack wanted a domestic diva, he was with the wrong girl. I hadn't been aware that it was high on his checklist. "I was in grad school up until a year and a half ago, living on cafeteria food. And now I'm spending long hours in the office."

"Never too late to learn," Maggie said. "I'll jot down my recipe for Yorkshire pudding before you leave; I've known Jack to eat three helpings. And treacle sponge, and shepherd's pie—even a simpleton could make that. I stuff the pie with minced lamb and mashed potatoes."

I felt like telling *her* to stuff it, but I merely nodded.

After supper Tracy cleared away the table, refusing my offer of help. "Save the foil!" Maggie called into the kitchen. We gathered in a capacious room that I would have called a den; there were large windows overlooking a frosty garden, a television, and several sofas and chairs. Jack lay on the floor letting Ollie trounce him at arm-wrestling, while Maggie sat in a chair by the fireplace and removed the Yorkie's sweater. Tracy passed around tea, which was chokingly strong. As I dumped in more milk, Sharon held up her silver spoon.

"Do you think they'll want it back?" she asked Jack.

"They probably do. More's the pity," Jack said.

I looked inquiringly at Sharon. "Jack and his friend Ned got into a lot of scrapes when they were young," she said.

"Julia wouldn't be interested in all that," Jack said. "Ah, you've beat me again." His arm whumped to the carpet beneath Ollie's full weight.

"I imagine she'd fancy this story." Sharon smiled. "Jack and Ned were always up to some barmy doings. They once got the notion to make a prank call to our local funeral parlor. They told the director that their uncle had died; he'd choked on a spoon that morning. The man got very worked up when they said they had him on ice in a large bin in the basement."

"That wanker," Jack said. "He'd complained to the cops just because we nicked one jar of his precious formaldehyde."

"Why'd you do that?" I asked.

"Thought it would get us high." Jack glanced at Oliver, who was soaking in every word. "Don't get ideas, young man."

"But tell her the kicker," Sharon said.

"Well, the director said he'd get a driver over right away to fetch the body," Jack resumed. "He seemed anxious to remove the 'remains'. So I said, 'But we can have the spoon back, right?' 'You want it *back*?!' he asked. I told him, 'Sure, but it's part of a set!'" Jack wound up, laughing.

"You always were up to no good," Maggie said. "Bringing

home insects, lizards, terrapins, and the like. I never knew what I'd find when I went to draw a bath."

"Tell her how you'd make the calls about the phone bills," Sharon prompted.

"We were just being kids." Grunting, Jack pretended to press back against Ollie, then collapsed on the carpet.

Sharon leaned toward me. "When he and Ned were around fourteen—their voices had just changed, so they sounded like grown men—they'd stay up late and look up people's numbers in the phone book. They'd ring them up in the middle of the night. Jack would get on the line and tell them there was a problem with their phone bill, and they needed to fetch it so they could go over it. The poor sods would be rummaging through their desk drawers, desperately looking for their paperwork at two in the morning."

"More like three," Jack said.

"Then when they came back on the line, Jack would make them go through each itemized call, one by one. He'd say they hadn't paid their bill. They'd insist that they *had*. Then he would tell them that a mild electric shock would be sent through the phone if they didn't pay what they owed by nine o'clock the next morning. If they really gave him a hard time, he'd put on his 'supervisor'—Ned—and drag them through it all again."

"One guy got so mad, I thought he'd have a stroke," Jack mused, scratching his chin.

"That's awful." I tried to hide my smile.

"Remember when you two burnt down Mr. Atwater's shed?" Maggie looked up from combing the Yorkie's topknot.

"That wasn't Ned. That was Peter." Jack sat up and crossed his legs. Ollie scooted next to him and crossed his legs in mirror imitation.

"How did that happen?" *I'm getting the real inside scoop, here in England,* I told myself.

"We were just having a smoke. A spark caught one of the hay bales," Jack said.

"How old were you then?" I edged my ankles away as Randall came sniffing around.

"He was twelve. The whole thing went up like a Guy Fawkes bonfire." Maggie pulled the sweater over the Yorkie's head, making it squeak. "I had to go and plead before the magistrate. Lucky thing he wasn't thirteen, or he would've been sent away to the delinquents'."

Wow, he had a wild childhood, I realized. *I guess that makes sense, given what he was up to in his twenties.* I tried shoving Randall away, but he reared up on my leg again.

Jack grinned. "You still remember, don't you, old boy?"

"Look, he's dancing!" Ollie cried. "Tell her about shooting the fish!"

"That's enough," Jack said as he pulled Randall off me. "Dredging up all this useless stuff about the past."

"I'd like to hear about the fish." I used the linen napkin to discreetly wipe saliva off my knee.

"All I did was fire one off a roof," Jack said.

"You never cared for Reverend Northrup." Maggie took a dainty sip of her tea.

"One Sunday Jack got in trouble for carving B-O-L-L-I-X into a pew," Sharon chimed in.

"Northrup was a tosser. He always had it out for me." Jack scratched Randall's belly, making his leg twitch. "And his curate, Carter, was a window-licker."

"Carter's done much better since he got back from reformatory," Maggie commented.

"Anyway, Jack decided to get Rev. Northrup's goat," Sharon continued. "He had this giant slingshot. I was little, but I still remember it. He bought a huge carp from the fishmonger's and climbed up the rainspout onto the rectory roof."

"It wasn't a carp. It was a pike," Jack said.

"A pike then. He loaded the fish into his slingshot and waited until the Reverend was coming out of his office," Sharon continued.

"You should have heard him scream," Jack said to Ollie. "Just like a woman: *'Cor blimey! I've been shot!'*" he exclaimed in a high-pitched, old-lady voice. "I scrambled down the other side of the roof like me pants were on fire. Guess that taught *him* to mind his loaves and fishes."

Everyone laughed. I loved the way he sometimes lapsed into his native Cockney, using *me* for *my*. "I had no idea you were such a troublemaker," I said. Suddenly I had to smother a yawn.

"That was the least of it," Maggie said drily. "You two had better turn in. What time are you going to knock her up?"

I stared at her. Jack had mentioned that his Mum would like more grandchildren, but suggesting it so blatantly on my very first visit . . .

"No certain time. We'll probably sleep in," Jack said. *It*

must mean something different over here, I thought. Really, all this British terminology was very confusing.

"*I'll* knock her up!" Ollie shouted, jumping around. "I always get up bright and early!"

"That he does," Sharon said wearily. "Six a.m., like clockwork."

"See that you don't," Jack said. "Julia and I need our beauty rest."

"I thought you were tired, but you had a second wind," Jack said as we lay back, recovering. He was sprawled beside me on the bed, one leg flung over mine. I ran my finger up his damp chest, still heaving from his exertions.

"Just like Randall," I said. "He really is stinky."

"Ah, he's old. I love that dog. He was me best mate." I could see the little boy in Jack's faraway expression; I adored that look of his.

"Your mother's kind of intimidating," I ventured. "I don't get the sense that she approves of me." I turned to face him and straightened his chain with the lightning bolt. He never took it off; he'd told me his Mum had given it to him for good luck when he first started out with the band.

Jack put his warm hand on my waist. "She'll come around; just give her time. She has no choice." He smiled, creating those sexy lines at the corners of his mouth.

"Was she hoping you'd marry Caroline?" The ghosts of all the other women he'd been with haunted me at times, particularly when we were in bed. Jack was so . . . *practiced.* Which made him a great lover, but also brought up the obvious: that he'd been with hundreds of other girls before me. And based on his reputation, he'd left them all panting for more.

"I dunno. Maybe. Mum fancied me marrying into the peerage. As if that would've happened." He shrugged, and with an effort I kicked those other women out of the bed.

"It must be nice to be home again," I said. "Although this isn't the house you grew up in."

"Yeah, that was on the other side of the tracks. I bought this for Mum when I earned my first real dosh. She was on the outs with her second husband by then. I was glad the wankstain wouldn't be living off the fruits of my labor. He gave me hell when I was in my teens."

"You seem close to Maggie though." I traced the line at the side of his mouth, and Jack pretended to snap at my finger.

"I was bit of a mama's boy, in my own way. I was brought up with a kind of benign neglect, I guess you'd call it. She didn't pay me much attention until I got in trouble. Which was fairly often. Then she'd tear a strip off me. But she was more into Sharon's business, her being a girl." Jack looked at me. "You didn't have that kind of mothering, did you?"

Jack knew of my fraught history with Dot; her running around with various men, beginning when I was fourteen and my father moved out. My Dad had accused her of having an affair with her boss at the hardware store where she'd worked at the time. Until recently, I had always thought their breakup was her fault. Only this past fall did Dot explain that my father had always been jealous and possessive, and had accused her of having affairs before. But she had sworn to me that she'd been true to him up until the day he vanished; the supposed tryst was simply a figment of his imagination.

I sighed. "Not exactly. It was more like I was trying to mother *her*. Making sure she got back home from the bar in one piece; helping her juggle the bills."

Jack traced the curve of my hip. "I still think you ought to try to locate your dad."

I felt a familiar pang. "I'll think about it. But he hasn't gotten in touch with me for ten years. Why would he want to hear from me now?"

"You never know what's going on with someone. Maybe things have changed." He stretched his arms and yawned. "Want to get a little shut-eye? I'm knackered."

"Me too. I'm really glad to be here with you." I snuggled into his chest and fell asleep.

We didn't rouse ourselves until late the next morning. Jack pulled back the heavy bedroom curtain and stared at the torrential rain. "It's pissing," he said. "Good day for a drive."

"Where are we going?"

"You'll see."

After some tea and toast in the quiet house—Maggie had taken the children to town to give their mom a break, and Sharon was resting upstairs—Jack located a key hanging in the cupboard. He outfitted us in Wellington boots and "macs" from a hall closet. Grabbing a giant umbrella, we set out across the back fields until we came to a small barn. Jack unlocked it and beckoned me in. There in the gloom was a gleaming, elegant car complete with leather steering wheel and hood ornament.

"That's my Rolls," Jack said. "I leave it here for safekeeping." He opened my side and let me in, then climbed into the driver's seat. "I'll take you for a spin around the track."

"Why don't we drive on the road?" I asked, reaching for my seatbelt.

"You won't need the belt. We're just going to stay in the field."

"I'd love to go to the village." I'd been curious to see more of the surrounding area.

"We can do that later. Actually, I'm not supposed to be driving."

"Why is that?" I asked.

"I got busted over here in the Seventies. More than once. The last time, they took away my license."

"You're kidding. You aren't allowed to drive?"

"Not in England. But the farmer that owns this land doesn't mind. I pay him for the use of the shed."

"I see. How long were you in jail?" He'd mentioned this once before, but I hadn't pursued it.

"Only a week, but it was pretty nerve-wracking. If Caroline's dad hadn't intervened, I could have done real time. Back then they got all worked up about a little stash of dope."

Something else to know about Jack, I thought. *I'll have to ask him more about it later.* He started the car and we bumped along the muddy track, rain bucketing down, drumming on the roof.

"Feels good to get behind the wheel again," Jack said. "Let's see if the radio still works."

He fiddled with the dial, and Bob Marley's "One Love" came on. Jack smirked. "That's the 'Hotel California' of Jamaica; their version of elevator music."

"What would it be in England?"

"Probably one of ours." He gunned the engine, and the car spun a little in the mud. "The times I used to have in this baby . . . Here's where we're going." He pulled into a grove of trees and parked, leaving the motor idling, heater on. Then he took off his mac, opened the door, got out and jumped into the back seat.

"What are you doing?" I asked.

"Why don't you join me?"

Rather than get drenched, I climbed over the gear shift. Jack pulled me onto his lap facing him and gave me a kiss that left my whole body simmering. "Let's get you out of these wet things." He undid my raincoat and slid it off, then began unbuttoning my blouse.

"You don't want to go back to the house?" I asked as he pulled down my bra strap.

"Mmm. We haven't done it in a car yet," he murmured, licking my nipple, making it pop.

"What if someone comes?" I asked, aroused by his circling tongue. I reached down to stroke him, ramrod-hard in his jeans.

"It's pissing rain; no one will come. Well, you'll probably come." He raised an eyebrow and unzipped himself, shoved down his jeans and lifted me up. I gasped as the full length of him filled me. "I probably will, too." He held my waist with his strong hands, slowly moving me up and down.

"God, you feel good," I whispered, feeling him grow even harder.

"It's a turn-on in a car, isn't it?" Jack's breath came faster as I used my thighs to move up and down. He cupped my rear and brought his other hand around to stroke me slowly, teasingly. I pushed against his long fingers, wanting more as we picked up the pace. I rode him, feeling each stroke deep inside. His fingers turned my whole being into a molten liquid need. I could hear him gritting his teeth, holding on as I started to pant. I had to stop moving; I needed to feel each motion of his hand, his tingling, lingering touch.

Jack gently strummed against me, unbearably slowing down. My hips jolted forward, begging for release. Just as I was practically sobbing, he pressed his fingers harder and drove up into me. My cries went on so long and loud, my throat felt sore.

I was still catching my breath when Jack grasped my hips. He pumped me up and down, faster and faster, plunging farther inside with each powerful thrust. I felt him tighten, making my inner muscles clench. He held me hard to his chest as he gave a wild cry, throbbing inside me. Then he stroked me softly and made me come again in a great, heaving aftershock.

"Now that's what they mean by a religious experience," Jack said as we lay tangled together on the back seat.

"We've steamed the windows up." I pointed to the foggy panes.

"I should think so." Jack shut his eyes. "I could go for a nice little kip right now."

"We'd better get moving before we breathe too much carbon monoxide." I sat up and put on my bra.

"Just let me lie here a minute. God, you Yanks are always raring to go."

"Do you feel more British when you're over here? I notice you use more slang. Ouch!" I bumped my head on the overhead light as I tried to pull up my jeans.

"I dunno, I guess so. I've lived so many places, it probably all blends in. And New York's a mix of everything. Oh, Ollie wants to come for a visit before we go on tour. I told Sharon he could come for a fortnight, but she's got to ask the old wanker if it's okay with him."

I quailed at the thought of Oliver running wild in the loft for two weeks. "What will he do while I'm at work and you're in the studio?" The Floor was going to start rehearsing again as soon as we got back.

"He can come along and watch me. I always told him he could stay with me when he turned six. You'd like that, wouldn't you?" Jack gazed at me through his thick eyelashes.

"Sure. I mean, he is . . . kind of a handful. But he's adorable," I added quickly.

"Yeah, he's full of beans. I can't wait to have him all to myself in the city. Sharon puts a bit of a damper on his spirits, if you know what I mean."

This version of Ollie was dampered?

The rest of the visit went by in a flash. The last night, Maggie caught me alone in the den. "I hope you've been comfortable," she said. "I know it may not be what you're used to in New York."

"It's beautiful here," I said honestly. "I really appreciate your having me. I was so glad to get to meet you."

"You're the first girl Jack's brought home in a quite a while. Since Caroline. I always thought he'd marry a nice English girl, but I can see he's quite smitten with you." Maggie gave me a dry smile.

This was nice to hear, although she didn't seem ecstatic about it. "I'm pretty smitten, too."

"I don't believe I ever told Jack this, but I was going to name him 'Julia' if he was a girl," Maggie said thoughtfully.

I was surprised at the coincidence. "That's amazing. Do you mind if I tell him?"

"Why not? It's the truth." Maggie surveyed me for a moment. "You know, I'm not getting any younger. I'd really like to have a chance to get to know my grandchildren. *Jack's* children."

"Oh! We haven't gotten that far along. I mean, in the planning, or—or anything. We've only been together half a year," I stammered. *Has Jack said something about it to her?* I wondered.

"Well. I know you're quite the career girl, but Jack needs someone who can focus on him. Caroline was very good at helping him pack for his tours, keeping his schedule organized, making him home-cooked meals. He spends so much time on the road that he gets tired of restaurant food." She eyed me for a moment. "And to be frank about it, he makes enough money so that if you two do settle down, you'd have absolutely no need to keep working. I had to work when Jack was growing up, and he hated being alone in the house. Sharon came along much later with my second husband, you know."

"Yes, he mentioned that," I said, taken aback by the unsolicited advice.

"At any rate, Jack had better get going if he doesn't want to be old when he has children. Kids take a lot of energy. Look at Ollie; he's the spitting image of Jack when he was a boy."

I gulped; this was what I'd suspected. "I'll keep that in mind."

Later, Maggie was instructing Tracy in the kitchen as Jack and I sat with Sharon near the parlor fire. "This visit went too fast," Jack said to his sister. "I need to get back here more often. Do you think Mum is doing all right?"

"I think so. I come with the kids as much as I can, and she's got the garden club. And her bridge group. And her friend Dilly redecorating every time you turn around." Sharon sighed. "Did you know Mum's having our coat of arms looked up?"

Jack snorted. "Is there a crest for horse thieves?" He leaned down to scratch Randall's back as Sharon and I laughed.

"So what d'you say, Ollie can come stay with us in the city? You know he'd love it," Jack urged.

"Well, he'd only miss a week of school since the new term doesn't start until the end of January. I guess so," Sharon said. "But Julia, don't let Jack stuff him with sweets every chance he gets. Try to set a regular bedtime," she pleaded as

Jack plugged his ears and started humming. "And make him hold your hand when you cross the street. Please?"

"He'll be safe as a chick in a nest," Jack said, taking his fingers out of his ears. "Too bad you can't come along too," he said to Randall. "You and I had many an adventure, didn't we, old boy?" He leaned down and let the dog slobber all over his face. Then he stood up and came over to me. "C'mon now, gimme a kiss," he said with a grin.

Chapter 3

PRIVATE IDAHO

After our stay at his mother's, Jack and I flew from London to the secluded island of Mustique for New Year's. Jack—or to be accurate, Mary Jo, at his request—had booked us an amazing cottage on an isolated beach, from which we would celebrate the dawning of 1982. There was no love lost between me and Jack's crabby manager, but I had to admit, she knew her stuff in terms of vacation paradises. My mom was flying in from Pennsylvania later that day. She would have her own room in a separate compound, within walking distance but far enough away that we could have some privacy.

On the winding road from the airport Jack chatted with the driver, whom he obviously knew from previous visits to the island. I stared out the window as we flew past coconut trees, fragrant bougainvillea and blossoming hibiscus, and luxurious villas situated behind ornate iron gates. I bit my tongue to keep from asking Jack if he'd been here with Caroline, or what other girlfriends he'd brought here in the past.

The driver pulled up to a large two-story beachfront house surrounded by stately palms that belied Jack's description of a "cottage". When I stepped out of the car, my eyes were momentarily dazzled by the sun. The air was wonderfully humid after the dry radiator heat of England, and scented with a heady hint of frangipani. The driver carried our luggage inside and left us with a set of keys. The entrance was spacious and airy, salmon-pink-tiled with potted plants and huge ceiling fans slowly circling.

"This is amazing," I breathed. Growing up in small-town Pennsylvania, an exotic vacation had been a sweaty five-hour drive with Dot to the South Jersey shore. In my two and a half years in New York City, I'd only made a couple of day trips with girlfriends by train to Jones Beach on Long Island. Sugar-white sand and balmy breezes were entirely out of my league.

Jack kicked off his boots. "Nice, isn't it? Let's get our suits on and hit the beach."

I followed him upstairs to a huge room dominated by a king-sized bed made up with a snowy cotton coverlet. Through open doors I went onto the veranda, which overlooked a sparkling pool. Beyond it was a thatched hut and the beckoning azure of the ocean. Jack came up behind me, already in his swimsuit. "C'mon, let's get some sun."

"I'm just taking it all in. I've never been anywhere like this before," I said.

"Good thing we came, then."

I fished my bikini out of the bag and went into the bathroom to change, self-conscious about my pale skin in the skimpy suit. Jack's eyes lit up when I emerged. "Very nice," he said. "Let's go. If we don't leave now, we'll never make it out of here."

We went downstairs, grabbed towels and suntan lotion in the foyer, and stepped out into the radiant sunshine. A narrow sand path led to the wide white stretch of beach. The strand was entirely empty as far as the eye could see. Jack and I spread our towels and laid down under the brilliant sky.

"Ahh," I said, basking in the sensation of warm sun on my skin. "This feels amazing. Especially after all that snow." There had been a blizzard right before we left England.

Jack turned on his side, head in hand, his dark eyes shadowed. "This detour was a very good idea. You know, the beach is totally deserted," he said, slipping his finger under my bathing suit strap and sliding it down my shoulder. "Why don't you take your top off and get some sun?"

I sat up. "I don't know. Do you think anybody's around?"

"Nope."

"Okay. I guess I'll try it." I reached for the clasp and unhooked myself. It was strange to feel the ocean breeze on my bare breasts.

"You'll need some of this," he said, squeezing lotion into his palm. He rubbed it on me, taking particular care with my nipples. "I wouldn't want the girls to get burned."

I stretched out as he sat gazing down at me. "Now that's a pretty picture. I could go for a total tan myself." He pulled off his suit and lay on his stomach next to me.

"Do you want me to rub some on your back?" I asked.

"In a second." He shut his eyes and was still for a minute, then put his arm around me and started kissing my neck. "I knew this wasn't going to work."

"What?" I glanced around. I really didn't want to be stumbled upon by some beachcomber. Or by Dot, whose flight was arriving any minute.

"I should have known I couldn't keep my hands off you." He pushed up and got on top of me, his bare chest against my sun-warmed breasts, his tousled head silhouetted against the bright blue sky.

"I have a feeling we're about to get very sandy," Jack said. He began tugging down my bathing suit bottom.

"Shouldn't we go in?" I asked.

"Relax, baby. Not a soul here except us."

Sunburned and sticky, we put our suits back on and waded into the cool water, then walked hand in hand to the house for a siesta. I felt more relaxed than I had in ages; the stress of work—and worrying about whether his mother had liked me—was sloughing off with each caress of gentle ocean breeze. Even my highly-charged boyfriend seemed content to kick back. As we were drifting off to sleep beneath the ceiling fan, the phone rang. I grabbed it and took it out onto the veranda.

"I just got in," Dot said. "Boy, this place is fantastic. It must have cost Jack an arm and a leg." Hearing the strike of a match, I pictured her, hair dyed a brassy shade, lit cigarette sending up plumes from the resort ashtray.

"It's beautiful, isn't it? I feel so lucky to be here." Shading my eyes, I gazed at the view.

"How was your visit with his mother?" Dot lowered her voice dramatically, although I knew she was alone in her hotel room.

"I think it went well. Maggie's a little bossy and obsessed with her dogs, but I think she liked me all right." I wasn't going to mention what she'd said about wanting more grandchildren; I knew Dot would take that and run with it. "I forgot to ask, did you wind up getting off early on Christmas Eve?"

"No, Erwin had me and Marie doing inventory again. I don't know why; it's not like the pipe fittings are going to walk out of the place by themselves." My mother worked at a plumbing supply store in our small hometown of Pikesville, Pennsylvania. She complained about her boss nonstop, but she liked chatting up the customers, who were mostly well-built construction guys.

"I can't believe he had you doing that up until the last minute."

"It was okay. We had eggnog in the storage room, and then we went to Buck's afterwards." Buck's Bar and Grill was my mother's local hangout. "This hotel is great though. The concierge told me there's a luau tonight, so I went ahead and booked a table for us," she continued.

I plopped down into a white chair, then immediately jumped up as the iron-hot metal branded my thighs. "I don't know if Jack will want to do that, Mom. He usually has to keep a low profile."

"For goodness' sake, Julia. It's the islands. Everyone's laid-back here; I doubt anyone will even notice him. Let the man have some fun."

"I think that just about does it," Jack said after signing his thirtieth luau program. The minute we'd stepped into the seating area, people started whispering and pointing. They'd lined up three-deep beside our table, wanting autographs. I felt badly about it, but Jack was being a good sport.

"I had no idea he was so internationally known," Dot whispered to me. She tugged at her pink tube top.

"Pretty much worldwide," I whispered back. Finally the manager came over and cordoned off our table so Jack could have a bite to eat. The highlight of the evening came when the musicians, in the heat of their final number, beckoned Jack onto the low stage. Since there wasn't a guitar, he gamely took a place at the bongos as the limbo-la began. Three sheets to the wind after her fourth Fuzzy Navel, Dot was at the head of the line, going down low with the best of them.

When we got back to the cottage, the stars were sparkling above the wide bowl of vast dark ocean. Jack and I walked barefoot on the beach, the moon looming over the endless span of water like a great shimmering moth. The sensations were intoxicating: the soft night breeze, the rushing sound of the waves leaping and subsiding on the shore, Jack's arm around my waist.

"I'm sorry about tonight," I said. "Dot got a little carried away." She'd wound up doing a suggestive grind with a muscled ukulele player.

"We all need to cut loose sometime." Jack's smile flashed in his tanned face. "Tomorrow I've rented a motorboat so we can go off by ourselves for a bit."

"How beautiful," I said the next day as Jack moored the boat in a quiet lagoon. Arcing palms dipped long green fingers into the turquoise water, and I could see silvery fish flitting around on the surface. Jack looked sultry, dark eyes and hair set off strikingly by his bronzed face and chest.

"Let's get in," he said, shoving down his swimming trunks. He stood naked on the side of the boat and executed a neat dive. His sleek head popped up like a seal's. "C'mon in, the water's fine."

"Okay." Gingerly I sat on the edge and dabbled my toes. There were hardly any waves, and the seawater was clear and cool. I pushed off, going under. When I surfaced, Jack started untying my bikini top. By now I knew better than to protest.

"Just don't lose it," I said, laughing. I reached down and grabbed him. "I think someone's happy to see me."

Jack draped my bikini around his neck so it hung down in back. "Let's go closer to shore where we can stand up." We swam to a rock outcropping and stood in the chest-deep water, soft sand enveloping my feet. The sun beat down mercilessly on the top of my head, but below chin-level, the water was perfect. Jack gave my neck a teasing lick. "Salty," he commented. Reaching down, he ducked his head below the surface and tugged off my bottom. I stepped out of it so he could come up for air. Jack put his arm through the leg hole and shoved it up on his shoulder.

"That's a smooth move with the bikini," I said, thinking again of Caroline and all my other predecessors. "You've done this before, haven't you?"

"No comment."

"Is there anything you *haven't* done?" I asked.

Jack thought for a minute, water swirling around his chest. "I've never had sex with a man. Or an animal."

I laughed. "Well that's good, I guess."

Jack got that slightly glazed expression that meant he was turned on. "You look like a mermaid with your wet hair and those blue, blue eyes." He lifted me up by my elbows. "But I'm glad you're not. If you were a mermaid, I couldn't . . . do . . . this."

Chapter 4

STIR IT UP

We had been back in New York for a week. Following the balmy bliss of the islands, I'd had a hard time re-adjusting to icy sidewalks and crowded subways. But now I had to focus on my career, which after gaining an initial head of steam, currently seemed stalled in its tracks.

I had been promoted this past fall when I'd signed up a memoir by former sitcom star Isabel Reed. Since then I'd acquired a few books of my own, while also continuing my assistant duties for my boss, the publisher. It was far from an ideal situation—most people who made editor didn't have to keep doing the clerical stuff—but Harvey claimed he didn't have the budget to hire anyone else. For the time being, I was stuck.

"Time for the editorial meeting, Julia." My friend Meredith, our managing editor, put her head in my office door.

Meredith and I took our seats at the conference table. Edgar, a dignified older man who handled arts and crafts, sat next to me. Senior editors Charlie and Kate took their seats. Harvey hustled in, brandishing the bestseller list.

"Freeman Fyfe's just dropped off the list," Harvey said, referring to the house's one big author. I had edited Freeman's last novel, which had stayed at the top of the charts for several months. "We've got to find another brand name. Kate, what do you have this week?"

"Roxanna stopped by with yet another manuscript," Kate answered.

"That's not writing; that's typing," commented Edgar.

Everyone looked at me in commiseration. Roxanna Stokes was a pale, emaciated novelist with a devoted following. The problem was, every four months she showed up at the office with another 700-page doorstop in a shopping bag. It was a house tradition that the junior editor got first crack at her books; I had only just finished whacking back her latest masterpiece.

"Is it true she never sleeps or eats?" Charlie said.

"Who cares? They sell, so let's keep her cranking them out," Harvey said. "Julia, you'll need to clear your plate for the next few weekends. What about you, Meredith?" Unusual for most managing editors, Meredith acquired her own titles as well as handling all the copyediting.

"I have a historical about a flapper who turns to prostitution," she said. "It started out well, but the second half's a mess. I'll keep reading to see if it's salvageable."

"Don't bother. I turned that down three months ago,"

Kate chimed in.

"Okay, so you can skip the sloppy seconds," Harvey said. "Have any of you taken a gander at the list?"

"Four money guides in the top ten," Charlie said. "People are frantic to climb out of this recession."

"Not to mention the diet craze," Harvey added. "The *I Love New York Diet* moved up to number eight. You can never be too thin or too rich—remember that."

Meredith rolled her eyes at me. "If nothing else, he's original," she muttered.

"This week's entry in the weight-loss category is yet another grapefruit diet," Charlie said. "Half a fruit in the morning, the other half at lunch, and at dinner you get a celery appetizer with your broiled grapefruit entrée. After three days, they probably have to put you on intravenous."

"I have good news," Kate said. "We just upped the print run for *Cherishing Your Inner Child.*"

"Yes, and now your author's demanding a twelve-city tour," Harvey said. "If he doesn't watch out, I'm gonna kick his inner child's little butt. Edgar, what's new?"

"I have in a very smart guide to cross-stitch embroidery," Edgar said.

Harvey frowned. "Don't pay more than two grand for it."

Edgar's titles turned a tidy profit, since the gardeners, crewelers, and crocheters of the world were always hungry for new books on their craft. But they were never glam enough to interest our boss.

"Julia? Anything?" Harvey said.

I glanced down at my papers. "I have an intriguing proposal on something called the internet. It's about computers communicating with each other. The National Science Foundation just developed a network that connected three colleges."

"But what's the point?" Harvey asked. "Nerds yakking about what's stewing in their petri dishes?"

"They think it will have practical uses eventually," I said with a familiar sinking feeling. "A grad student has come up with electronic mail. You type in a message and send it by computer."

"Why bother with that when you have phones?" Kate said. "I don't get it."

"I don't either, but it's kind of fascinating," Charlie said. "I'll take a look at the proposal."

"Don't waste your time. There's no audience for weird science," Harvey pronounced as he got up to leave.

Glumly I gathered my notes and filed out behind the others. A few minutes later, Harvey stuck his head in my door. "You may as well get going on that needlework contract," he said. "Another one for the effing knit and purl shelf."

"I will," I said, keeping my eyes on my typewriter.

Feeling discouraged, I fed quarters into the vending machine and went back to my desk. Along with my promotion, I'd been given a tiny expense account to take literary agents out for occasional lunches. As a result I'd received some submissions, but it was still hard to actually acquire a book. Harvey was mainly interested in celebrity authors or knockoffs of bestselling diets. And since I was new at it, the agents tended to send me their B- or C-level proposals, things that had already been rejected by more senior editors at other houses. Naively I'd thought that once I got promoted, I'd be rolling in acquisitions.

As I was eating a cracker, the phone rang. "Julia Nash," I mumbled through peanut butter.

"Hello, Julia. This is Ted Rathbone from Hawtey House. I saw in *Publishers Weekly* that you acquired Isabel Reed's memoir. Smart move on your part," he said. "I was also talking to Freeman Fyfe's agent; she says you're an ace with a red pencil."

"Oh! Thank you." I felt a flutter of hope in my chest; Rathbone was editor-in-chief of the prestigious midtown publisher.

"Someone just gave notice, so we have an opening. Would you like to meet with me?"

An opening! At Hawtey House! "I'd love to," I said, trying not to squeal. "When should I come?"

"I don't have a lunch on Thursday. Do you want to stop by around one?"

I clutched the receiver. "That would be great."

"See you then."

I sat for a moment staring at the piles of paper on my desk; the overflowing inbox with Harvey's scribbled letters waiting to be typed. I'd always heard that junior editors had to switch houses in order to be taken seriously. *Maybe I'll finally get out of here!* I thought. Jack would be at the studio by now; there was no way to reach him. I couldn't wait to tell him my news.

But back at the apartment that night, I wound up telling Dot first. Jack was putting in long hours rehearsing for the band's upcoming eight-week tour. Harvey had given me permission to take all of my two weeks' vacation in early March, in order to join them midway through. Jack had been miffed that I couldn't come for longer. He didn't seem to get the restrictions of being a working stiff with a boss, and limits to how much time off one could take. I'd finally made him understand that I couldn't just up and leave for a month, and expect my job to be waiting when I got back.

Four to the Floor would start their 1982 tour in San Francisco and end up at Madison Square Garden, or "MSG" in band lingo—which made me think of Chinese takeout. The group was composed of Patrick, lead singer and bass player; Jack, guitarist and back-up vocals; Mark on drums; and Sammy, the only American in the group, on keyboard. The guys had formed the band in London over a decade ago, and then exploded in popularity after their first U.S. tour. I was excited that I'd get to see them perform once more when they arrived back in New York for their final concert; particularly since the Garden was the biggest show of all, and the culmination of the thirty-city extravaganza.

So far, the only time I'd ever seen The Floor onstage was late last summer when they gave a couple of concerts in L.A. Normally they hit the road immediately after a new album came out, but this tour had been delayed by several months because of a financial deal cooked up by Patrick and their manager, Mary Jo. One of the concert backers was promoting a new deodorant that was supposed to heighten men's sex appeal, and the ads would be featured prominently on the show's posters and tickets. Jack, Mark, and Sammy had been making bad jokes about it ever since the ink on the contract was dry.

When I got in from work around seven, I dumped my backpack on the front table, careful not to jostle the wire-mesh cage of praying mantises. Jack had been so excited a few days ago when the eggs gave birth to dozens of the little creatures. He'd jostled me awake at 2 a.m., his expression like an excited little boy: "C'mon, Julia, they're hatching!" I'd stumbled out of bed and followed him to the kitchen. We had watched their tiny bodies emerge from the egg case and dangle by fragile threads. For a while we'd tried to count them, eventually giving up as they multiplied. I went back to bed, but Jack stayed up until the very last one made its appearance.

The phone rang as I was looking at the insects scrambling around in their cage. When I answered it, my mother's voice came on the line.

"Where's Jack?" was the first thing out of her mouth.

"I'm fine, how are you?" It was a little annoying how much Dot liked my boyfriend, but my sarcasm went right over her head.

"We're still doing inventory. We should be done by tomorrow."

"I hope it goes fast. What are you reading this week?" I asked.

"Paulette loaned me a new one of Joyce Sutter's. An English maiden gets captured by these buccaneers and has to work in the ship's galley. Her fiancé tries to rescue her, but by then she's fallen in love with the head pirate."

I zoned out as she rambled on about the plot. ". . . and then they feed her true love to the sharks. But it turns out, it was a guy who just *looked* like him—"

"Sounds like a good one," I interrupted. "Have you lost your tan yet? Mine's completely gone."

"Mine's faded too. That was so much fun; I loved spending time with Jack. We'll all have to take another trip together soon." Dot had been singing Jack's praises ever since Mustique. "By the way, have you tried my Apple Brown Betty recipe?" She'd included it in her Christmas card.

"Not yet. I don't get home from work until seven most nights."

"You have plenty of time to cook on the weekends. You know, the way to a man's heart—"

"I know, I know. It's through his stomach." I parroted one of her oft-repeated wisdoms. "Jack's not really a big eater. Although he did go for seconds at his mother's house."

"I imagine he'd eat if you made him something good, instead of ordering takeout all the time. A man gets tired of that kind of thing."

"All right, Mom, I'll try to get it together to bake something," I said dubiously. What was it with these mothers and cooking? I had no experience whatsoever in the kitchen. "Guess what: I have an interview." I told her about the call from Hawtey House, and then she went off on a tangent about her co-worker's daughter's attempts to collect child support.

"Well, I hope Marie's daughter can work it out with her ex," I said. "I'm sure it's hard, being a single mom. I know it was for you. Hang tight with the inventorying."

"I'll talk to you tomorrow," she said.

I got a beer out of Jack's nearly-empty fridge and selected a vintage 45 by my favorite blues chanteuse. His amazing collection of albums took up one whole wall in the loft, facing the sofa and armchairs grouped around a glass-topped coffee table. Formerly this table had been coke-chopping central, but lately he'd been laying off it at home. I had a feeling he still did some at the studio, but I appreciated not having it right under my nose—so to speak.

I placed the record on the turntable and gently lowered the needle. Billie Holiday's "The Very Thought of You" came on, a lilting melodic swoon that was only enhanced by the crackling of aged vinyl. I went into Jack's bedroom—which I now sort of thought of as *our* bedroom—to change. As I went to brush my hair, my gaze fell upon the brightly colored lei draped over a corner of the mirror. I picked it up and put it over my head, inhaling its faint coconutty scent. If I could snap my fingers and go back in time, I'd still be lying on that sun-drenched beach, applying lotion to Jack's shoulders.

Chapter 5

SHAKE, RATTLE, AND ROLL

"Are you free for lunch? I have some news," I asked my best friend, Vicky. Even though I'd shut my office door, I kept my voice down.

"Harvey flashed an undercover cop in the park?" she deadpanned. Vicky was well acquainted with my boss's habit of harassing young women. She used to work at my company before she'd moved on to a more impressive midtown publisher.

"Even better. I have a job interview!"

"Meet me at the Athens. I can't wait to hear about it."

I left my building and walked up Park Avenue to the Greek diner halfway between our offices. Despite the slippery patches of ice, I tried to keep moving in the urban weaving-between-people stride that I'd learned to imitate. I'd also cottoned to the trick of not looking directly at people, while at the same time checking out everyone within arm's reach. The brusque tempo of New York was a far cry from the plodding pace of my small hometown, but I'd had to quickly acquire some street smarts after I'd moved here. The alternative was being eaten alive.

My face stiff from the chill wind, I pushed through the Athens' door and slid into a cracked vinyl booth, snow melting in trails down my boots. A burst of cold air announced Vicky's arrival. She came toward me, a furry babushka obscuring her eyes. She yanked it off and gave me a smooch on the cheek. "So what's this about an interview? Tuna salad, hold the fries, please," she told the waitress.

"Ted Rathbone from Hawtey House called! I'm meeting him at his office tomorrow. He'd heard that I acquired Isabel Reed, and Freeman Fyfe's agent gave me a recommendation too. Wasn't that nice of her?"

"Fantastic! What are you planning to wear?" She ran her hands through her blonde pixie cut.

"I thought my black suit with a white blouse."

"Too conservative. Hawtey likes a little more flair in their editors. Why not meet me after work and we'll go shopping for a suit? And I don't mean a second-hand throwback from Unique Boutique. Why not get one of those new jackets with the big padded shoulders? Your boyfriend will pay for it." The waitress approached with our food, and we moved our hats and gloves to make room.

"Okay, but I'll buy it myself. He gave me all those new clothes at Christmas—and about sixteen garter belts. Plus that first edition of *To the Lighthouse*; he must have spent a fortune on it."

"So what? You're living with the guy. He's rich, for Chrissakes. And you've got to do whatever it takes to get this job." Vicky took a bite of tuna salad.

"Jack was happy for me when I told him about the interview. He's probably sick of hearing me bitch about Harvey."

"He knows your boss is a letch. Do you have your resume printed up?" she asked.

I dipped a fry in catsup. "Of course. I'm not that clueless."

"Listen, you have to really talk yourself up to Ted Rathbone. Tell him how you went after Isabel's book. Brag about editing Freeman and all of Harvey's authors. Lay it on thick; this is your big chance."

"I know, I know. I'm nervous enough already. So who are you going out with this weekend?" Vicky was never at a loss for male companionship. She had dated Sammy, Jack's band mate, for a few months last summer, but broke it off when he groped a groupie at the Mudd Club. Ever since they'd stopped seeing each other, she'd been flitting from one guy to the next. She never seemed to get her heart broken, being blasé about relationships in a way I'd often wished I could imitate.

"I'm deciding between three guys," Vicky said. "One's a Wall Street banker who's kind of a bore, but he takes me to nice restaurants. The other's a starving artist who's great in the sack. The third one's a P.R. type that Emily wants to hook me up with, but I'm not sure I want my boss arranging my social calendar."

"*Emily's* setting you up on dates now?" I asked.

"She's sent me on a few. I think she views it as networking. Anyway, when is Jack's nephew coming?" She signaled for the check.

I groaned. "Next weekend. Oliver's staying for two solid weeks."

"You said he's a live wire," Vicky commented as she studied the bill.

I got some cash out of my bag. "That doesn't even begin to describe it. I'm kind of dreading it, but Jack's thrilled." I recalled what Maggie had said. "Before we left England, his Mum made this little speech about how she's getting older and she wants to know her grandchildren. Specifically, Jack's children."

Vicky's eyes widened. "You didn't tell me that. Does Jack want kids?"

Jack had once mentioned to me that he wasn't sure if he could make babies, since he'd never gotten a woman pregnant in all his years of sowing wild oats. But that was private information. "I think he might, in sort of a vague, non-specific way. But he's always in the studio or doing interviews, or in meetings about album covers and tours. And I'm in the office all day. Who'd have time to raise a child? Plus, we haven't even talked about marriage. It's way too soon for any of that."

Vicky smiled. "Doesn't sound like his Mum thinks so."

"How'd the Hawtey meeting go?" Meredith asked the following week as I put some jacket copy on her desk. I had told her in confidence about my interview.

"I think really well. They're seeing a lot of people, but Ted Rathbone wants me to come back in a couple of weeks and meet the publisher." I didn't want to get my hopes up too much, but I had a good feeling about this. "Ted seemed very friendly. Although he spent more time reminiscing about when he was editor of the Harvard newspaper, than he did asking about my own editing. But I guess it's a good sign if he wants a second interview."

"That's fantastic, Julia! I'll keep my fingers crossed. And how goes it with your handsome boyfriend?"

I knew I could trust Meredith not to tell anyone I was with Jack. I'd kept a lid on it all last summer when I first started seeing him, and was glad I had when we'd broken up in the fall. I decided to keep it a secret when we got back together, only telling Vicky and Meredith. I wanted to make absolutely sure we were really staying together before I let the cat out of the bag.

"Things are good. He's putting in long hours, rehearsing for their upcoming tour. Anyway, since he's been working so hard lately, I thought it would be nice to make him dinner one night."

Dot's comment about "the way to a man's heart" had stuck in my mind, as well as Jack's mother's heavy-handed hints about his love of home cooking. I knew that Meredith knew her way around the kitchen, since she handled most of our cookbooks.

"Sounds like a plan," she said.

"But I've never made anything more difficult than spaghetti. What would be an easy meal that I couldn't screw up?"

"Oh, there are lots of options." Meredith took off her half-rims and rubbed the bridge of her nose. "What kinds of things does he like to eat?"

"I guess pretty much anything; eggs, pizza, filet mignon. I'd like to make him something kind of romantic, but it can't be the least bit complicated."

"I know exactly what you should do. Why not make Cornish hens? They're just little roast chickens, and they look great when they're nicely browned. You could do that with some wild rice and green beans. Then you could pick up a fantastic dessert at a pastry shop. That's all you really need, along with a good bottle of wine."

"How do you cook a Cornish hen?" I envisioned myself, hair pinned up and wearing a flowing dress, relaxing jazz on the stereo, putting a delicious plate of food before Jack in a glow of candlelight.

"It's simple. You just stick it in the oven for an hour and a half, on three-twenty-five. Throw a little butter on top, then toss in some carrots for the last forty-five minutes. A ten-year-old could make it."

"That sounds doable," I said.

On the way downtown after work, I stopped at a grocery store. I picked up two Cornish hens, a box of wild rice, some butter, a bunch of carrots, and a can of green beans. I didn't bother going to a pastry shop, but on impulse I grabbed a tub of vanilla ice cream, just in case Jack had any room for dessert. I also put a foil pan in my basket since I wasn't sure if he had any poultry-roasting equipment. The little chickens were surprisingly pricey, but I figured he could get a second meal out of the leftovers. I didn't bother buying wine, as alcohol was the one thing Jack was completely stocked up on.

I felt like a real chef, getting ready to make a fancy meal all on my own. Dot had rarely cooked after my father moved out, so I'd had no training in this area. That timeframe from age fourteen to when I'd left for college had been so awful that I'd made a conscious effort to forget most of it. What I did recall of our meals post-Dad involved warmed-up pizza or a can of soup. Often I'd dined alone on PB&J while waiting for Dot to get back from the bar. But now I figured, How difficult could it be to throw a meal together, when people all over the country did it almost every night?

When the elevator opened, I could hear Jack playing something mournful. The plaintive notes lingered like the scent of burning leaves in an autumn breeze. He had stuck the guitar pick between his lips, and was strumming the strings with his fingers. I loved that intent look of his, as if the only thing in the world that existed were the sounds he was making. The only other time he got that look was in bed.

Noticing me standing there, Jack put down his guitar and came over, his shirt unbuttoned, jeans riding low on his lean hips—sexy as hell. From the way his choppily layered hair stood up in back, I knew he'd been wrestling with a new tune. I was tempted to drop everything and run my hands down his muscled chest.

"You brought groceries?" he asked, peering into the bags before taking them from me. I followed him into the kitchen.

"I thought I'd make dinner instead of ordering takeout.

Don't peek, it's a surprise."

"This *is* a surprise," Jack said, putting the bags on the counter. "I could go for something homemade."

"I'm psyched about this thing I'm going to cook. How's the new song coming along?"

Jack made a frustrated noise. "It's like pink smoke. Every time I think I'm getting close, it drifts out of my grasp. But I'm done for now; want me to put on some dirty blues? How about a little Bo Carter?" He came near and put his hands on my hips. "I'm the banana in yo' fruit basket, baby. You can squeeze my lemons, and I'ma eat yo' cherry pie," he sang in his black blues voice, making me laugh.

"Some Bo would be great. Okay, let me get going on this." I shooed him out of the kitchen. "Meredith told me exactly what to do. I'm just going to get something in the oven."

I turned the dial to 325, unwrapped the Cornish hens and dropped them into the foil pan. They make a loud *thunk* as they landed. After cutting some chunks of butter on the birds, I stuck the pan in the oven and placed the box of rice and can of beans on the counter. I put the ice cream into the freezer, which was totally bare except for a bottle of vodka. Then I took the rubber-banded bundle of carrots and started washing them in the sink.

"Now which one reminds you of me?" Jack asked, coming back into the room. He looked over my shoulder as I scrubbed.

I pretended to think about it and poked through the bunch. "This one," I said, holding up the puniest carrot I could find.

"Hey, that's the runt of the litter. Surely I'm better than that. What about this?" He pointed to a thick, nubby stub.

"Nah. Maybe this." I held up a gnarled tuber.

"Ooh, that's ugly."

"Actually, here you are." I pulled out the longest one. "Except you're much bigger around."

"Well thank you, I guess." He gave a wry grin, creating those handsome creases around his mouth. "I try to please."

"You *do* please."

"I could tell. Baby, last night you were squeezin' me john-son so—"

"I get the picture," I said.

"We could do that again, as soon as we eat." He examined the carrot. "I've always wondered what it would be like to have two," he said, stuffing it into his jeans. "How does that look?"

I laughed at the twin bulges in his crotch. "Very strange. But kind of intriguing."

He grabbed me and walked me backward. "Imagine what I could do with two of these," he said, lifting me onto the countertop. "Just think of the possibilities."

An hour and forty minutes later, I remembered the hens. "I've got to check on dinner," I said, sitting up in bed.

Jack smiled at me lazily. "Hurry back."

"No, I need to get going on things. It should be ready in about half an hour." Meredith had told me to let the poultry sit while I prepared the side dishes.

"All right, after dinner then." Jack got up to put on his

jeans, *sans* underwear as usual. "Let me know if you need any help."

I pulled his "Better Living Through Chemistry" tee-shirt over my head and went into the kitchen. I would have thought there would be a nice roasting smell by now. I opened the oven and checked the hens, but they didn't look the slightest bit brown. I felt inside the oven; *Yep, the heat's on.* Using two kitchen towels, I lifted the foil pan and put it on the stovetop. The chickens felt cold to the touch. *What am I doing wrong?* I opened the oven door and put my hand in again. Definitely there was heat. *Maybe Meredith forgot how long they take to cook.*

I put the pan back in the oven, turned the temperature up to 400, and put water on to boil for the rice. The chickens would probably be another twenty minutes, which was exactly how long the rice needed to simmer, apparently. So that would actually work out fine. I figured the green beans would only need about ten minutes to heat up. Really, this whole cooking thing seemed to be about timing.

I boiled the rice on high as the box instructed, and turned the burner down low. Only then did I notice that I was supposed to use *two* cups of water for every cup of rice. My mother never measured anything, so I didn't realize you were supposed to. *Oh well, it looks about right. I'll just boil off any extra water at the end.*

Jack came into the kitchen for another beer. "I was going to ask you to open some wine," I said. "To go with dinner."

"Sure. What are you making?" He pulled a bottle of white out of the fridge.

"Take a look." I opened the oven a crack.

"Is that squab?" he asked, peering in, his thick hair falling into his eyes. "I *love* squab. I haven't had that in ages."

"I guess it's squab. Meredith called it something else." *If he wants to call a Cornish hen a squab, that's fine with me. I wonder if a squab is a pheasant.*

"When will it be done? I worked up an appetite back there," he said, jerking his chin toward the bedroom.

"In about ten minutes." I checked on the rice; there was still a lot of water in the pot, so no rush on that. I decided to go ahead and heat up the green beans. "Can you find me your can opener?"

Jack started yanking drawers open. "I must have one in here somewhere," he said. After an exhaustive search, he concluded that he did not. "I'll get those beans out. Hand me the towels."

I gave him two dishtowels and he stacked them on the counter, then put the can on top. He went to get a big knife and jabbed it into the lid. Bean juice squirted all over the place.

"Don't hurt yourself," I warned. "It's not worth it. We don't have to have a vegetable."

"You went to all this trouble; I'm gonna get it open." Jack pulled out the knife and punched it in again. Finally he got half the lid cut through. He pried it up and poured the contents into a small pot.

"There's your beans," he said, presenting it to me with a flourish. I clicked a back burner and put them on the flame, then opened the oven door again and slid the pan toward me.

The hens, or squabs, were getting brown on the outside, but beneath the dark patches they were still pink.

"Good, they're finally cooking." I turned it down to 350. "That should be ready in a few minutes."

But over the next quarter-hour, as I moved the pan back and forth on the rack to check, they just didn't seem to be getting done, as far as I could tell. I could still see patches of pink below the skin, which was now very dark; almost black.

"Is the oven working?" I asked. "It feels like it's on, but I think it might be a hundred degrees off. This is taking forever." The water for my rice had long boiled away, and I was keeping it warm in its pot. I had turned off the beans too, as they had started to percolate in their juices.

"It worked fine the last time Sammy used it for those slice cookies," Jack said. "He put it on whatever temperature they cook at, and they were done in ten minutes flat."

"Maybe something's happened to the wiring since then. Something's definitely wrong." I slid the pan across the rack yet again, astounded to see that the meat still did not look white beneath the blackened crust.

Jack tossed his beer bottle and poured us both a glass of wine. "If they're not done soon, let's order something. I'm starving."

It was a logical idea, but it sort of pissed me off. "It'll be ready soon. You really should get the oven looked at."

Jack shrugged and took a gulp of wine. I downed mine and opened the oven door again. This time when I dragged the pan across the rack, something dripped and smoke began belching out. Quickly I slammed the door as the alarm began to shriek.

"Can you shut that off?" I shouted over the din.

Jack pulled a chair over to the wall and banged at the alarm with a spatula. It fell and hung dangling from a wire, mercifully silenced. "I'll get the super up here to fix that, and also check the oven," he muttered.

"Maybe I should call Vicky. She cooks once in a while." I went to dial her number, glad to escape from the kitchen for a minute. To my relief, she picked up the phone.

"Hi, it's me. Listen, I'm at Jack's. I'm trying to roast some Cornish hens . . . No, it was Meredith's idea," I replied. "But they don't seem to be cooking. The rice and green beans have been ready for ages."

"Maybe you didn't defrost them enough. How long did you leave them out?"

"What do you mean?" I asked. "I brought them right home and put them in the oven."

"Julia, were they frozen?"

I thought for a moment. "They did seem kind of hard."

Vicky made a strangling sound.

"Don't you dare laugh! I've spent three hours trying to make this damned meal. And now smoke's pouring out of the oven because I rubbed a hole in the foil pan, I checked it so many times." Over in the kitchen, Jack was waving a towel around.

"Here's my advice: Eat vegetarian tonight."

"I think I'll go ahead and serve them, and we'll see."

I hung up and went back to the kitchen. When I opened the oven, it emitted an odiferous puff. Jack stifled a cough behind his hand.

"I'm going to take this out and check if it's cooked enough. At least we can have the other stuff if it isn't."

I put a towel under the pan so it wouldn't leak black drippings on the floor, and put it into the sink to drain. I got out two plates, speared a charred hen onto each, and scooped a good portion of the rice and green beans on the side.

"Why don't we eat on the couch?" Jack said.

"Yes, it's way too smoky in here." We carried our plates out front, Jack pouring us each another glass of wine. I watched as he cut into his chicken and put a piece in his mouth. He chewed slowly and swallowed.

"Not bad," he said, taking a big sip of his drink. "Not much different from the last squab I had."

Heartened by his reaction, I took a bite of mine—and immediately spat it out. "Oh, that's horrible!" I seized my glass and took a huge gulp to wash out the execrable taste. Burnt to a crisp on the outside, the meat was raw and, amazingly, still cold beneath its blackened surface. "Don't eat it! You might get sick." I snatched up both our plates, took them to the kitchen and threw the meat into the trashcan. I scraped the rice and beans onto clean dishes and brought them back to where Jack was sitting.

"At least we can have the rest of our meal." I took a forkful of the rice. A gummier mess I'd never had in my mouth; gummy and, I realized, somehow still uncooked, as I crunched down on several tough grains.

"Don't bother trying to eat this." Tears came to my eyes.

"The beans are delicious," Jack said, chewing a mouthful.

"Oh, it's all awful." I jumped up and took our plates to the kitchen.

Jack followed me in. "Maybe something *is* wrong with the oven. I'll get somebody to look at it. All right with you if I order Chinese?"

"I'll have some too. It's probably not the oven; Vicky said I should have defrosted the hens first."

Jack shrugged. "That never would have occurred to me, either."

The next morning, Meredith stopped by. Quickly I slid the *Post*, my secret vice, inside a copy of the *New York Times*.

"How'd it go with the Cornish hens?" she asked.

I hesitated for a moment. "They caught on like a house on fire."

Chapter 6

KID

"Crikey, look at all the bugs!" Oliver shouted. We'd just gotten back from picking him up at the airport with Jack's driver, Rick. Although it was only late afternoon, I already felt tired. Ollie had peppered us with questions about what we were going to do ("Anything your heart desires," Jack said with a fond smile); whether he could see the Statue of Liberty ("I'm sure that can be arranged"); and if he and Jack could shoot a fish off the Empire State Building ("Err, probably not"). Once we got through the tunnel, Ollie began exclaiming about the sights on Manhattan's slushy streets.

"What's that guy doing?" He pointed to a man carrying a dripping stick with a dirty sponge taped to it.

"That's a squeegee. He wants to wipe the windshield with it," Jack said as Rick edged the car forward at the stoplight. The man followed, gesticulating angrily.

"Why doesn't Rick let him?" Ollie wanted to know.

Rick turned around in the front seat. "Because he'll only make it dirtier."

"What's he doing now?" The guy had grabbed the radio antenna and was bending it down toward the hood.

"He's upset that he didn't get a tip," Jack said as the car roared through the red light. "Next time, give 'im a fiver," he added to Rick.

Now that we were in the apartment, Ollie was gesturing wildly at the praying mantises, making the tiny green creatures scrabble to the opposite side of the mesh cage.

"That was my Christmas present from Julia." Jack went to stand beside him. "Isn't it great?"

"Can I play with them?" Ollie looked up at Jack, his brown eyes sparkling, one eyebrow lifted. If I didn't know better, I, too, would have thought he was Jack's love child.

Jack put his hand on Ollie's shoulder. "They're too young to play with, but maybe we can let one out of the cage for a while next week, when they're bigger. They're fun to watch."

"I love bugs!" Ollie shouted.

The mantises scuttled frantically into a corner, piling up on each other.

"Indoor voice, please, Ollie," I said, recalling what Sharon had repeatedly told him.

"I don't have an indoor voice!"

After a bowl of spaghetti with butter, two ice cream cones, and a giant lollipop, Oliver chased Jack around the apartment playing tag as I tried to get some editing done in the bedroom. Jack came in, panting. "I think I've finally worn him out," he said. "Time to get him to bed." He went into the walk-in closet and came out with sheets and a pillow. Although Jack's loft was huge, it had only one bedroom, so we planned to put Ollie on the fold-out couch.

"I'll come say goodnight." I put my pages aside.

"Want to read him some *Henry and Beezus*?" Jack had been working with a dyslexia tutor for several months, ever since his reading problem was identified. Now he was making his way through the Beverly Cleary novels, which I had loved as a kid. I hadn't met the tutor yet; she came in the early afternoons when I was at work. She must be really good though, because Jack had made incredible progress.

"You don't want to read it yourself?" I asked.

"Why don't you? Me eyes are a bit fagged." He switched to his native Cockney.

I got the book and went out to the couch, which Jack had already unfolded. We spread the sheets and Ollie clambered in between us. After a few pages, he climbed onto my lap to better see the pictures. I could feel his heart beating against my chest like a little wild animal's. I wasn't sure if he'd want me to, but I cuddled him close until his head began to nod. It felt nice to hold his small, warm body. Jack's arm was around my shoulder, his long lithe frame stretched out beside me.

"Let's get him tucked in," Jack whispered.

As I eased Ollie onto the sheets, his eyes popped open. "I always sleep with Budgie. Did Mum remember to pack her?"

"I'm sure she did. It's his favorite stuffed animal," Jack

said to me. He knelt to poke through Ollie's bag and then straightened up. "I don't see it in here. You'll be all right without it."

"I can't sleep without Budgie!" Ollie sat up, wide-eyed. "She's my lovey!"

"Hang on." Jack hurried back to the bedroom. I was starting to feel bleary, having gotten up at five a.m. to finish reading a manuscript. Jack came back with something yellow and frizzy bundled under his arm. "This is *my* lovey," he said. I saw what it was; the scuzzy blonde wig that was usually crammed onto a shelf in his closet. "I'll let you borrow it while you're here. It's nice and soft, isn't it?" He rolled it into a ball and tucked it in next to Ollie. "I call her . . ." He looked at me for help.

"Frowsy?" I suggested.

"Blondie," he said firmly. "Her name is Blondie."

"She's nice and soft," Ollie murmured, snuggling into the wig. His eyes began to close. Jack put his finger to his lips, dimmed the lamp, and gestured for me to follow.

"God, all day I've been dying for it," Jack said as he picked up speed. I felt the sinews shifting in his back, his shoulders flexing with tension. "I can't hold off much longer."

"Try not to make any noise," I said, grabbing him tightly.

"He won't wake up. Ahh . . ." Jack's voice became a moan. It rose in pitch as he moved faster, building toward his climax. "I'm gonna—"

The doorknob rattled. "Uncle Jack!"

I snatched at the sheets as Jack quickly pushed up off me.

I managed to cover my chest before Jack opened the door, holding a tee-shirt over his groin. Ollie burst into the room. "What happened? I heard someone crying!"

Jack plopped down on the edge of the bed. "I was just—having a dream." He rubbed his face tiredly.

"Can I stay here? Blondie's itchy."

Jack looked at me. "I don't think we'll get any rest otherwise."

"All right. But can he sleep on your side?" I whispered.

"Sure." Jack moved to the middle of the bed. "C'mon, Ollie. It'll be like that time we went camping."

Ollie scrambled onto the pillow next to Jack. "I knew this trip was going to be great!"

I awoke at my usual early hour, feeling Jack's warm hand cupping my breast. *Mmmm, he probably wants a quick toss before I go to work.* Instead of being tired, I was really in the mood for it. I stretched, arms over my head in the darkness, feeling my nipple harden as his fingers squeezed me gently. I rolled to my side to reach under the covers—and jerked away as a small body snuggled against my hip. *Oh my god, I forgot Ollie was in bed with us! He must have switched places with Jack in the night.* I removed the sleeping kid's hand from my boob and slid out from under the covers. *Good god, I almost . . . * I shook my head at the thought. *He'll have to stay on his side of the bed tonight. Maybe I can barricade myself with pillows,* I thought as I got dressed in the bathroom.

They were both still asleep when I tiptoed out of the apartment for my early-morning jog. Before I left, I tucked a twenty-dollar bill into my sneaker tongue; a New York City runner's trick so I'd have something to hand over if I got mugged. I came back an hour later, my face numb from the cold. Quickly I showered and left for work, leaving Jack and Ollie snoring lightly on the pillows.

When Jack called me at the office around noon, I told him what happened.

"He's a breast man, just like his uncle."

"That's not funny. Do you think he can sleep on the couch tonight?" I asked.

"I dunno. We can try it. I'm going to take him to Odeon for lunch, and then to the studio. Mark's going to let him bash around on the drums."

I couldn't picture Ollie sitting still for long at the fancy restaurant. "Drums sound like just the ticket," I said. "Let him get his ya-yas out."

After several days I was getting used to Ollie being at our place, but it was taking a toll on Jack. Not that he didn't love spending time with his nephew. Over the weekend we'd gone to the Museum of Natural History (Jack wearing a floppy hat so he wouldn't be recognized); to Serendipity on the Upper East Side for ice cream, where Jack got mobbed by a bunch of teenage girls; and on several outings to the studio, where Ollie was allowed to have at Mark's drums and Sammy's keyboard.

After we finished a late breakfast on Sunday, Jack got on the phone with Sammy. "I owe you one," I heard him say before hanging up. "Me knob's turning blue."

"It's only been four days," I said.

"Four and a half. Sammy's taking him to the zoo. It'll be fun for Oliver, and even more fun for me." Jack waggled his eyebrows suggestively.

I had to admit, I was ready for a little adult time too. Jack roused Ollie from his cartoon-watching and got him dressed in warm clothes. "Do they have elephants?" he asked as Jack pulled a sweater over his head.

"No elephants. But a very cool panther, I've heard."

"Why aren't you coming?" Ollie asked. Jack zipped him into his coat.

"Julia has to do some editing, and I have to concentrate on this song. It's only for a few hours," he said.

There was a knock, and Sammy entered the loft blowing on his fingers. His sandy brown hair was shoulder-length, and his soul patch had flecks of snow in it.

"Cold as a witch's ti—hey there, young fella!" He came up to Ollie and rumpled his hair. "Ready to shake up the wild animals? How are you, Miz Julia?" he asked in his Marietta, Georgia drawl.

"I'm good. Thanks for this," I said.

"Sam-my! Sam-my!" Oliver chanted, pulling on his coat-tails. "Did you bring me some sweets?"

"I may have something in here for you," Sammy said. He reached into his pants pocket and pulled out a joint. "Whoops, wrong pocket. You ready to rock an' roll?"

"Yeah!" Ollie cried.

"Don't rush back," Jack said, plumping Oliver's hat on his

head and escorting them to the door. "Take your time. Go out for lunch after. On me."

"All right, I got it. Julia, I want him good and relaxed when I get back," Sammy replied with a grin.

I blushed. "I'll do my best."

"Alone at last." Jack shut the door. "Now come here. I have a vision of what I want to do to you. You're gonna get very hot and sweaty before it's all over."

After a little nap, Jack rolled onto his back and lit a joint. "De ganja make de mon happy." He inhaled deeply, held it in for an interminable minute and then blew an acrid-smelling cloud toward the ceiling. "I'm afraid to smoke around Ollie; Sharon would skin me alive. Want some?"

"I'd better not. I have to get some work done this afternoon," I said. The few times I'd tried pot, it had really knocked me out.

"Maybe it would *help* with the editing." Jack took another big suck of the joint, sparking the tip. "Puts me in the mood to make music."

"It would put me in the mood to go to sleep. After I giggled for about an hour."

"That's what you always say. Are you ever able to read just for pleasure, or are you always thinking while you're reading? Being an editor, I mean." Jack gazed at me through his eyelashes.

"It is a little hard to turn it off, even when I'm reading for fun. I'm usually analyzing the word choices the author made. How about you, when you're listening to other people's music?"

"Nah, I can't listen without critiquing it. I'm always think-ing: How'd they do that? Or else, why on earth *did* they do that?" He held out the joint. "But you don't want to have a toke with me? Why not let go a little?"

I smiled. "I think that's what I just did."

"Yes, you did seem to enjoy yourself. Especially that last time. Something to be said for synchronicity."

I felt my face flush. "It was amazing. You do things to me that I wouldn't think were possible. No one's ever made me feel so great in bed."

Jack put his hand on my thigh and squeezed. "Good. Let's keep it that way."

Swept up in a tide of feeling, I had to say it. "Jack. I love you."

He took one last hit and put the tiny nub in the ashtray. "Me too. Although sometimes you could use a little loosen-ing up."

I was sitting on the couch, red pencil in hand, editing a bel-ly-slimming guide that Harvey had signed up. Jack was in the middle of the loft strumming his acoustic guitar, a smoldering spliff in the ashtray. He'd play the same chord sequence over and over again, slightly differently each time. I marveled at his ability to keep bashing away until it sounded right to him. Sometimes he asked me which way I thought was better, but usually I could hardly tell the difference. His ear was so finely attuned that infinitesimal changes were life and death to him.

Seeing that it had gotten dark outside, I glanced at my

watch. It was five o'clock. I wondered when Sammy and Oliver were coming back; the zoo closed at four in the winter.

Fifteen minutes later they walked in, Ollie holding a wreath of deflated helium balloons.

"I only lost track of him for a little while." Sammy peeled off his scarf.

"We saw the panther! He was sleeping the whole time," Ollie said. "And the monkeys really liked me. I fed them scads of peanuts! This old geezer told me they'd had enough, but we gave them another bag. Then he ratted me out, and I had to stop."

Ollie quit talking and got a funny look on his face. "Phoar, Uncle Jack, what's that smell? Did someone faff?"

"Your uncle was having a cigar," I said, fanning the air. We probably should have opened a window while he was having a toke, but I would have frozen to death.

"Got any more of that wacky baccy? I could go for a cee-gar myself," Sammy said.

Jack merely shook his head and helped Ollie out of his coat. "I see you got some balloons. Did you have fun?"

"Can you take me back tomorrow?" Ollie said. "I want to feed the monkeys again!"

"We'll see," Jack said. "Bring those balloons over to the sink. I know a good trick we can do."

"Here goes the last one," Jack said.

Sammy handed the balloon, dripping and bloated, to Jack, who held it out the window. "Ready, aim . . ."

"Fire!" Ollie screamed.

"Bombs away!" Jack released it, and I heard it splash on the sidewalk twelve stories below. The three of them giggled and high-fived like they were all six years old.

"That's it for the fun and games." Jack wiped his wet hands on his jeans.

"But I want more games!" Ollie cried. "I never get to do this stuff at home!"

"It's your dinnertime," Jack said. "Maybe later."

"I'd better get out while the gettin's good. I'm supposed to pick up Lara at nine." I heard Sammy mumble something to Jack, and his answering laugh. Sammy often said that he needed a steady girlfriend, but his behavior indicated otherwise. Sometimes I wondered if Jack missed being out on the town, trolling for women. But if he did, he didn't let on, and I was determined not to second-guess him the way I'd done in the past.

"Have fun," I said as Sammy shrugged into his coat.

"Oh, I will." He gave me a wink.

After we dined on sugar pops cereal, Oliver sat in bed next to Jack as he read *Henry and Ribsy* out loud. I finished loading the dishwasher and stood in the doorway for a moment. Jack's dark head was bent toward Ollie, who snuggled into his shoulder, staring sleepily at the page. *Jack's so sweet with him*, I thought. *He really would make a good father.*

Jack continued reading: "'I'm not making faces,' said Henry. 'I'm wiggling my loose teeth.'" He shut the book. "And that's it for tonight's selection."

Jack looked up, and our eyes met across the room.

Something in his expression created a well of emotion in my chest. I wanted to hold the warmth of that perfect moment—Jack cuddling Oliver, me about to get into bed next to him, the close family feeling; something I'd missed so much ever since I was fourteen—in my heart forever. I tried to hush the inner voice telling me it couldn't last.

Chapter 7

MINDLESS LITTLE INSECTS

On the way downtown, I stopped at the grocery store to get some biscuits for Oliver. He'd asked for them several times, but I didn't know what kind he liked, so I got the whack-em tube as well as a box of mix. When I got to the loft, Ollie was sitting at the kitchen table with a squeeze bottle of glue, making a sculpture out of guitar picks and Zig Zag rolling papers.

"Hi Ollie, where's Jack?" I dumped my backpack on the couch.

"Back here." Jack came out of the bedroom wearing jeans ripped at the knee, pulling a long-sleeved tee-shirt over his head. I caught a glimpse of his ridged abdomen before he drew it all the way down. *God, it would be nice to be alone together tonight.* But Oliver was still sleeping in our bed.

"I have to go to the studio. I probably won't get back 'til

one or two," Jack said. "You okay hanging out with Ollie?"

"I guess," I said uncertainly. I had planned to do a lot of work tonight, assuming Jack would be around to entertain his nephew. I also wanted to concentrate on tomorrow's interview at noon with Hawtey House's publisher, Perry Stroud. I'd never met Perry, but Vicky said he had a rep for being snooty and difficult. I wanted to anticipate any tricky questions he might ask about my resume, or the list of books that I'd edited. "Didn't you rehearse this afternoon?" I asked Jack.

"Robin had to move my tutoring session to later; she was out shopping with some friends. She didn't leave until a few minutes ago."

"How old is Robin?" From what Jack had said, I'd always pictured her as kind of frumpy; not the type to socialize much.

"I think in her thirties. Or maybe twenties, I'm not sure." Jack laid his guitar case on the couch and gently cradled his Gibson inside. "Oh, and she brought over a lasagna. Maybe you and Ollie could heat some up for dinner. I had a piece; it's really good."

"Why did she bring food? I didn't even know you liked lasagna."

Jack put on his coat. "Neither did I, 'til I tried it. She said she likes to cook."

Did Jack complain to her that I'm a disaster in the kitchen? Maybe I should meet this tutor. "What does she look like?" I asked.

"I dunno. I haven't paid much attention." He zipped the case and shouldered the strap.

"She's a stunner!" Ollie said. "But I thought she'd never leave."

"Which is what I have to do, or we'll never be ready for this tour." Jack rumpled the top of Ollie's head and gave me a distracted kiss on the cheek.

"Could you try to get home a little earlier? My interview with Hawtey is tomorrow. I need some time to collect my thoughts." I was annoyed that he'd forgotten. At times his all-consuming focus on his music made my own career seem like an afterthought. With the upcoming tour, I knew the demands on Jack were urgent—but mine were just as important to me.

"Oh, that's right." Jack gave me a guilty look. "I'll try. Patrick and I have to work out this thorny bit in one of the songs. He wants to do it his way, and I want to do it the *right* way. Same old story." Jack rolled his eyes. "But we'd better get it sorted, or they'll be throwing rotten veg at us."

I doubted that; The Floor's fans were rabid and adoring. But my concerns must seem piddling compared to letting down hundreds of thousands of concert-goers. "Well, please get back as soon as you can. This interview's really important to me."

"You'll fix Ollie dinner? He wasn't hungry earlier." Heading to the door, Jack ignored my last comment.

"Sure. And I bought him some biscuits." I pulled the tube out of the bag.

"What's that?" Oliver said.

"Didn't you say you wanted them?" I asked.

"He meant cookies," Jack said. "I'll pick some up on my

way home."

Then why didn't he say he wanted cookies? I thought as I shoved the tube in the fridge.

Neither Ollie nor I felt like having the showoff's lasagna. I slathered butter on his spaghetti, and we sat at the kitchen table with the mantis cage between us. Then he wanted ice cream, so I scooped out a big bowl. "What did you do today?" I asked as he stirred it into a chocolate soup.

"I watched TV while Uncle Jack was asleep. Then I turned up the sound, and he woke up." Oliver's big brown eyes met mine.

"He didn't get mad, did he?" I asked.

"No, just quiet. We went out for pancakes. Then we went to a record shop at Sint' Marks."

Jack liked the vintage 45s at St. Mark's Music Exchange. "Did you get anything good?"

Ollie's brow furrowed. "We had to leave because I dropped one. I didn't mean to break it!"

"I'm sure it was okay."

"The guy was mad, but Uncle Jack paid him. Then we came back here 'coz the reading lady was coming, but she was late."

I couldn't quite conjure up a picture of the reading lady. "What did she look like? You said she's beautiful?"

"She got cheesed off when I wouldn't go in the bedroom. But I wanted to play out here!"

"What color is her hair?"

Ollie scrunched his face in concentration. "Can't remember." He went back to stirring his ice cream.

"What's your favorite thing about New York so far?" I asked him.

"I liked the zoo. And the water balloons." He looked a little sad.

"Are you okay, Ollie?"

"I like it here. But I miss Mum." He fiddled with the latch of the cage.

Poor little guy; of course he missed his mother. "Want me to read to you?"

"Sure!" Oliver hopped up and went to fetch the book. He climbed in my lap as I began reading, my chin brushing the top of his head, breathing in his little-boy smell. It felt really nice, just the two of us in the quiet kitchen, the only noise the sound of my voice and the occasional scratching of the mantises. After a couple of chapters, Ollie was getting wiggly.

"Had enough for now? I can read some more before you go to sleep."

"That one's climbing on top of the others!" He put his face close to the cage.

"I'm going in the bedroom for a while to do some work. You'll be okay out here?" I was hoping I could squeeze in an hour's work.

Ollie didn't answer, so I left him gazing at the insects.

I slid into bed and stacked the nonfiction proposals on the pillow next to me. If I speed-read, I could get three or four done quickly, and also try to come up with some semi-intelligent questions to ask in my interview. Vicky had said it was a good idea to bring up a few things that showed I'd done my research on the company. I began rapidly flipping the pages.

An hour later, I still didn't hear any noise from the front of the loft. I had finished the reading, and had just started jotting down some notes for my interview. *Guess I'd better go check on him*, I thought reluctantly. I put my pen and paper aside and headed toward the kitchen. As I went past the fireplace, my foot crunched on something. I lifted my bare heel and with my fingernail, scraped off a dried piece of grass. I took a closer look—*Oh my god!*

On tiptoe I ran into the kitchen. The cage door was open. Ollie turned toward me, several mantises in his hand.

"Ollie! What did you do?"

He gave me a sheepish look. "They wanted to play with me."

"They're going everywhere!" I cried as the little green creatures hopped off the table and onto the kitchen counters, the parquet floor. I ran over and flipped the cage door shut, but only a few were left inside. *Jeez, I didn't know they could fly!*

"I'll help!" Ollie stood up.

"Don't move! Sit here." I pressed his shoulders down into the chair. "You might squish them walking around. Just sit still, okay? Let me put these two back in the cage." I took the ones he was holding and placed them inside. *Damnit!* The rest seemed in a frenzy to escape. I scooped a few off the counter, opened the cage door a crack and slid them in. Closing it, I went to snag a couple more off the floor. Those that were flying seemed to be the larger ones. Just as I nabbed a few from the glass coffee table, the front door opened.

"The power went off. A truck hit a pole at the corner of Eighth," Jack said as he propped his guitar case on a chair. "Did one get out?" he asked, seeing what I had in my hand.

"More than one."

"What happened?" Jack took off his coat and ran his hands through his hair, making it stand on end.

"We had a little accident. I was in the bedroom trying to get ready for my interview, and—" I looked at Ollie, who'd come up behind me.

"I didn't mean to!" he said tearfully.

Jack sighed. "Let me get the dustpan. We'll catch more that way."

"I'll get it!" Ollie shouted, running toward the broom closet.

"Bring it over here. I see a few on the amp." Jack had him hold the pan while he gently nudged them in. Once some of the larger groups were taken care of, we had to go after individual bugs. The airborne ones were incredibly fast; we took paper cups and chased them through the apartment.

Ollie raced around the table, his brown eyes sparkling with excitement. "This is the best night of my whole life!" he exclaimed.

Two hours later, I surveyed the living room. We had captured a lot of the insects, but I had a feeling many more were still loose. The cage didn't look nearly as full as it had before. There was no way we'd round up all the bugs by two a.m., if ever. I hadn't had any time to prepare for my interview, and now I was going to be exhausted for the big day.

"I'm going to turn in. I'm wiped out." I put down my cup and went toward the bedroom.

"Let's all hit the sack. I'll buy a butterfly net tomorrow," Jack muttered as one whizzed past his ear.

Stifling a yawn, I answered the phone yet again. I took a message for Harvey and went to the office kitchen to fix myself another mug of instant coffee. *I really need to perk up*, I told myself. My interview with Perry Stroud and Ted Rathbone was in an hour.

As soon as Harvey left for his lunch date, I bundled into my coat and took the subway up to midtown. I'd borrowed Jack's eye drops to get some of the red out, but I still felt haggard. We had chased the bugs until midnight, and then Oliver was so wound up that it was hard to get him to sleep. I hadn't been getting much shut-eye anyway with Jack in the middle of the bed, flinging his octopus arms as he tossed and turned.

I got off at the 50th Street stop and walked the couple of blocks to Hawtey House. The building was an impressive skyscraper with several security guards in the lobby; much fancier than my current office. The elevator zoomed up to the fourteenth floor, where I took a seat in the overheated reception area. The room was so warm and I was so exhausted, I almost nodded off in the twenty minutes I was kept waiting. Finally a harried-looking young woman came to escort me to the corner office. It was huge, with one window fronting the avenue and another facing uptown. A silver-haired man in a crisp dress shirt and navy blue suspenders rose from behind his desk.

"Perry Stroud," he said, shaking my hand briskly. "So you're the one who signed Isabel Reed for her memoir. How'd it turn out?"

"It needed a fairly heavy edit, but I think it's in good shape now." I perched on a chair across from his desk as he took his seat. "She's been great to work with."

"I was never a fan of her show, but I guess it was aimed at a juvenile audience. We don't do many of those B-list celebrity memoirs here." Perry crossed his arms, his pale eyes surveying me coolly.

"Well, um, it's the only one I've signed up so far," I stammered. "Ted mentioned that you want to add some more commercial books to your list."

Perry scowled. "Ted and I don't always see eye to eye on the direction of the company. We've done quite well with literary titles for the fifteen years I've been at the helm. We've had eight Pulitzers and four National Book Awards; although lately not as many bestsellers as we'd like. But I think there's a way to accomplish that without catering to the lowest common denominator." Perry paused and straightened a cufflink. "Speaking of which, Ted tells me Freeman Fyfe is a fan of yours."

I tried to ignore the insult. *Focus*, I told myself. *This is your one chance to get out from under Harvey.* "Yes, I worked with Freeman on his two most recent novels. The first one got up to number three, and stayed high on the list for several months. It's going to net over a hundred thousand in hardcover." To my satisfaction, this elicited a raised eyebrow. "His new book's coming out in August, and we think it will hit number one. I worked really hard with him on the pacing, and I came up with the title. Which he loved." I drew my resume and list of books out of a folder and handed them over to Perry, who dropped them on the desk without a glance.

"That's funny, I'd heard Fyfe's numbers were down," Perry observed. "Your publicity department must be a bit slow on the uptake. It doesn't do to get sleepy."

At the word *sleepy*, my mouth started to stretch wide in a yawn. *Stop that, you idiot!* With superhuman effort, I was able to stifle it.

"Julia! So glad you could come." Ted Rathbone entered the room, pushing his glasses up on his nose and extending his hand. "I was just telling Perry about your initiative with Isabel Reed's book. Julia read in Page Six that Isabel was doing a memoir about her sitcom years, and set up a meeting with her. After that, she signed up the book," he said to Perry. "We could use more of that can-do attitude around here."

Perry still looked distinctly underwhelmed. Frantically I tried to think of something I'd worked on that might impress him, or at least wipe that superior expression off his face. I sat forward in my seat. "I've done some serious nonfiction too. Harvey had me edit a book about the Korean War; it had fascinating research on the Battle of Inchon." I swiped at a bead of sweat on my upper lip.

"You do much military history?" Perry smirked.

"That was the first one I'd ever worked on. But it turned out well; it just got a starred Kirkus review."

"Julia's very versatile. She's done everything from—" Ted

picked up my resume and perused it. "Toilet training to diet books to astrology guides. And I see a nice range of fiction, including Roxanna Stokes." Ted's eyebrows shot up above his glasses.

"Any literary fiction?" Perry said, glancing out the window. *Why did he have me come, if he's so bored by my list?* I wondered.

Clearing my throat, I made one last attempt. "I've worked on some smaller literary novels. We don't have any big names, other than Freeman."

Perry snorted. "I wouldn't call Freeman Fyfe a big name. I thought his last book was a yawn."

Oh, no! I felt my mouth irresistibly stretching open. Cursing myself, I put up my hand and faked a cough.

"I hope we aren't boring you." Perry frowned.

"Not at all!" I said.

"Well. Anything you'd like to ask us?" He looked at his watch.

I knew I should say something, but I couldn't pull my thoughts together. "Not at the moment," I mumbled.

"Thank you for coming." They both stood up, Ted looking rather abashed.

"I'll be in touch," Ted added.

I blurted "Thanks," and rushed out. "*That* went well," I said to myself on the ride down.

"How'd it go?" Jack asked when I walked in the door. The power still wasn't back on in the studio, so he'd been home all day with Oliver. The apartment was a train wreck; dirty dishes on the counter, newspapers and cereal boxes spread around the living room, Ollie's socks and tee-shirts on the floor.

"Not too great." I shucked off my coat.

"Why not? The first guy liked you so much." Jack gave me a concerned look.

"Ted said they'd call me, but I'm not going to hold my breath. The publisher wasn't too impressed with my books. He implied that they aren't literary enough. Not to mention that I was so wiped out from last night, I practically yawned in his face. And I didn't have a single intelligent thing to ask about Hawtey House."

Jack hooked his thumb in his belt loop. "They're insane if they don't hire you. You work your arse off," he said, conveniently ignoring how last night's fiasco had affected my performance. But I was too tired to get into it.

"I guess they're looking for someone with more high-minded tastes." I went back to our room to change. Oliver was on the bed watching cartoons, an empty bowl next to him. I took a tee-shirt and jeans into the bathroom.

When I came out, Jack put his arm around my shoulder. "We have just the thing to cheer you up. Tell her, Ollie."

Ollie jumped up and down on the bed, making the spoon in the bowl clatter. "We're going to play hide and seek!"

"I promised him if he'd let me have some time with the guitar, we could play." Jack took a good look at me. "On second thought, Julia might be too tired, Ollie. We can wait 'til another night."

"No, I'll play with you. It'll take my mind off today," I said.

"Blow me!" Ollie cried, springing higher on the bed.

"Best not to say that. It means something different over here," Jack said. "Okay Julia, your turn to hide first. We'll go out front and count to ten."

After they left, I stepped into the tornado of Jack's walk-in closet without turning on the light. When I first moved in, I'd made a stab at organizing his stuff once I'd hung my meager wardrobe in a corner. But Jack simply threw everything he'd worn onto the floor, half the time missing the laundry baskets. His housekeeper was doing the wash more often, so at least at some point it all got clean.

In the dark, I squatted down under several pairs of his pants that were actually on hangers. I heard them shout "Ten!" and tucked my knees up to my chin.

"Let's find her, Oliver!" I heard their footsteps, and then rustling as they moved around the room. "Is she under the bed?" Jack asked.

"Nooo," Ollie answered.

"How about in here?" The closet door swung open.

"I don't see her." Ollie's little feet in socks were next to Jack's big bare ones.

"Tell you what. You go check out front, and I'll look around here for a bit."

Ollie scurried out of the room, and Jack came in and shut the closet door. "Hmm." He crouched and put his hands through the pants legs. "What have we here?" he said, palming my breasts. "I think I've found a beautiful girl in my closet." He stuck his head through the dangling pants. "Maybe he'll stay out there for a while." Jack sat on the floor and pulled me onto his lap. "Just sit on this for a minute."

I melted into him as his lips met mine, my stomach doing flips. *God, I've missed this . . .*

Bam! The door crashed open. "You found her!" Ollie exclaimed as we jerked apart. "Why didn't you call me?"

Jack slid me off his lap and stood up. "I was going to. Julia and I had to talk about something."

"That wasn't talking! That was *kissing!*"

Because of who Jack was, we were allowed to see Oliver onto the plane. He was in the front row of first class, looking very small sitting alone in the middle of three empty seats. Jack tipped the flight attendants to ensure that he'd be watched over, and then autographed a stack of luggage tags for them.

"We've got to leave now. Have a good flight, and mind the nice attendants." Jack checked Ollie's seatbelt and gave him a kiss on the cheek.

Ollie threw his arms around Jack's shoulders, clinging tightly. "You're aces, Uncle Jack! You too, Julia."

When Jack stood up, I saw tears in his eyes. I leaned down and gave Oliver a hug. "I'm glad you could come. I'll miss you."

"Call me as soon as you get home," Jack said. "Love ya'."

The plane's engines revved. We went down the icy metal steps and into the waiting car.

"I've got an idea," Jack said later that night. "Playing with Ollie put me in mind of it. Let's play hide and *strip*. Whenever I find you, you have to take off a piece of clothing." He grinned. "Draw it out a little."

"That sounds interesting." I was amazed he was still in the mood; we'd spent all afternoon in bed. But if he was up for it, I was game.

Jack went around the apartment turning off all the lights. He got a flashlight from a kitchen drawer. "I'm gonna count to ten out here," he called, lying back on the couch and using his hand to strobe the light on the ceiling.

In the dark, I hurried into the bedroom. The closet wasn't very original, but I couldn't think of anywhere else last-minute. Spying the empty hanging wardrobe he used for his concert gear, I stepped inside and zipped it up. *He'll never find me here*, I thought, standing perfectly still. I could feel my heart pounding in the pitch-black interior, a faint lingering scent of pot perfuming the lining.

"Aah!" I screamed, doubling over as I was suddenly grabbed at the waist. Jack lifted me up and slung me over his shoulder. Laughing, I tried to kick his butt from inside the bulky garment bag. He dumped me on the bed and slowly unzipped the zipper. "Not too imaginative," he said as my face appeared. "In fact, as a penalty, you'll have to take it all off at once."

Chapter 8

I CAN'T STAND UP FOR
FALLING DOWN

The next morning, a Sunday, Jack was unusually quiet. We ate a late breakfast in bed listening to Albert King belting out "Born Under a Bad Sign," followed by Blind Lemon Jefferson's "Matchbox Blues" and "Tight Like That" by Tampa Red. When Jack got in the shower, I stretched my legs across the mattress, luxuriating in the peace and quiet.

The water stopped, and I heard the screech of the medicine cabinet. Jack stood in the doorway, toweling his hair.

"Listen, maybe you could go off these at some point. See what happens." He held up my birth control pills.

I felt hot and cold all at once. *I can't believe it—he wants to get married! And I'd been thinking I should just enjoy it while it lasts. He really wants to stay together forever!*

A tidal wave of emotion brought tears to my eyes. My mind skipped ahead to a vision of Jack in an elegant black tux, his long hair in sensual contrast to the formal attire, waiting for me at the end of the aisle. *I'll be Mrs. Jack Kipling—no, wait—I won't change my name. We'll be Julia Nash and Jack Kipling, together for eternity . . .*

Jack was staring at me, waiting for me to say something. "Jack, I'd love to!" A big grin spread across his face, and I realized I'd better clarify. "I mean, eventually. But we'd need to do some planning, right? I mean, to figure out all the details."

He sat next to me on the bed. "What details? We could start tonight." He put his hand on my thigh.

Suddenly it hit me: *He isn't talking about marriage—he just means getting me pregnant. For all I know, he only wants to prove that he can.* Since he'd told me none of his previous girlfriends had ever had a baby, maybe this was merely a test run. My mind leaped ahead, seeing myself as a twenty-something single mother, living on child support in my narrow loft on Broome Street. An infant in a dirty diaper crawling around on the floor. Mary Jo sighing as she wrote out the monthly check. A memory of Dot intruded, sitting at the kitchen table after my father left, trying to juggle the bills.

"Actually, I'm very flattered that you'd ask, but we should probably hold off for a while. I mean, we haven't even been together for a year yet. And I'm trying out for this new job."

Jack frowned. "I'm thirty-three. Time's going by. I want to know if I can make a baby."

Typical, I thought. *He only sees it from his point of view.* "But I'm just twenty-four. And anyway, once you'd 'made a baby,' what then? Who'd stay home with it?"

Jack's deep brown eyes pooled into mine. "I've got plenty of dough. You wouldn't have to work."

I stared at him. *What planet has he been living on? He thinks I'd give up my career?* "Jack, I *want* to work. I love what I do; you know that. I feel like I was born to do it."

"Wouldn't it be great to have a little Ollie running around underfoot?" he asked.

I gulped. If we ever did have a kid, chances were, he'd be a wild child. "Right now I'm enjoying just being with you. Anyway, wouldn't that be getting the cart before the horse?"

He seemed to have no idea what I was talking about. *It's exactly as I thought; marriage hasn't even occurred to him. I guess it's too middle-class a concept for a rock star.* "Never mind. Let's talk about it some other time, okay?

Jack got up and started putting on his jeans.

"I've never even taken care of a dog, much less a child. Neither have you," I added quickly. "You said your mother fed all your pets, growing up."

He looked down at his chest, buttoning his shirt. Then he sat and jammed on a pair of boots.

"Where are you going?" I asked.

"Out." He stomped to the front of the loft. I heard him pick up the phone and call Sammy.

"Fine," I said after the door slammed. *I guess Mr. Kipling's used to getting exactly what he wants.*

After tossing and turning for hours, I fell asleep around three. But every noise from the street made me jerk awake, thinking it was Jack coming in. Finally I realized that he wasn't going to. *Is this the way he's going to react every time I don't agree with him? That doesn't bode too well for our future*, I fretted as I threw off the covers and got out of bed. It was five a.m.; the corner diner would be open. I could have breakfast there and head in to the office early. I didn't want to be here when he came back.

I passed a bleary day at work. Every time the phone rang I jumped at it, spoiling for a fight—but his call never came. *I guess his true stripes are showing; the first time he doesn't get his way about something, he bails out.* We hadn't yet discussed his habit of staying out late at bars with the guys—or, for that matter, monogamy. I had assumed it was part of the package of living together, but maybe that was just another of my middle-class ideas—like the concept that one might get married before one got knocked up.

Several times I picked up the phone, then slammed it back down. *Why should I call him? He's the one who started it!* Suddenly my indignation turned to despair. *Jack is the first man I've ever been so intensely in love with. I'll never feel this way again. Am I insane to throw away what any other girl would give her eye-teeth for?*

Then I caught myself. *My entire identity is wrapped up in being an editor. Who would I be, if I gave up my career?* Sure, the more established editors were able to leave the office at 5:30 and go home to their kids, but I was just starting out and had to prove myself. It took a while to acquire a strong list of books, and that involved late nights and long weekends spent editing. How could I do all that and deal with a baby too? And as much as Jack seemed to think he wanted one right now, would that turn into one of his spur-of-the-moment ideas that he'd later wish he could back out of? If so, where would that leave me?

Exhausted from second-guessing, I forced myself to stay late at the office. I didn't want to seem anxious to see him, and also I dreaded the showdown. At eight I trudged home from the subway in yet another heavy snowfall. Nervously I pushed open the door.

Jack was sitting on the couch, an open whiskey bottle on the glass-topped table. He nodded at it. "Want a shot?"

The casual comment made my blood boil. "Where'd you go last night?" I kicked off my dripping boots.

Jack looked surprised at being questioned, but that was too bad. "I hit a few bars with Sammy," he said, coming over to me. "I got in at five. I must have just missed you; the bed was still warm."

I crossed my arms. "So, we have a difference of opinion about a huge thing—especially for me—and you just leave? Does that mean we'll get along great, as long as I agree with everything?"

Jack ran his hand through his hair. "I was ticked off. You're entitled to your opinion."

As if we were deciding what to have for dinner. "We're talking about my career—something that would change my whole life."

"I know." He gave me a dark look. "It's *always* about your career."

"It's just as important to me, as yours is to you—hard as that may be to believe. Besides, if you walk out on me over one disagreement, I'll *need* a career to fall back on. Because our chances of staying together aren't looking too good!" Hot tears surged behind my eyeballs. *Don't cry,* I told myself. *You'll seem weak.*

"Do you know how many girls would—" He stopped himself.

"Would what? Be dying to have your baby?" Jack shrugged, but I knew that was what he meant. "Maybe you should be with one of them. A sweet, fawning admirer who goes along with everything you say. I'm not that person, Jack."

"*That's* for sure. If I wanted that, I could've had it a million times already. But I like a challenge." He gave a wry smile. "And you're definitely a challenge."

I thought about that for a moment. "I'll take that as a compliment. I guess."

"But seriously, don't you ever want children? You can still do your editing."

"You don't know how much it means to me. It's not some little pastime," I said heatedly.

"Sure I do," Jack said. "I see how you slog away at it. It's the first thing you think of when you wake up in the morning, and the last thing you do before you go to bed."

"Not necessarily the last thing." To try to make peace, I reached out and gave him a little squeeze.

Jack put his hands on my shoulders. "I'd take care of you, baby. You wouldn't have to worry about supporting yourself."

I pushed his hands away. "What is this, the 1950s? Am I

supposed to have dinner waiting on the table, or something?"

"A pot roast wouldn't be bad, once in a while." Seeing my expression, he added, "You know I'm kidding. But I think you care more about your work than you do me."

"That's not true. Anyway, why does it have to be one or the other?"

He gave me a contemplative look. "All right. I admit I shouldn't have left last night. But I want you to think about it. No pressure." He lifted his hands. "Just give it some thought."

I didn't want to say I'd already thought about it. "Okay. I will."

Chapter 9

GIRLFRIEND IS BETTER

⟩ ══⟨

"Wow, so he wants you to have his baby." Vicky gulped the last of her margarita and signaled for another. The Broome Street Bar was rowdy tonight, jukebox booming, packed with its usual artists and downtown types. "You said he was impulsive, but that takes the prize." She licked salt off the rim of her glass, her catlike green eyes reflecting the light from the mirrored bar.

"Having Oliver stay with us must have triggered it. But he hasn't even mentioned marriage. And I'm just starting this new job."

I had been shocked when Ted called to offer me the position at Hawtey House; I'd given up hope after Perry Stroud had acted so unimpressed in the interview. I had a sneaking suspicion that maybe their first choice hadn't accepted. But, I told myself, perhaps that was just Perry's personality.

Maybe he'd warm up to me once he saw how hard I worked. Regardless, I was on cloud nine. I'd be a full editor instead of a junior underling, and finally free of the mind-numbing clerical duties. Bidding adieu to Harvey would be the icing on the cake.

Jack had been genuinely thrilled for me, and had a bottle of champagne chilling when I got in last night. We'd dressed up and gone to Caliban for dinner, and later he made the most amazing love to me. I thought the baby thing might come up again, but he didn't mention it. We had survived our first big spat as a live-in couple; I wondered how long the air would stay cleared.

"Earth to Julia." Vicky waved her hand in front of my face. "Does Jack understand how hard it is to move up? Practically nobody's hiring with this recession."

"He knows Hawtey's my big chance." I stirred my vodka tonic with a finger and licked it. "But he's eight and a half years older than me, and he's reached the height of his profession. So for him, the timing's great. But then again, maybe having a kid is something he *thinks* he wants, but hasn't really thought through."

"And what Jack wants, Jack gets." Vicky narrowed her eyes. "Too bad there isn't some way to compromise." She scooted her stool closer to make room for a guy with THIS SIDE UP tattooed on his neck.

"I've worked so hard to get this new position; I can't let it slide through my hands. I'm going to have to acquire like crazy, and my first list of books will just be coming out next year. Besides, I am so not ready to have a baby."

"I guess there *is* such a thing as a nanny," Vicky commented.

I raised my voice as the jukebox got louder. "I'd love to have children eventually, if we stay together—but now isn't the right time. Oliver is cute, but boy, is he a bundle of energy. I almost blew the interview, I was so wiped out from chasing the bugs he let escape. Apparently Jack was the same way when he was a kid." I thought for a moment, and smiled. "Actually he still *is* pretty energetic."

"I'm not even going to ask what you mean by that, Ms. Nash." Vicky crossed her long skinny legs on the stool. "On that topic, did I tell you, I had the strangest experience last week. I was at a party for an author at the Explorer's Club, of all places. His book is about Alaska. Everyone had to pose for pictures in front of this huge stuffed polar bear." She rolled her eyes.

Vicky's publicist job often took her to glamorous places, but she'd become jaded. "That sounds kind of cool," I said.

"These two different guys in suits kept coming over to talk to me. I was just focused on shmoozing the critic from the *Times*. But it was like they were competing for me, or some-thing." Vicky acted as if she was surprised, but she'd been hit up like that before.

"Not a new situation for you. So what happened?" I asked. A Pretenders song blasted from the jukebox, and I swayed my foot to the beat.

"The party was wrapping up, and I went to get my coat. The first guy started walking me to the door. I just figured he was leaving the same time I was. Then when we got outside, he had the nerve to say, 'I knew you were going to go home with me from the minute I laid eyes on you.'"

"What a jerk!" I downed the rest of my vodka.

"Luckily the second guy came outside right then. I looked at the first one and said, 'No, I'm not. I'm going home with *him*.' I walked over to the other guy, and we got into a taxi."

"Did you really go home with him?" I hoped the answer was "no".

"Nah, I wasn't that attracted. I asked him to drop me at my place. He wanted my number, so I gave it to him." She reached for her wallet. "I may see him this weekend, or I may stay in and catch up."

"Let me pay. I'm feeling flush with my new salary." I put some bills on the bar. "The only downside is that now I'll have to take the subway to work, since it's too far to walk. Jack offered to have Rick take me in the mornings, but can you see me getting out of a car with a driver?"

"Why not? *I* wouldn't have a problem with that," Vicky said.

"Everyone would think I had a sugar daddy. I'm still keeping it a secret that I'm with Jack. If people found out, they'd think that was why I got the job."

Vicky made a face. "Jeez, Julia, you and your scruples. Anyone else would be shouting it to the rafters."

The next morning, I went to tell Meredith about my job offer. She put down her watering can and hugged me.

"I'm so thrilled for you! That's great; you really deserve it. But I'm going to miss you around here. Promise me we'll have regular lunch dates?"

"Of course we will." I felt a little teary-eyed.

"I'd love to be a fly on the wall when you tell Harvey," she said. "And I hate to ask, but I need one last favor. Could you edit this book on Ayurveda before you go? I've sat on it for three weeks already."

"Sure thing, I'll start on it tonight. What's Ayurveda?"

"A kind of yoga technique. It'll be a good topic to have under your belt before you head off to Hawtey," she added. "They have some woo-woo on their list."

Harvey turned pale when I told him. "You aren't even giving me a chance to make a counter-offer," he said in a testy tone of voice. "I can't believe you're jumping ship before we publish Isabel's memoir."

"I have to take this opportunity. I'm sure you understand," I replied coolly.

He frowned. "Hawtey House has pretty high standards. Are you sure you're up for it?"

"I think they want to broaden their range beyond pure literary stuff. Anyway, they must think I can handle it if they hired me." I relished his look of chagrin. *Now that I'm leaving, he's ready to give me more money. Well, he can take his counter-offer and shove it!*

"Be sure to tie up all the loose ends before you go," Harvey said with a scowl. "And don't think you can come crawling back here if it doesn't work out."

"I wouldn't dream of doing that." *Jerk.*

Jack was in an amorous mood that night, but I barricaded myself in the bedroom with the Ayurveda manuscript. After an hour of trying to parse the author's headache-inducing prose, I went out to where he was sitting on a stool, shirtless. He was strumming a Muddy Waters tune on his electric guitar, wearing headphones—or "cans", as he called them—so I could concentrate. I put my hand on his shoulder, and he slipped them off.

"All done?" he asked with an anticipatory look.

"Could you come here for a minute? I could use your help with something."

"Sure, baby. I could come here," he said, putting his hand between my legs, "or here," tracing my lips with his finger, "or anywhere you want. But it'll take more than a minute."

"Let's hold that thought for now." He propped his Telecaster on a chair and followed me into the bedroom. "Can you lie down? I need to try to figure out all these confusing chakras," I said.

"I'll do it if you take your top off," Jack bargained. He stretched out on the mattress and put his hands behind his head.

"Deal." I shrugged out of my blouse, leaving on my bra. I took the manuscript page with the diagram and placed it on his bare chest. "Let's see. There are seven chakras: the crown, brow, throat, heart, solar plexus, navel, and root," I mused, comparing the illustration to the page of text in my hand. "But here he calls it the third eye—no comments, Jack—so that has to be fixed." I marked the page with my pen.

"People really believe this crap?" Jack asked.

"It's huge in California. All this stuff starts out there and then spreads east, like a virus. Okay, he says the energy centers are also in the hands and feet, but he's left that off the chart." I made a notation on the page resting on Jack's chest. "The channels can be blocked—"

"I think one of mine is blocked," Jack said, starting to turn toward me.

"Hold still for a second. There are thirteen srotas or body channels: the rasa vaha srota, rakta vaha srota, mamsa vaha srota . . ." I looked from the text to Jack's supine form, trying to make sense of the mumbo-jumbo.

"How do they expect you to keep all this straight?" Jack asked. "One week you're editing a book about thinner thighs; the next, it's this bullshit."

"Meredith said that if I want to get ahead, it's good to be a generalist," I replied. "Hold on—the marmas are the pressure points. You make a gentle circular motion to release toxins." I revolved my finger on his stomach.

"Ooh, that tickles. Hey, I have something that needs to be released." He pointed to the bulging crotch of his jeans.

I sighed. "This is supposed to relax you. Can you try to focus on your toes now? I need to see if this pressure point aligns with your feet."

"Sorry, baby. I'm trying, but it all seems to be going to my cock."

"You're hopeless," I said, laughing.

"Actually I'm hope*ful* that you're done with this for the night."

"I'm almost finished. Let me just make a few more notes." I took the chart off his chest and perched next to him.

Jack sat up and rifled through the rest of the manuscript.

"This looks interesting." He showed me a diagram.

"That's a yoga pose. The downward dog."

"I even like the name of it; the doggie pose. I can definitely get into that," he said, taking the pages out of my hand. He stood up and grabbed me, turning me around and hiking up my skirt as I giggled. "My chakras are already feeling better," he added, pulling my underwear to the side. "Now my mamma-slamma is gonna jamma into your sweet little mamsacunnahasa . . ."

Half an hour later, a fine sheen of sweat covered my skin. We sat perfectly still in bed, looking into one another's eyes. My legs were wrapped snugly around Jack's hips, his thighs supporting mine. My entire body felt like it was singing. We were pressed so close together that every time his muscles tightened, a pulsing started in my core. I gave a sharp intake of breath as another ripple surged through me.

"Did Caroline teach you this?" I gasped.

"Shhh. What does it matter?" Jack whispered. He licked a drop of sweat as it trickled down my cheek.

"Did she?" I insisted.

"Caroline couldn't spell 'tantric'. It was a chick from Berkeley. Now shhh."

He pulled me even closer. I couldn't have uttered another word.

My eyes popped open at seven-thirty. I tried to ease off the bed without waking Jack, but he reached out and grabbed me by the waist.

"Where do you think you're going?" he asked, locking his hands so I couldn't get up.

I rolled over to face him. "I'm late as it is."

"Don't go in today. You've been working all hours." I adored his British pronunciation, saying *bean* for *been*. "Why don't you call in sick?"

"I have so much to do." I was torn; he looked so handsome with his thick, disheveled hair and sleepy-lidded eyes, dark lashes brushing his cheekbones. I felt like kissing my way from the hollow of his neck to his nipples; running my tongue down his taut abdomen, pausing for a moment to tease him . . .

"Call in sick. Just once." He sucked on my earlobe, giving me an involuntary shiver.

"I really should go in," I breathed, picturing all the stuff piled on my desk.

"Let me call for you. What's Harvey's number?"

It's so tempting to stay. After all, what can they do to me? I'm leaving in a week.

"Give me the number," he growled. "Or I'll have to extract it from you."

I smiled. "Okay." He reached for the phone and dialed as I recited it.

Jack cleared his throat. "Harvey Lowenthal, please."

I rolled my eyes; this had to be a disaster.

"Hello. Julia's not feeling well. Uh-huh. Very hot to the touch." He moved his free hand down my belly and slid a finger in me. I bit my lip to keep from laughing. "She probably does have some type of fever." He made eyes at me, finger pulsing. "Yes, I've been giving her plenty of liquids." Evil grin. "I'll be sure to give her lots more hot liquids. She might be in tomorrow; don't know yet."

He hung up the phone. "I've given you lots of nice liquids this week, haven't I?" he said, climbing on top of me. "I think he fell for it."

I wrapped my legs around his waist. "I don't know, *hot* liquids might have been a tipoff."

"See, I have a vast amount that I've been storing up for you. And I really need to give them to you," he said, beginning to move over me. "It'll make us both feel muuuch better. But I don't know how much it'll cool you off."

Later, hair wet from our shower, we went into the kitchen. Jack was humming the Muddy Waters tune bare-chested in his jeans as he made breakfast. I poured some juice and took a bite of my eggs, which were delicious. "It's weird not to be at work in the middle of the week," I said. "I've never played hookey before."

"We've got to break you of that habit. You know what they say; all work and no play." Jack sat down and stirred his tea.

"After what we just did, I don't think you can say I'm 'no play.'"

"That's for sure." Jack put down his spoon and looked at me. "Why don't we get a dog today?"

"A *dog*?" I repeated.

"You said neither of us has ever taken care of one. I figure we could try." He crossed his arms and tilted his chin in a challenge.

I thought about it for a minute. *Maybe a pet would take his mind off impregnating me.* "I guess I could take it out early in the mornings when I go for a run. Then when you get up, you could walk it again. Could we find one that's medium-sized?"

Jack smiled. "I'm sure they'd have whatever size we want."

On the way home from the SPCA, the large black puppy threw up twice. Rick handed me some paper towels, and I dabbed at the leather seat as Jack murmured soothingly and stroked its head. From the minute its nose poked through the bars of the cage, we'd been hooked. "Reminds me of the time I got busted," Jack said with a grimace as he carried the dog to the waiting car. "We had to break you out, didn't we, buddy?" The attendant had said it was a terrier mix, but given the size of its paws, I had a feeling it might be part Lab.

Inside the loft, we sat on the floor as the puppy bounded back and forth between us. Suddenly it squatted and made a big puddle. I cleaned it up as Jack hooked it to the leash. "We'll have him trained in no time," he said as the dog lunged into the elevator.

While Jack was out, I called Dot. We caught up for a few minutes, and I told her our latest news.

"A puppy! What for? You're at work all day," she exclaimed.

I wasn't about to get into the baby thing. "Jack had a lot of dogs growing up. And he really misses Oliver, so this will sort of fill in the gap."

"When are you going back to England? It would be good to spend more time with his mother," she said.

"He hasn't said when he's going back. They're getting

ready for this big tour, and I'm joining him midway through. I only have one week off now, with the new job."

"I'd try to get more time off, if I were you. You know all those girls will be throwing themselves at him."

I didn't need to be reminded of that. "I can't ask for more. I was lucky Ted would give me a week, so soon after I start. I kind of implied I had a family commitment."

"I guess it's better to make your new boss happy. You don't want to be left hanging if it doesn't work out with Jack," she said direly.

There she goes, always looking on the bright side. "I'm aware of that, Mom."

"I don't know that living with him is such a good idea," she continued. "You know what they say: Why buy the cow when you can get the milk?"

I pictured Jack surrounded by a bunch of mooing heifers. "I know, you've told me that before." *Many times.* "But it was kind of the next step."

"The next step would be a wedding."

Another theme she liked to harp on. "We'll see. And there's something else: Jack wants me to get in touch with Dad."

There was silence on the line. "Your father? Why?" Dot finally said.

"He thinks it would be a good idea, since I haven't seen him in so long. I'm not sure if I'm going to, or not. But if I decide to, do you have an address for him?"

"That's a *horrible* idea," she said emphatically. "And I don't have his address."

I didn't know whether to be relieved or disappointed. "Well, I guess that takes care of that."

"I'd tell Jack to drop it. I'll talk to you later; I'm meeting some people at Buck's." She hung up before I could say goodbye.

As I cradled the receiver, something caught my eye. I went over to pick up one of the concert tickets that had fallen out of the mirror's frame. FOUR TO THE FLOOR: LONG BEACH ARENA, Saturday July 18, 1971. *That's the year I was fourteen,* I realized. The year my father had left.

I stuck the ticket back into the frame and stared at my image in the mirror, wondering if he'd even recognize me anymore. I had changed a lot from that gawky, skinny girl with glasses. He'd never even seen me since I'd gotten contacts; when my eyes had come out from behind those thick lenses. Back then, I was still my insecure Pikesville self. The new me hadn't even started to emerge—not that I was the picture of confidence now. But I *had* managed to move to New York on my own, get a job in publishing, and make my way in an incredibly tough city that could chew you up and then spit out the mangled pit. And whether from indifference or other reasons I couldn't even imagine, my Dad had opted to miss out on all of that. *So why am I thinking of pursuing him?* I asked myself. *Just because Jack wants me to?*

My father is 45 now, I realized. He'd been 21 when he and Dot had me, and he was 35 when he left. *When he moved out, he was only two years older than Jack is now,* I realized with a start.

Just then, Jack walked in the door. I knelt and the puppy

trotted over, leaving wet brown footprints in his path. "Did you have fun?" I asked as I petted its damp head.

"He's a gas." Jack threw his coat over a chair. "What do you want to name him? I thought maybe Bhang. Or Ozone." He folded his long legs and sat on the floor next to me.

"I was thinking more along the lines of Othello. Or Icarus."

"Too fancy. What about Ribsy?" Jack said. "Good boy. Down." The puppy was standing on its hind legs, paws on his shoulders.

I looked at the wet tracks leading from the door. "What about Muddy?"

Jack lay back and the dog climbed onto his chest. "You wanna be Muddy?" he asked as it started licking his ear. "All right then." He held the puppy's head and looked it in the eyes. "Muddy it is."

Chapter 10

COLOR ME IMPRESSED

"First off, welcome to Julia Nash, who's joining us as editor." Ted pushed his glasses up his nose and nodded in my direction.

"Thanks. It's good to be here," I said shyly as everyone seated at the long conference table turned toward me. I was used to a much smaller group; here, fifteen people were gathered for the weekly meeting. A few smiled, some looked indifferent, and one or two looked positively unfriendly. I'd heard that the editors at Hawtey were pretty competitive with each other; Meredith and Vicky had both warned me to watch my back. But anything would be better than being a glorified secretary to a grabby boss.

The meeting began as the editors took turns bringing up books they wanted to pursue. Ted commented after each person made his or her pitch. The atmosphere did seem less collegial; more snarky and sharky. One attractive woman in particular seemed to shoot down everyone else's projects. When it was over, I went back to my window office, complete with a brand-new IBM Selectric typewriter and a big ficus plant. Jack, Vicky, Meredith, and Suzanne, the wife of Floor drummer Mark, had each sent me bouquets, so my room smelled like a florist's shop. I sat behind my desk and got ready to call a long list of agents to make lunch dates.

"Julia. I'm Erica Graham." It was the woman who'd put the kibosh on everyone's projects. She looked to be in her early thirties, had shoulder-length brunette hair, close-set eyes, and an aquiline nose. She struck me as very cool and polished in her fitted suit and heels. "I'd heard Ted had hired someone new, but he was being secretive, for some reason." She gave me a dismissive glance.

"Nice to meet you." I watched as she took in my bare bookshelves.

"Did you bring any of your authors over with you?" she asked pointedly.

I started to say that I only had a few of my own, but her haughty expression made me catch myself. "They couldn't get out of their contracts, so no. I didn't bring anyone with me. I'm looking forward to starting with a clean slate."

Erica seemed to consider this. "I suppose there's something to be said for a clean slate." She gave a little smirk as she left.

I was waiting at the elevator to go out for a deli salad, having sworn never again to eat lunch from another vending machine. A woman with curly brown hair pressed the button. "They take an eternity in these durn skyscrapers," she said. "I'm Cathy. I'm two doors down from you, in what's known as the manuscript graveyard."

I laughed. "Nice to meet you. This building's so much fancier than what I'm used to. My old office had only eight stories, and the carpet was circa 1960."

"You won't think it's so slick when there's a power outage." Cathy rolled her eyes. "That happened twice last year, and we had to walk down fourteen flights. Want to grab some lunch?"

"That would be great!" I was happy to have an invitation on my very first day. Cathy took me to a shoebox of a sushi place, and over California rolls we found that we had mutual acquaintances. We also compared notes on the literary agents we dealt with, and by the time we got back to the building, I felt that I'd made a new friend.

As we waited with a large group of people in the lobby, Perry Stroud came forward and pushed the elevator button. The door opened and I started to get on, but Cathy grabbed my arm. "Perry doesn't like anyone to ride up with him," she said under her breath. Sure enough, everyone who'd been waiting at least ten minutes held back; the door closed, and Perry rode to the eighteenth floor alone.

We all crammed into the next car, at the last minute making room for a woman wearing pink bedroom slippers. "Thanks," she gasped, edging in sideways, her hands bracing her beach-ball belly.

"How's it going, Brenda?" a guy asked.

"Only two months left 'til my due date. I'm gaining five pounds a week, but at least I've finally gotten over the morning sickness. Or should I say, the 24-hour sickness."

Everyone nodded politely as she got off on her floor.

"That's Brenda from accounting. She's had a rough time with this pregnancy," Cathy commented.

"Why was she wearing slippers?" I asked as we exited the elevator.

"Water retention. Her feet have gone from a size seven to ten and a half." Cathy stopped, listened, and then darted down the hall at the sound of her phone. "Stop by later!" she called over her shoulder.

The phone was ringing when I got home. I almost tripped over Muddy in my rush to answer it. "Jack?" said a woman's voice.

"He's not here. Can I take a message?" I asked, but the line went dead. Ten minutes later it rang again, and this time I was pleased to hear his half-sister on the line. Usually Sharon called Jack in the afternoon, given the time difference.

"You're up late, aren't you?" I asked. It was seven here, so it must be midnight in England.

Sharon sighed. "I couldn't get Oliver to bed. He keeps going on about the balloons in New York. Where did you get them?"

She sounded deeply exhausted. "Sammy bought them at the zoo; they were regular helium balloons. Did he tell you Jack filled them with water and they dropped them out the window?" I knelt, letting Muddy bump against me.

"Oh yes, he's all about wanting to do that. I keep telling him it's a different effect from two floors up, versus twelve. Did you ever catch all the mantises?"

"I think we got most of them. They're really fast; it could have happened to anyone."

"That's nice of you to say. Well, I'm going to try to get some sleep. Tell Jack I'll call him later this week. I hope we'll see you again soon, Julia."

"I'd really like that." I hung up and got Muddy's leash. "Come on, puppy. Let's go for a walk."

After we finished our takeout, I remembered to tell Jack about Sharon's call.

"I'll ring her tomorrow. But I promised Oliver I'd write to him." He put a piece of notepaper on an album cover and scrawled his message in capital letters. At the bottom, he drew a picture of a scruffy guy holding a guitar, and I added a P.S. about our puppy. "You really should try writing to your father," Jack said, licking the thin blue airmail envelope. "Does Dot have an address for him?"

The thought made my stomach clench. "She said she has no idea where he is."

"You know, my own Dad died three years ago, and I always regretted not getting to know him better. He didn't think much of my being a musician; thought I should get a *real* job. Even when I started making scads of money, he didn't really approve." Jack patted the couch, and Muddy jumped up onto his lap. "And he definitely didn't approve of the lifestyle. So we had our differences. But now I really regret not spending more time with him." Jack looked at me, his depthless dark eyes reflecting the low lamplight. "It might be good for you to track down your father; get to know him as an adult. Isn't it time you heard his side of the story?"

My mind was churning. I didn't want to stir up all the hurt, which I had thought I'd managed to tamp down. I had only made my peace with my mother last November, after years of blaming her for the divorce and all the bad things that followed. When Dot revealed that she hadn't had an affair with her boss—that my father had just been irrationally jealous—suddenly the man I'd put on a pedestal all my life fell to earth with a loud crash. Did I want to get involved again with someone who'd falsely accused his wife, and then abandoned his only child?

"I have an idea." Jack broke into my reverie. "Why don't I have Mary Jo hire a private detective to find him?"

"I wouldn't want to bother her with that. It's way outside her job description." And to be honest, I didn't want his manager poking around in my personal life. She and I had reached an uneasy truce since I'd moved in with Jack, but I'd never forgotten the look she gave me backstage at a concert last summer. It was one of deadly envy, as in: *I would feed you a poisoned apple if I could just get my hands on one.*

Jack frowned. "Her job is anything I ask her to do. I'm curious about the guy myself; it sounds like he had good taste in music."

I had told Jack some of my memories of my father: sitting with Dad on the front porch of our old house, listening to 45s on the record player he'd given me. Being swooped up in his arms and dancing whenever a great Motown song came on the radio. My favorite night of the week—Saturdays, when Dot was moonlighting as a cocktail waitress—when Dad would put me on a stool in my pajamas and wash my hair. I'd always felt closer to him than to my impatient and less cuddly mother, which made it even harder to believe it when he left me behind.

"Maybe you're right," I said. "But what if we find him, and he doesn't want to see me?"

Jack gave my thigh a squeeze. "Let's burn that bridge when we get to it. C'mon, Muddy," he said to the snoozing dog in his lap. "Let's go to bed. I'm zonked."

"Should we put him in the crate, like the shelter said?" I asked.

"Nah, let's let him sleep with us. I always had a dog in my bed growing up."

Chapter 11

EVERY DAY I WRITE
THE BOOK

"When I was editor of the Harvard newspaper, I always went with my gut," Ted said. I'd gotten used to his habit of working his Ivy League education into almost every conversation. "So if you're excited about this little book, go ahead and make a modest offer. Somewhere in the ten-thousand range. We have a hole in the upcoming list; we can rush it out and plug it in there."

I stared at Ted; at my former company, a "modest offer" was a couple grand. I'd felt a tingly premonition when reading the self-help manuscript, which was only a hundred pages long, and aptly titled *Little Things Can Be Big*.

"And be sure to get world rights. Our new rights director is champing at the bit for things to sell at Frankfurt this fall," he added, referring to the big book fair in Germany.

"Okay, I'll try." Thrilled to be making my first offer since I'd arrived at Hawtey, I got on the phone with the agent. Fifteen minutes later I was the proud owner of a guide to appreciating the smaller things in life, which often led to larger opportunities. The agent told me to go ahead and call the author, so I had a nice chat with the friendly insurance salesman from Omaha who'd written the whole thing on his days off.

I stopped by to tell Cathy my news. "Congrats! You're off and running," she said. "Take a look at this." She handed me a xeroxed form with Perry Stroud's name at the top.

"Perry's expense account?" I asked, wondering why she had it.

"His assistant asked me how to code it for accounting. Look at item number four."

I gazed down the list; lunch with this agent, that agent . . . *Boy, he spends a lot on meals.* Number four seemed to be a dry cleaning bill. "He puts his shirts on his expense account?"

"And see what he put for the 'Purpose' column? *To look good.*" She laughed.

"Huh. I guess that's one of the perks of being publisher," I said. "Along with riding up in an empty elevator."

Cathy nodded. "That isn't the half of it."

I was returning from my own agent lunch when a tall, well-dressed man jumped into the elevator at the last minute. "What floor?" I asked, since I was closest to the buttons.

"Fourteen. The same as you." The man seemed to look me

over. He was very handsome in a polished way; dark wavy hair, piercing blue eyes, open jacket with a crisp light blue shirt, Italian loafers. His tanned face seemed familiar. Suddenly I realized that it had been staring down at me from a huge poster in our lobby. Dermot Chase was one of Hawtey's biggest authors; that rarity who wrote highly acclaimed literary fiction, yet also managed to sell by the bucketload. His last novel had spent four months high up on the bestseller list.

"I don't recognize you from my last visit," he said, extending his hand. I shook it quickly, feeling nervous.

"Nice to meet you. I'm Julia Nash, the new editor. We're all big fans of your work here," I said, edging around the fact that I hadn't read any of his recent books. I had only made it through one of his novels years ago, and thought it was kind of pretentious.

"My previous editor has left for greener pastures," Dermot said. "It's good that Hawtey's getting some fresh talent. It doesn't do to get stale."

He held the door for me as we went into the lobby. "Good luck with your next book," I said in parting.

He smiled. "I expect I will get lucky."

I'd spent half an hour returning calls when my line buzzed. "Can you come in for a sec?" Ted asked.

"Sure." I grabbed a form that I needed him to sign and rushed down the hall. I was surprised to see our big author sitting in his office.

"Dermot tells me you met in the elevator, but I wanted to introduce you formally," Ted said, pushing his glasses up his nose. "Julia is the bright new star in our galaxy."

I flushed at his overstatement. "Nice to see you again."

"Dermot wants you to work with him on his next novel," Ted said.

"Oh, that would be great!" Incredibly flattered, I wondered what Ted told him about me. He'd probably mentioned that I was Freeman Fyfe's editor at my former house.

"Perfect," Dermot said, standing up. "I'm running off to do an interview for *The New Yorker*, but call me tomorrow and we'll set up a time to get together. I like to dig in and revise from the ground up." Dermot waved Ted off when he started to escort him, saying he knew his way out.

"I'm so excited," I said to my boss. "Thank you."

Ted frowned. "I'll have to finesse it with Erica. Initially she was assigned to him. She's already met with him several times."

I was confused. "Then why switch?"

Ted looked a little embarrassed. "Dermot was pretty insistent about working with you. I don't think there's any way around it now." He sighed. "Erica's going to have a conniption."

"I don't want to cause trouble." I dreaded starting off on the wrong foot with this woman, who seemed super-confident and aggressive in ways I couldn't even imagine. I'd hate to make an enemy in my very first month. And if Dermot wanted me to be his editor based on a chance meeting in an elevator—well, that was weird. But maybe his agent had heard I was a whiz with a red pencil.

"I'll fix it with Erica," Ted said. "You should set up a

meeting with Dermot as soon as possible. He requires a lot of hand-holding, and we paid a king's ransom for this new novel. It's slated for next spring, and of course it's late. So you're going to have a very full plate for the next few months."

I licked my dry lips. "I'll do my best."

The apartment was quiet when I got in. I opened a beer to have with the slice of pizza I'd picked up on the way home, assuming correctly that Jack wouldn't be there. I poured some kibble into Muddy's bowl and grabbed the phone on the third ring.

"Still swotting away at those manuscripts?" came a distinctive British voice. Suzanne and I had bonded last fall during my ups and downs with Jack, and I counted her as a real friend. Jack was great buddies with her husband, Mark.

"As always. How are you?" I asked. "Are you getting any painting done?" Suzanne was struggling to be an artist, along with the full-time job of managing and coddling her wayward spouse—who definitely walked to the beat of his own drum.

"The artwork has taken a backseat to getting Mark ready for the tour. Has Jack had his concert wardrobe dry-cleaned yet?"

I was surprised at the question. "I don't know. Doesn't Mary Jo handle that kind of thing?"

"She may have assumed you're doing it. Don't worry, I'll make sure it happens. Listen Julia, I wanted to talk to you. Is there any way you can come for longer than one week? It really gets crazy on tour; it would be good for Jack to have you there from the start. And you could help me keep the guys sorted." She paused, and I heard the flick of her lighter. "Plus you and I would have a great time together," she continued. "Mary Jo doesn't have much of a sense of humor, y'know? And I'm so sick of Patrick's ditzy tarts. He picks one up at every stop. Or two or three."

"I wish I could. I know it would be fantastic, but I can't get more time off." I took a sip of beer and scratched Muddy's head.

"That's what Jack said, but he seemed kind of ticked off about it. I thought I'd give you a heads-up, woman to woman. There are packs of girls with sharp claws, eyeing the guys like a piece of meat. I'll try to keep tabs on Jack, but it won't be easy." She took a puff of her cigarette. "I can't tell you what that scene is like; you have to live through one to believe it. Women bribe security and turn up naked in their dressing rooms with suitcases full of drugs—you name it."

This was sounding worse and worse. "Thanks for letting me know." I tried to get a grip. "I guess I'll just have to hope for the best."

"Okay, but don't say I didn't warn you."

I told her goodbye. Having lost my appetite, I fed my slice to Muddy.

Chapter 12

BAD TO THE BONE

"Surprise!" Dot crowed into the phone. I was making tea and toast for yet another solo dinner that Friday night, since Jack was still at the studio.

"Surprise what?" I crooked the receiver under my chin so I could spread the butter.

"You'll never guess where I am."

"Um, you're borrowing Buck's phone to make a call?" I pictured the cord stretched across the beer-splattered bar at her favorite watering hole.

"I'm in the Big Apple!" she exclaimed.

I sank into a chair. "Why—how did you get here?"

"I rode up with Darrell in his eighteen-wheeler. We've just started seeing each other."

I couldn't quite take it in. This past fall my mother had caught a ride with a trucker named Darrell who'd had a delivery in New Jersey. From there, she'd taken a bus into Manhattan to visit me. But I couldn't believe she was here now—and with a date. "Where are you staying?" I asked.

"A hotel on 42nd Street. Darrell got a deal on this place; a buddy of his stays here when he's passing through," she said.

"Mom, Times Square can be dangerous. What kind of hotel is it?"

"I didn't catch the name. Don't worry, there are lots of women coming and going. Some of them are dressed really fancy; Broadway actresses I guess."

They may be on Broadway, but they probably weren't in that profession. "How long are you staying?"

"Just two nights. I have to be back at work Monday. Darrell suggested we pop over here after he dropped off a load of lawnmower parts in Scranton."

I had a bad feeling about this. "Have you told him I'm seeing Jack?"

"I might have mentioned it. Don't worry, he's more into country music. I'm not sure he's even heard of Four to the Floor."

He's been living in a cave for the past fifteen years if he doesn't know The Floor, I thought. "So, what's the plan?"

"The plan? I'm planning to see you, of course. And Jack. He told me to come back and visit New York again soon. That was when you were in the bathroom at the luau."

I'd have to clue him in that Dot took everything literally. "Jack's not here right now. Why don't I take you and Darrell out for dinner?"

"We're going to stay in tonight; Darrell's pretty tired from all the driving. But tomorrow let's walk around downtown, the way you and I did last time. I want to show him the sights, especially that Washington Square Park. I told him about some of the crazy stuff we saw. He's dying to see it for himself."

"Sure, we can do that. Jack will probably be busy, but I'll take you around," I said.

"Well, I hope he can at least have dinner with us. I did tell Darrell he was going to meet a famous rock musician."

Just what I suspected. "Okay Mom, I'll try to arrange dinner. But please tell Darrell to be sort of low-key around Jack. He doesn't like kissing-up. He doesn't like talking about himself at all, especially to people he doesn't know well." I'd seen Jack clam up the minute he got a whiff of flattery; it really wasn't his thing. Unlike their lead singer Patrick, who seemed to soak it up like a dehydrated fern.

"Oh, I'm sure Darrell will be low-key. He's seen it all, driving his truck from coast to coast. He's a grown man, not some screaming teenybopper."

"Just one more shot to show the guys. They're not gonna believe this."

We were standing on an icy patch of sidewalk outside the Erotic Bakery in the Village. Darrell took yet another picture of the window display, which featured cannoli penises, strawberry tart breasts, and an array of other body parts done up in pastry. Then he handed Dot the camera and posed as if cupping one of the tarts, a lascivious grin on his face.

I'd already had my fill of Darrell. All morning he'd been

broadcasting his opinions about the clogged traffic, the weird people, the piled-up garbage, "the beggars" (as he called the homeless), and anything else that caught his eye. I was kicking myself that I'd forgotten the Bakery was on this block; we'd been stuck there shivering for twenty minutes while Darrell got his pictures. And from his comments about women passing by, he obviously considered himself a connoisseur of the female form. Which was pretty annoying, since his own figure was that of a bantam rooster: short, spindly legs topped off by a barrel chest, red face, and bulbous nose with spidery purple veins. Dot had said he was only a few years older than she was, but based on his looks, he had her beat by a decade.

"All right; why don't we move along?" I suggested. "Do you want to see some of the galleries on West Broadway? There are some great vintage shops on Prince Street. Or there's Canal Jeans, if anyone needs a new pair of jeans," I added desperately.

"Why don't we sit in one of these ca-*fés* and have a beer? My dogs are dead." Arms crossed high above his protruding belly, Darrell shook out his right foot, then his left.

"Okay," I said. "Let's have a light lunch, since we'll be having a big dinner." Jack was coming along tonight, after all. Darrell had stated that he only ate fried meat, and Mary Jo had found a West Village pub called Texarkana that served it.

"I can handle a big lunch." Darrell patted his belly. "No problemo."

"Darrell has a huge appetite," Dot said, making eyes at me.

After our meal, I flagged a taxi and dropped the love-birds off at their hotel. As I'd imagined, it was swarming with prostitutes. I had tried to convince them to let Jack pay for a room at the Plaza, but Darrell wanted to stay put. Dot ran upstairs and came back holding a pie that she'd baked for Jack at home and brought along with her. Unable to summon a cab for the return trip, I had to wend my way down the snowmelt-slippery steps and through the turnstile of the Times Square subway, cradling the cling-wrapped dish. The platform was jammed with panhandlers; I would have given the pie away, except Dot never would have spoken to me again. Holding it high so it wouldn't get jostled, I shoved off the train at Astor Place and made it to the loft by four. To say I dreaded tonight was the understatement of the century.

"I thought you said she was dating a man." Darrell eyeballed Jack, who was still wearing his sunglasses as he followed the maitre d' across the crowded restaurant toward our table. "That longhair looks like a girl."

"It's the style for these rockers," Dot said. "He's really very masculine."

"Shh!" I hushed her. Dot jumped up and gave Jack a big hug. Darrell remained seated, so Jack reached over to shake his hand, then sat between me and my mother. He took off his shades and rubbed the bridge of his nose. "So, did you take in the sights this afternoon?" His accent sounded even more British compared to Darrell's drawl.

"Julia dragged us all over Greenwich Village." Dot shook a cigarette out of her pack, and Jack held out his lighter.

"Yeah, we nearly froze our butts off," Darrell said. "But I did get to see your famous bakery."

Jack looked puzzled. "We passed by the Erotic," I said.

"Oh, that place." Jack signaled to the waitress hovering nearby. "Someone gave me a bunch of those things for my birthday once. Very lifelike, but they tasted awful."

A woman in a low-cut dress exposing creamy cleavage came over to take our drinks order, first informing us that her name was Serena, and that she was thrilled to be serving us tonight. Jack asked for a bottle of whiskey along with our beers, and Serena quickly returned with the drinks. She leaned over much farther than necessary to put the bottles down, making Darrell's eyes goggle.

"So you drive a truck," Jack said. "What's a typical route?"

Darrell reared back in his seat. "Hotlanta, the Big O, Beantown. Sometimes I haul out to the Big Shaky." He noticed Jack's confused look. "That's what we call Los Angeles."

"Oh, I love L.A. Do you spend time out there?" Jack asked.

"Nah, usually I have a return load. I just pop a few West Coast turnarounds and head right back cross-country."

Jack's antenna went up. "What's a turnaround?"

"You'd probably call them bennies," Darrell said.

"I'm familiar with those," Jack replied with a reminiscent air.

"Forty-two that, good buddy. Anyway, the last time I was coming back from the Left Coast, hauling a big reefer load, a Kojak with a Kodak pulled me over. I was doin' eighty in a double nickel."

"You carry *reefer* in your trucks?" Jack sat up straight in his seat. "Do you ever sell to individuals?"

"Negatory." Darrell shook his head. "A reefer's a refrigerator trailer. That cop got me with hand-held radar hiding behind his unmarked vehicle. Gave me a ticket for going twenty-five over the limit. I *told* him I was going into a downstroke."

"Ah, a double nickel's the fifty-five speed zone," Jack said. "I get it."

The waitress sashayed over. "I hope everything's all right." She took up Jack's empty beer bottle, nudging his shoulder with her breast.

Jack leaned away slightly. "It's fine."

"I'll be right back with your dinners," she added, not bothering to remove our empties.

"I think somebody likes you." Darrell grinned.

"Not my style," Jack said. "But very friendly."

"Roger that," Darrell said.

"I'm Jack. Roger's in The Who," Jack muttered.

"I hear you're going on tour soon." Dot ground out her cigarette in the bread plate. "Will you be anywhere near Pikesville?"

Jack nodded. "We've got a gig in Philly. I can have Mary Jo send you tickets if you want."

Dot sighed. "Erwin probably won't let me have off. But give me the date, and I'll ask."

"I'm not into rock," Darrell declared with a burp. "I'm a country man, myself."

"I dig country. Especially the older stuff," Jack said. "Johnny Cash, 'Ring of Fire.'"

"My favorite's 'If Love Was Oil, I'd Be a Quart Low,'" Darrell opined.

"I'm not familiar with that one," Jack said.

Serena appeared with our meals. As Jack picked at his overcooked prime rib, Dot pushed away her catfish platter. "I brought you something," she said to Jack, reaching into her purse. She pulled out a few faded photographs and passed them to him. "I thought you might like to see some pictures of Julia growing up."

"God, Mom, that's terrible." I recognized the third grade class photo of me with light blue cat-eye glasses, bangs chopped high on my forehead, my new front teeth far too big for my mouth. "Let me have it." I made a grab, but Jack swatted my hand away.

"What year was this?" he asked me.

"I was eight. I think that's the worst picture I ever took."

"That's some haircut," Darrell said, leaning in to look. "Who did that to you?"

"I did," Dot admitted. "We couldn't afford a beauty parlor."

"Good thing you didn't go into that line of work," Darrell said. "I'm gonna hit the little boys' room." He lumbered off toward the back of the restaurant.

"And here's one of her in high school." Dot passed another picture over to Jack.

My mother must have spent hours searching for the most ghastly photos she could find. In this one I wore the ubiquitous bell-bottoms of the era, skinny as a toothpick, thick brown glasses curtained by long, middle-parted hair. *Dorked-out hippie* would be a kind way to describe it.

"Couldn't you have found something a little more flattering?" I asked.

Dot shrugged. "I looked and looked, but this was the best one of the bunch."

Jack held the picture close, scrutinizing it. "Does Julia take after her dad?"

Dot shook her head emphatically. "Oh, no. He was really good-looking."

Jack cocked an eyebrow; I could tell he was trying not to laugh.

"Thanks a lot, Mom," I said.

"I was just telling Julia she should try to get in touch with him." Jack leaned back in his seat.

"Why would she want to do that?" Dot's furrowed brow caused a perverse resentment to rise up in me. Why *wouldn't* I want to find someone I'd once been so close to, I couldn't imagine spending a day apart from him? Who I'd run to meet in the driveway the minute he got off his shift at the factory? Who'd introduced me to the love of music that had shaped a huge part of my life?

"She could get to know him again. See what he's been up to," Jack said as he signaled for the check.

"I have no idea where he is now," Dot said. "It was really hard on Julia when Paul left us. I doubt it would do her any good to look for him now."

"Maybe he's missed me too," I blurted out.

"You always thought your father could do no wrong." Dot's expression hardened. "But it's time you faced the facts. It's been ten years, and he hasn't called you once. What does that tell you?"

Jack spread his hands. "All I'm saying is, maybe the guy has his reasons. It's worth finding out."

Dot frowned at the photos like she'd been dealt a bad hand of cards. "Anyway, that was Julia back then," she said as she stuffed them into her purse. "Now don't order dessert, Jack. I made you a pie. Julia took it home this afternoon," she said as Darrell returned to the table.

"You carried it all the way from Pikesville?" Jack asked.

"It sat in my nice warm lap the whole time in the truck."

Jack initialed the check and left some cash for Serena. Since he didn't bother carrying credit cards, all the bills went to Mary Jo. He donned his sunglasses, and we hurried past the other diners whispering and pointing. Luckily Rick was waiting nearby with the car; a big crowd was waiting to get into the restaurant, and people started to recognize Jack as he went past.

As we sat stalled in Times Square traffic, Rick caught up with Dot, whom he'd met on her previous visit to New York. Darrell just glowered out the window. Finally we pulled up in front of their garish neon-lit hotel. Dot kissed both Rick and Jack on the cheeks, and climbed out.

"Tomorrow we'll get our own ride," Darrell said as he slammed the door.

Jack laughed. "I guess Bubba doesn't like competition."

"What an asshole," Rick said. "Why is your mother seeing someone like that?"

"So how's my downstroke?" Jack paused mid-motion. I gazed up at him, my hands gripping his shoulders.

"It's amazing," I breathed. "But god, Darrell's awful. I haven't been subjected to one of her Romeos in a long time. I'm glad they're leaving tomorrow."

"He didn't seem to be into the city all that much. Or your mother, for that matter."

Suddenly I wasn't in the mood for lovemaking. I slid away from Jack and turned toward the wall. "What did I say?" he asked.

"Nothing. It's just depressing to see her with someone like that. It reminds me of all the awful men she went out with after my father left."

Jack turned me over to face him. "You said she got around. I know that was hard on you." He regarded me with his fathomless brown eyes.

"She always seemed so desperate, like she'd do anything to catch a man. Picking up guys from Buck's, and god knows where else." I winced at the memory. "I couldn't believe my Dad never came back for me. It was like the rug got pulled out from under my whole life." I didn't mention what had always run through my mind: *If your own father doesn't want you, then why would anyone else?*

Jack traced the curve of my cheek. "It was pretty bad after my own Pop left, too. After they split up, Mum had to take a full-time job. I hated coming home from school to an empty house. I always told myself I'd make enough money so my own kid would never have to do that."

This gave me a queasy feeling. Was he saying he wouldn't have a child with someone who had a career? "Did Maggie like working?" I asked.

"She loathed it. She would've loved to have been home with me, but it wasn't until awhile after she remarried that she could quit. Sharon was little, but by then I was a teenager." He scowled. "I moved out before her douchebag of a second husband threw me out. Then after *they* divorced, I was able to buy Mum the house she's in now." I lay there in silence, taking it all in.

"So." Jack took me by my shoulders. "Are we gonna look for your Dad, or not?"

"Let me think about it some more," I said.

Chapter 13

POPSTAR

Unzipping my coat, I stuffed my damp gloves in my pocket as the elevator whooshed up to the penthouse. I hoped Jack was home, but I knew the band was in furious preparations for their upcoming tour. According to him, rehearsals had been anything but smooth.

I pushed through the front door and stopped in my tracks. A woman was on the couch with Jack—*Oh my god! Her head's in his lap!*

Jack turned around and saw me. He pulled the woman up to a sitting position.

"Julia, this is Robin." He got up and came over to me. "She felt something in her hair. I thought it might be a mantis."

The tutor—who was very attractive, I noticed—was calmly gathering her papers from the coffee table.

"Did you find anything? Or did *she* get what she was

groping for?" I asked as Muddy anxiously circled us.

Robin was pulling on her coat. I took a good look at her; lush brunette hair and plenty of curves under her clingy sweater. Jack had always implied she was rather plain. Tucking in her scarf, she glanced at me.

"Lesson's over; we've done *everything* we wanted to do," she said with smug emphasis. "That was great, Jack. I'll see you Thursday." She brushed past me on her way out.

Well, bully for you. I stared at Jack. I figured he wasn't dumb enough or sleazy enough to fool around with someone in the loft, particularly since he knew I'd be home at any minute. But I was interested in what he'd have to say.

Jack sighed. "It wasn't what it looked like. She felt something crawling in her head." He gave a wry smile. "As opposed to giving *me* head."

"That didn't look too good. In fact, that was the definition of 'compromising position'." I put my hands on my hips. "What if I'd come in five minutes later; what would I have seen then?"

"Keep your knickers on. Nothing happened." Jack crossed his arms.

"Did she keep *hers* on?"

"C'mon, Julia." Jack turned on his heel and went toward the kitchen. "She's helping me with the reading. That's all there is to it," he said as he opened the refrigerator. It was annoying that he thought he could just blow off my concerns.

"What would you do if you came home and found *my* face in some guy's lap?"

"What d'you think? I'd kick seven shades of shit out of

him." He rummaged in the fridge and returned with a bottle in each hand. "Here, have a beer. Tell me about your day." He indicated a spot next to him on the couch, but I sat at the other end. From his fleece-lined bed Muddy warily pricked his ears.

"My day went pretty well until I found you two together," I said.

"Look, if I was going to fuck somebody, it wouldn't be her." With this not-entirely-reassuring statement, Jack snapped his fingers. "Come here, Muddy." The puppy trotted over. As I stroked his soft black head, he buried his nose in my crotch.

"Hey, dog, that's my spot." Jack pulled Muddy away by his collar. "What happened at work?" He took a gulp from the bottle and fixed his deep chocolate gaze on me.

I took a swig of beer. "My day was almost as exciting as yours seems to have been."

Jack made a "keep it rolling" gesture, so I resumed. "Today I got *Little Things Can Be Big* into production, since we're rushing it out. And I didn't get a chance to tell you with Dot around, but I got assigned a new author. New to me; not to Hawtey. One of our big bestsellers."

"That's great, Julia. Who is it?" Jack put his arm around my shoulder. Even though I was used to his touch, it still sent an electric jolt through my body. I took in his sexy five o'clock shadow; his long dark lashes that would seem almost pretty if not for his decidedly masculine features. *No wonder he melts women in all seven continents*, I told myself. *Not to mention his uppity tutor.* The thought of her made me decide to do a little lesson-teaching of my own.

"This writer's a real big shot: Dermot Chase. He's our most important author, in fact. I ran into him in the elevator, and he decided on the spot that he wanted me." I waited a beat. "To be his editor."

Jack removed his arm. "How old is this guy?"

"I'd say early forties. You've probably seen his picture in the paper; he's really photogenic. They always run huge ads whenever he has a new book out. I have to set up a meeting with him right away. He said he likes to work very closely together." *Put that in your bong and smoke it*, I told him mentally.

"I thought they just send the manuscript to you, and then you mark it up."

"With a big author like him, I guess it's pretty hands-on. I'll probably have to meet with him after work," I said. "But since you're in the studio so late most nights, it won't really matter. I imagine I'll be home by the time you get in."

Jack frowned, but what could he say? It was pretty much tit for tat. "Do you want to order something for dinner?" I asked.

"Patrick's coming over. We have to nail down some details about the tour. Mark and Sammy will probably stop by, too."

My pulse leapt; I dreaded having his world-famous band mate here. Patrick always seemed to look down his nose at me, assessing me with contempt and slight disgust—the way you might examine a stray hair floating in your soup. Of course that hadn't kept him from trying to seduce me in a restaurant bathroom last summer, but I'd always thought that was just a way to get Jack's goat. The two of them seemed to be in an ongoing competition over—as Suzanne once put it—everything from who got the hottest girl to who wrote the best lyrics; who had the coolest clothes to who could hold the most liquor.

"What time are they coming?" I got up to feed Muddy, thinking maybe I could take him out for a walk to avoid Patrick. The puppy leaned against me as I reached for his dish. Something was sticking out of his mouth. I held his chin and removed—*ugh!*—a small green matchstick. Quickly I tossed the mantis leg into the garbage so Jack wouldn't see.

"I've already fed him, and he's done his business. On the rug again, but I cleaned it up," Jack said.

"Oh. Okay." *Too bad—that would have been a great excuse to vacate the premises.*

"Patrick should be here any minute. For a while there today at the studio, we were working on this new song." Jack got a faraway look in his eyes, as he did sometimes when talking about music.

"Have I heard this one yet?"

"No, it's brand new. But it's really coming together. When Patrick and I can just sit down and play, without all the bullshit . . . It's like when two strings are vibrating on different wavelengths, but eventually they come together and get in tune. When that happens, it's the best thing ever— even better than sex." Jack smiled. "And you know how much I like that. I wish it could be that way all the time with him."

"It must be amazing when it is," I said.

"Yeah, but he always claims I come up with better stuff when I'm gutted. I wrote 'Bent, Not Broken' in that frame of mind." He named The Floor's saddest ballad about having lost love and even the will to go on. "Sometimes I do think I write the best songs when I'm knocked-down and drug-out," he continued musingly.

Assuming he hadn't felt that way lately, I wondered how it affected his songwriting. Or his feelings about me.

The buzzer from the doorman sounded, and Jack went to answer it. A few minutes later, Patrick came in. I could smell his cologne from across the room; a signature scent that Jack said he had specially made up for him in Paris. Patrick unwove his cashmere scarf, took off his coat and tossed his fur hat on the table, smoothing his perfectly feathered blonde hair.

"Fucking freezing out there," he said in his upper-crusty London accent. He removed the sunglasses he'd worn to avoid being recognized in the lobby. Despite the wintry chill, he had the year-round tan of the extremely privileged.

"What else is new. Did you bring the tape?" Jack asked.

Patrick plopped down on the couch and pushed Muddy away from his wool pants. "Shit. I thought you had it."

"I left it there, since you wanted to redo your vocals for the trillionth time." Jack sat in an armchair.

Patrick's blue-green gaze flicked over me. "Fetch me a drink, will you sweetheart? Gin with a dash of bitters. D'you have any Tanqueray?"

"Get your own. You know where it's kept," Jack said as he stretched his legs.

"I'll get it." I'd rather keep busy than have to make small talk with his cranky lead singer. I fixed the drink, going heavy on the bitters, opened another beer for Jack and brought it over with the bottle of whiskey I knew he'd want.

"We've got to finalize the stops on the tour. Should we bother with Ohio this time around? It's so inconvenient." Patrick took his drink without thanking me, and handed Jack a typed itinerary. "We could fly right over, go straight from St. Louis to Philly."

"We could do. But the fans would probably riot," Jack said.

"That's just 'coz you like Cincinnati Patty." Patrick smirked.

Jack glanced at me. "That was Sammy."

The door banged open. "Patty's a complete minger!" Mark waltzed in, Sammy in tow. "It's Dallas Alice that's the mutt's nuts." The men tugged off their coats as Muddy barked. I went over to calm him down.

"Hello, luv." Mark kissed my cheek and rifled the snow out of his spiky yellow hair, exposing dark roots. *Suzanne needs to give him a touch-up,* I thought. They had met when she was a stylist in London, but she had long since stopped working in salons. Now she only practiced on Mark, changing his hair color every few weeks.

"Hello. Is it still snowing?" I asked.

"It's cold as a lawyer's heart," Sammy drawled. He grabbed me, leaned me back and pretended to make out with my neck as I giggled. "Come on, you know you're tired of that limp teabag over there. Time to try a Georgia king snake, baby."

"Lay off her," Jack growled. "She's had a long day at work."

"How's the new job?" Sammy asked, releasing me.

"It's great. I just signed up my first book: *Little Things Can Be Big.*"

Sammy stared at me. "You mean like those ads in back of the *Village Voice*? I didn't know your company did that kind of thing."

I laughed at his shocked expression. "No, it's nothing like that."

"Ignore him, his head's in the gutter," Jack said.

"Got any Vitamin T?" Sammy asked, sprawling in a chair. "I need some lubrication."

"I'm fresh out of tequila; pass him the Wild Turkey. We've been having a chin wag about the schedule," Jack added.

"I thought it was all set." Mark grabbed Patrick's drink off the coffee table and drained it in one gulp. Sammy lit a huge joint and handed it around.

"It still needs finessing." Patrick took a hit and gave it to Mark.

"He's changing it up last-minute. Just like the lyrics," Jack said.

"You two aren't still on about that, are you?" Mark poured shots of whiskey and opened a beer. I settled into a chair as they discussed the tour. Patrick only wanted to do twenty-five cities, complaining that his voice wouldn't hold out, but Jack was pushing for thirty.

"If I can get it finished, I'll do my new song in the middle of the set," Jack said. "That'll give you a break."

"Oh, that. I guess you could, if we're desperate for something to fill in." Patrick looked distinctly underwhelmed.

Jack glared at him. "Don't bite your arm off."

"Yeah, show a little enthusiasm." Mark passed the joint and scratched his head, sending his roosterish yellow hair pointing in all directions. "Did you hear Nicky Headon's leaving The Clash? They've kicked him out 'coz he won't give up the junk."

"Who cares?" Jack flicked an ash and rubbed it into his jeans.

Patrick looked bored. "How sad to hear of such a ... schism."

"Bless you!" Sammy said.

There was a knock at the door, and I got up to get it. A tall, stick-thin redhead in a long leather coat strode inside. "I was working on a painting and lost all track of time," Suzanne said, bussing my cheek. As I took her coat, the men continued their conversation.

"Let's leave them to their bitching." She followed me into the kitchen and I poured us both a beer. Suzanne made a face as she sat at the table, so I moved the mantis cage to the counter.

"Bugs give me the willies," she said. "I hope Jack appreciates you indulging his twisted ways."

"I don't mind, as long as they stay put. How's the painting coming along?" I asked.

Suzanne tsk'ed. "This is the first time I've done any in over a month. With all the concert preparations, I just haven't had time. And Mark's such a sodding infant: *Where's my orange jeans? Can you touch up my hair? Did you order the nylon-tipped drumsticks?* She ran her hand through her spiky red layers, her skeleton earrings swaying.

"I hope you'll be able to get back to it, once the tour's over. Your opening was so great." I'd attended her first solo show at a gallery on Spring Street last fall.

Suzanne picked at the bottle's label. "It's driving me crazy. I feel like I had my big breakthrough, but now I'm back to ironing Mark's shirts. How about you? You seem to have time to work, and also be Jack's love slave." She smiled, showing upper gum in a way that was appealingly childlike.

"I guess. Although lately the work part seems to be overtaking the romantic part. By the time he gets home, I'm usually sacked out. Then of course he's asleep when I leave for the office in the morning."

Suzanne touched my hand. "Well, I admire your drive. But keep in mind that these guys are big babies. They expect everything to happen *when* they want it, *how* they want it— almost even before they've *realized* they wanted it. 'My wish is your command' type of thing."

I hadn't really seen that aspect of Jack yet, but she seemed to know what she was talking about. "Okay, forewarned is forearmed, I guess."

"Hey, Suzie! Can you bring us more beer?" As if on cue, Sammy's voice came from the front of the loft.

"And another whiskey!" Mark called out.

"See what I mean?" she said. We grabbed a few bottles and took them to the men.

Patrick stood and smoothed down his pants. "I've got to go. Stephanie's picking me up at eleven." He named the most recent supermodel in his collection. "Later, you lot." He fitted his hat on his head and grabbed his coat. Sammy hummed "Somewhere Over the Rainbow" as the door closed.

"*Stephanie's* picking me up," Mark imitated in a high-pitched voice. "It's not like she's all that hot. Why'd you let him cut back on the tour?" he asked Jack. "It doesn't make sense, if people want to see us. He's always got to throw a spanner in the works."

"Better to let him think he's getting his way, while he's still at 98.6," Jack replied. "I'll tell Mary Jo to leave it as it was."

"Who told him he's in charge?" Mark said.

"You know Patrice; he always wants to control everything. And I just want to *lose* control." Jack stretched his arms over his head and yawned.

"That's for sure," Sammy said. "All right, I'm gonna make like a prom dress and take off." He took one last big draw of the roach—the third or fourth of the evening—and rose to get his coat. "Julia, I don't know what you see in these crumpet-suckers. Any time you get bored, you've got my number."

"And I'm gonna make like a dog and flea." Mark petted Muddy's head and got up to go.

"Both of you make like birds, and flock off," Jack said. Suzanne blew him a kiss, hugged me goodnight, and ushered Mark and Sammy into the elevator. I could hear the echo of their voices singing "Love Me Tender" as it descended.

After they left, I started dumping the ashtrays, the fug of pot making me a little woozy.

"Just leave all that," Jack said.

"I don't want Muddy to get hold of it." I gathered the bottles and took them to the kitchen counter, the puppy at my heels. "So how *was* Cincinnati Patty?"

"Oh, that was our last tour, two years ago. Those backstage types aren't really my speed." Jack came up behind me and nuzzled my neck. "Not like my Pikesville Coupe-de-Ville. She goes from zero to eighty in under three minutes."

"Don't those Cadillacs have huge rear bumpers? That doesn't sound too attractive." I turned around and pressed my body into his.

"You're a Rolls, baby. Now let's roll on back to bed."

"What does that feel like?" Jack moved up beside me and propped his head in his hand. "I've always wondered what it's like for a woman. You make so much noise; I love watching you writhe around."

My face flushed. "I don't know. My body sort of lifts out of itself. It's like I'm floating high above the bed."

"That sounds kind of trippy. It looks so intense." He traced an infinity symbol around my nipples.

"Oh, it is," I said. "It's like wave after wave of the most intense pleasure I've ever had."

"I picture a flower opening up." Jack spread his fingers wide. "And I'm a honey bee, drowning in pollen."

"How about you?" I asked, curious about what he'd say.

"I see colors; yellows and reds. Bursting all over. Sometimes I hear snatches of music." His warm brown eyes regarded me. "Lately I've been picturing what could happen if we let those little swimmers up there. Give 'em a chance."

"But I've just started a new job. That would be like asking you to get pregnant right before you go on tour."

"I wouldn't mind that." Jack rolled off the bed and pulled on a tee-shirt. He stuffed a pillow under it, grabbed a guitar and strummed it over the bulge. "See? Piece of cake."

I laughed, relieved he was making a joke of it. Barking, Muddy leaped up and tugged the pillow out from under his shirt. Jack switched off the light and got into bed. After a moment, he turned toward me.

"Hey. Mary Jo's found a private detective to try to locate your dad. All right with you if I give her the go-ahead?"

God, I'm really not ready for this. But he isn't going to drop it, I realized. "Okay. But if he finds him, it's up to me whether or not I want to contact him. Right?"

"That's right. For now, it's just to see where he is."

"I guess it'll be good to know for a fact that he's still alive. Even if I decide not to get in touch." I was pretty sure I wouldn't want to take that step.

"I'll tell her to hire him, then." Jack reached over and turned off the lamp.

As I listened to his breathing even out, I thought about what it would be like to see my father again. Would he have a good excuse for not writing or coming to visit? Had he been injured or incapacitated in some way, so he couldn't even call? But I knew that wasn't very likely. As I pulled the covers up to my chin, a memory hit me of my father tucking me in at night when Dot was working late. The faint scent of his aftershave as he leaned in to kiss my forehead. The way he'd pause in the doorway and say, "Goodnight, sweetheart." That always made me feel so safe, as if nothing in the world could hurt me.

I punched my pillow and turned to face the wall. The last birthday of mine that he was there for was the summer I turned fourteen. I always felt so unattractive with my thick glasses, but he'd tried to build me up. "You're my beautiful girl. Someday you'll wake up and see how pretty you are." "You're so smart, Julia. I know you're gonna go places." For my present that year he'd made me a bookshelf, smoothly sanded and lacquered, sturdy enough to hold encyclopedias. After he left and we had to move to a much smaller rental, Dot made me leave it behind.

Chapter 14

LET IT BLEED

"Hello? Oh, hi, Mom," I said, stretching the cord so I could sit on the couch. "No-no, Muddy." I removed the coil from his mouth. Our teething puppy had gnawed everything from table legs to armchair corners. Jack now had to be careful where he laid his guitars.

"So you still have that dog?" Dot asked. "What does it do while you're gone all day?"

I scratched Muddy's belly as he stretched out next to me. He really had grown in the past two weeks; Jack thought he might hit sixty pounds eventually. "Oh, he chews stuff, mostly. Sleeps in his bed. He's so cute, though. He gets super excited when one of us comes in the door."

"I don't know why you wanted a pet. Who's going to take care of it when you're on tour with Jack?"

"I'll have to put him in a kennel for that week. Mary Jo is looking into it."

"That's the manager you don't care for," she said.

"Yes, but she's indispensable to Jack. She takes care of all the details he's too busy to deal with," I said.

"I'd keep my eye on her. Do you think he'll be good while he's away?" Dot asked.

That very thought had been plaguing me lately, aggravated by the run-in with his tutor. "He'd better be, if he wants me to stick around."

But how would I know? I asked myself. *He'll be on the road for almost four weeks before I show up, and then several more after I leave.* The Floor would be hitting every major arena in the country—with all the enticements of women, drugs, non-stop adoration and partying. From the little he'd told me, it sounded like a three-ringed circus.

"What have you been up to lately?" I interrupted my uneasy line of thought.

"Darrell and I broke up."

I heard the quaver in her voice. "I'm sorry, Mom. But I have to tell you, I don't think he treated you very well. To be honest, he seemed really obnoxious."

Dot sighed. "I know. But it's hard when you're older, Julia. You'll see. Men aren't exactly knocking down my door."

"Well, they should be. Hold out for the right guy."

"That's easier said than done. Anyway, I'm heading over to Buck's for a while. Say hi to Jack for me. When do they leave?" she asked.

"Tomorrow night. I'm going to miss him so much."

"Tell him I said good luck. And to behave himself."

The next day was insanely busy; I hardly had a moment to think about Jack's impending departure. I returned about thirty calls from agents, sat in two interminable meetings, and had a long chat with my friendly Omaha author, who always signed off the same way:

"Remember, Julia, little things . . ." He paused, waiting for me to fill in the blank.

"Can be big!" I smiled to myself, recalling Sammy's interpretation.

The topper was that just as I was ready to leave the office, I started my period. I felt like crying; this would definitely put a crimp in my plans to give Jack a great sexual sendoff. I got a tampon out of the machine and then raced down to the subway. Despite Jack's urging, I rarely used cabs for my commute, instead taking the dirty, dangerous, but much faster train.

When the local roared into the station, I wedged myself between a clump of straphangers. A woman with a huge unwieldy belly pushed her way inside. Looking like she could give birth at any minute, she stared hopefully at three seated businessmen in suits, who only raised their newspapers higher.

Watchda closindaws, came a voice over the crackly speaker. *Nex' stop, the deuce.* The train lurched forward, and she almost lost her balance.

"Want to grab hold?" I asked.

"Thanks." The woman squeezed in next to me and gripped

the pole as more passengers shoved on and off. "Mayor Crotch" was scrawled on one half of the sliding door; when it closed, it met up with "Sucks". *Turty-turd an' Lex,* came the disembodied voice.

The woman fanned herself and rapidly unbuttoned her coat. "Only one more month to go. I've already gained forty-six pounds. I used to be a size eight, but now I just can't seem to stop eating."

I nodded politely. "And none of these assholes ever give me a seat," she added.

"I guess chivalry is dead."

"You can say that again." We swayed through several stops, the car becoming less crowded as we progressed downtown. She grimaced as the train juddered over a rough patch of track and came to a screeching halt.

I let go of the pole. "Well, this is my stop. Good luck with—with everything," I said as she finally claimed a seat.

I chatted with the doorman until the elevator came. Riding up, I was hit with a pang of disappointment that I was on the rag. Why couldn't it have waited 'til tomorrow?

Jack was in a hurricane of packing, shirts and belts and rolling papers strewed everywhere, open suitcases on the bed. He grabbed me, and in a minute we were both breathing hard and tearing off each other's clothes. Jack shoved the suitcases to the floor and started kissing my breasts.

"Ohh," I said, feeling a little tender. "I have bad news. I started my period today. Let me do something nice for you, though." I started to sit up, but Jack pushed me back on the pillow.

"I don't care, baby. I'm gettin' in there." His lips tantalized my nipples, tongue swirling sensuously.

"But I just started a few minutes ago. Of all the rotten timing."

"Don't care." He inched his way down my belly.

"Let me at least get some towels," I said.

"I've got plenty more sheets."

He ran his tongue up my inner thigh, wrapped the tampon string around his finger and pulled it out. Then a butterfly landed on me lightly and sought my nectar, becoming more and more insistent until I was filled to the brink with sweetness. Again and again my cup almost overflowed. It began to trickle over the lip as the drops became a stream and the waves started crashing. I was rocked in the sway of a huge swell that took me far, far away. Just as I was starting to make my way back, he entered me and rode the tide until he filled me with his salty spume and collapsed with a long, lingering moan.

We breathed in syncopation for a while, recovering. Jack opened his eyes and smiled at me, his face smeared scarlet.

"You look like you've starred in a horror movie," I said. "Want to get in the shower? I'll strip the bed."

"In a minute. That feel good?" he asked.

I found a clean spot on his nose and kissed it. "Better than good. Astounding. Stupendous. Earth-moving. Galaxy-shattering. Thank you."

"Any time, baby. I ain't afraid of a little red."

"I should say not; you just took a bath in it. Let's get in the shower before I get stuck to the sheets," I said.

He started the shower as I put the sheets in the sink to soak. Jack came toward me, walking Frankensteinish with arms outstretched.

"Heeere's Johnny!" he cackled in a schizo voice. "Redruuum . . ."

I laughed. "I was so afraid after I read *The Shining*, I never saw the movie." He opened the shower door and we got in under the spray. Jack lifted his face to the water as a pinkish stream ran down his chest.

"I went to a screening with Mark and Suzanne. Mark and I were about to pee our britches, we were so scared." Jack wiped his neck with a washcloth. "We kept going out to get snacks, to avoid the terrifying scenes. On the other hand, Suzanne, that cold bitch, sat there calmly taking it all in, not the least bit perturbed. Man, this stuff really sticks to you," he added, scrubbing at his hands.

After we dried off, I put on his "Things Go Better with Coke" tee-shirt, and Jack wound a towel around his waist. We remade the bed, ordered pizza, and ate listening to "Rebecca" by Big Joe Turner and Bull Moose Jackson's "No Mercy." We kept the conversation light, but his departure weighed heavily on my mind. After our meal we started fooling around again. His towel was propped up by a tentpole; I undid it and began smooching his abdomen.

"Let me give you something to remember me by," I murmured as Jack shut his eyes and groaned.

I lay there memorizing his face as he slept; his thick dark eyelashes and eyebrows, expressive even in slumber; the creases at the sides of his sensual mouth; the fine lines at the corners of his eyes. Jack stirred and peered at me.

"I could go for thirds. Not that the first two times weren't brilliant." He got up and rifled through a drawer. "Want to put this on?" He held up one of the scraps of lingerie he'd given me for Christmas.

"You want to do it again already?"

"What can I say? I'm a sex machine, baby." He did a James Brown hip-shimmy.

"God, you really are. Just give me a minute to catch my breath."

I didn't say what I was thinking: with his insatiable drive, how was he going to be chaste for three and a half weeks? Especially with all those gorgeous women throwing themselves at him. I knew he wasn't into the groupies, but he'd dated plenty of models, movie stars, and other fancy hangers-on.

"What if you get stoned on tour and some woman comes along?" I blurted out.

Jack drew the garters up my leg. "Weed doesn't affect me that much anymore."

"I hope you won't do a lot of coke." I knew he used it on the road to keep his energy up—and because he liked it.

"It's good you're coming midway through. Keep me on the straight and narrow."

I hope he bears that in mind when he's at Party Central, two thousand miles away.

Jack kissed me, creating a ripple from my breasts to my toes. As we made love one last time, I took in every lush sensation, storing it up for the coming drought.

I had told Ted I'd be in late the next morning. I helped Jack with last-minute packing, cramming a few more packages of guitar picks into his carry-on since he always lost them. Rick came up to collect the luggage, and we all rode down together. As Rick loaded the car, Jack and I kissed and kissed out on the sidewalk with pedestrians gawking and cabs honking and messengers pedaling and hungover punks walking their dogs. Finally we pulled apart. Jack gave me one last look, and darted into the backseat.

At least I had something to distract me that day. A literary agent had sent me a late-night talk show host's humor book, which I planned to bring up in the editorial meeting. When my turn came, I quickly described the project and its potential, given that the show had millions of viewers.

"Isn't his audience kind of young?" Erica cut in before I'd finished my pitch. "I wouldn't think a bunch of college sophomores would spend their allowance on recycled jokes."

My hackles rose. "A lot of adults watch it too; I have the statistics. And over half of the book will be brand new stuff from his writing staff."

"I'm just not seeing it." Erica folded her arms with a snarky smile as several others shook their heads.

"I think it would be huge," Cathy chimed in. "I know tons of people who love his show."

"I agree. See me after the meeting and we'll cook up an offer," Ted concluded. "The show's headquarters are down the block. We'll get together with them once we own it."

Just as we were leaving, the managing editor stuck her head in. "It's tip sheet time again!" she sang out as everyone groaned. "I need one for each of your titles by end of the week. The marketing director wants them well in advance of sales conference."

I was familiar with the dreaded tip sheets from my previous job. For every one of our books, we had to fill in a zillion pre-publication facts, and wing it on whatever was still TBD. Supposedly the sales force used them to get bookstore orders, and those numbers determined the first print run. It would be nice not having to do Harvey's this time around.

Erica caught up with me on the way out. "I would think you'd be too busy with your new prize author to acquire anything right now. Dermot Chase is quite a handful."

"I'm sure I can manage," I said coolly. I felt like adding, *Mind your own business,* as I continued down the hall to Ted's office.

"Try to pre-empt this late-night book for a hundred thou," he said, polishing his glasses on his shirtsleeve. "Perry will complain, but this is just the kind of commercial stuff we need. Come see me if the agent wants more."

I could hardly believe my ears. "Great! Oh, and I'm getting together with Dermot after work. He's handing over the first batch of chapters."

"Very good; keep me posted. One bit of advice about this TV guy: I'd keep a distance from these celebrity types. Be friendly, but don't ever believe they're your friends. There's a big difference."

He has no idea how close I am to a real *celebrity*, I thought. "I'll keep that in mind."

"When's your family reunion again?" Ted asked.

I didn't correct him. "Middle of March."

"Congrats on your big acquisition!" Cathy exclaimed. "I heard you got it for a hundred-fifty."

"Thanks. I'm still in a daze. We're meeting with the show's head writer next week. I guess I have to do a tip sheet for it, since we're pushing it out in the fall." I stared at the stack of forms on my desk. "What should I do for a description of Dermot's novel? He hasn't even finished the first draft."

"Just make it up. The reps never read those things anyway."

Cathy had told me that Perry Stroud hardly ever came down to our floor—unless he was visiting Erica, since she did all the "important" books. But after lunch, our publisher stepped into my office holding a paper cup. I was just winding up a call with the head writer of the TV show, who was excited about the deal. It turned out Stuart wrote all the host's jokes and would be the real author of the book, which suited me fine. Even on the phone, he was hilarious. I hung up and quickly slid my copy of the *Post* under the *New York Times*, knowing Perry would look down on such light reading.

"So, you've signed up a little humor book," Perry said. He went over to the window, parted my ficus and gazed out at the skyscraper canyon. "Ted said it'll be ready by fall, but we have a lot of big titles on that list. *Serious* books." He leveled his gaze at me. "I don't want to clutter up the imprint with frivolous junk."

My face burned. "I was just talking to the head writer. He's already written half of it."

"Hmph. And you're dealing with Dermot Chase, I hear." Perry took a sip of his coffee.

"Yes, I'm meeting him tonight. He's delivering some chapters," I said.

"Erica's an old hand at mollycoddling important authors; I don't know why he wanted to switch. Do you think you can get it out of him in time? We have a lot riding on this one."

"He seems eager to get going. I'll start on it right away." I felt like adding, *I can't write it for him.*

Perry dumped his coffee into my ficus. "See that you do." On his way out, he put his empty cup on the corner of my desk.

I had thought I'd just meet with Dermot in the conference room, but he suggested grabbing dinner. Since Jack was away, I figured, Why not? There was reason to rush home. And after all, I was supposed to give my new author the white-glove treatment. I was surprised when Dermot suggested Elaine's, the Upper East Side actor-and-writer haunt; I'd pictured someplace more low-key. But that was fine, because I could put the meal on my expense account. Hawtey had given me a nice fat allowance that I hadn't even begun to make a dent in.

I got to the restaurant early out of nerves, checked my coat and waited for Dermot to show. His piercing blue eyes met mine as he came through the door, flashing a big smile. Beneath an elegant coat and jacket his shirt was undone a few buttons, revealing a tanned chest. I was glad I'd worn the stylish interview suit Vicky had helped me pick out.

"So good to see you," he murmured, bussing my cheek. Not realizing he was going for the other one, European-style, we bumped noses. "I hope I haven't kept you waiting."

The spicy hint of his cologne lingered pleasantly in my nostrils. "Oh no, I just got here."

Dermot handed his coat and briefcase to the coat-check girl and went to embrace the restaurant owner, who held her cigarette aside for his kiss. "Elaine, this is Julia, my talented new midwife. She's going to extract this novel from me, come hell or high water."

"Your usual spot's ready," Elaine said without giving me a glance. As she led us through the dark room, famous faces gazed at me from the book jackets plastered on the walls— and from a few tables, as well. I dropped my eyes to avoid breaking the cardinal rule in Manhattan: Never stare at a celebrity. Dermot stopped every few seconds to speak to people he knew as I stood awkwardly beside him. Finally we were seated, and he asked the waiter for a bottle of Burgundy. *Is it okay to put alcohol on my expense account?* I wondered.

"So, Julia. You're a fresh face in the grizzled publishing world. What brought you to New York in the first place?" Dermot spread his hands on the table, ringless but for a large onyx set in gold.

I fiddled with the menu tassel. "Originally I came here for grad school, but then I decided I'd rather be an editor than go for a Ph.D."

"Wise choice. I arrived fifteen years ago, determined to

write the great American novel. Little did I know, I'd wind up writing three of them." Again the sexy flash of those white teeth in his bronzed face. "Which one's your favorite?"

"Um, *Oblivious Journey*?" I named the only book of his that I'd read. I took a sip of wine to collect my thoughts. *I'll have to do some catch-up skimming over the weekend,* I realized. Seeing that he was waiting for something more, I added, "I really loved it. But all of your works are such important contributions."

"I'm glad you feel that way. Yes, we're ready," he said to the waiter. Hoping to keep the tab down, I ordered one of the cheaper entrees, while Dermot went for the pricey steak tips. *I guess I won't get in trouble for expensing this fancy dinner,* I thought as the waiter took our menus. Harvey used to complain if a bill hit forty bucks.

Dermot waved at someone across the room, and then focused on me. "This new novel has been tough to jumpstart," he said, twisting his onyx ring. "I'm having trouble with one of my female characters, Penelope. She's about your age, so I'm hoping you can give me some insights."

"Insights into . . .?" The last drops of wine slid down my throat like scarlet silk. *It even tastes expensive,* I thought as Dermot refilled my glass.

"The inner workings of the mind of a twenty-four-year-old woman. What makes her tick. What turns her on." He raised an eyebrow as the waiter set our plates in front of us.

I was happy for the interruption. With the wine I'd drunk and Dermot's forceful blue gaze, I was feeling discombobulated. Stalling, I took a bite of overcooked pasta.

"Do you think you can help me with that?" Dermot persisted. "I need details that will really flesh her out. *Intimate* details."

"Oh, sure! I'll try to put all that into the notes." I took another sip of wine and tried to focus on the reason for this dinner. "You have some pages to give me?"

"You'll soon have it in your hot little hands." Dermot speared a steak tip and brought it to his lips. "Since this is the first time we've worked together, you should know that I get heavily involved in the design. I can be a bit obsessive about the typeface, the chapter ornaments. You should probably get your people going on it; I've been known to change my mind numerous times. Same thing for the cover."

I gulped; at my previous house, we never ran the interior design by authors. They were lucky to get a good gander at the jacket before it went to press. "Okay, I'll get the art department started." I put down my fork as Dermot polished off his steak.

"You know, the Book Awards are coming up next month. I'm pretty confident my latest novel's a shoe-in," he said.

I knew that Dermot's first book had won the prestigious award. "I imagine Ted has reserved a table. I'll ask him about it."

"You'll have to come, too." Dermot put his hand over mine and gazed at me. His eyes seemed to radiate a searing heat; they really were an amazing shade of blue. "It would be a good opportunity for you to mingle with the *hoi polloi*," he added. "We'll have to get you out and about more, Ms. Nash. I hadn't even heard of you before you started at Hawtey

House. You don't want hide your light under a bushel."

In spite of myself, I blushed. "I'll try to go." I envisioned myself at the fancy annual ceremony that everyone-who-was-anyone in publishing attended. Of course, I'd never been to one in the past; assistants weren't invited unless they were helping check people in at the door.

The waiter brought the bill, and I reached for it. "It's on Hawtey," I said, and Dermot didn't give me an argument. I tried not to gasp when I saw the amount: almost two hundred dollars.

Dermot smiled. "Elaine always gives me a break on the tab. She adores writers. That couple over there in Siberia—" he nodded toward a pair seated near the kitchen who were obviously out-of-towners—"will make up the difference."

How unfair to them, I thought as I signed the bill. We got our wraps from the coat-check girl, and Dermot gave her a five as he took his briefcase. "This was great," I said as we stepped onto the icy sidewalk. "Do you have the pages? I thought I'd start digging in tonight."

Dermot pinned his gaze on me. "I'm still polishing, but you'll have them by next week."

I can't believe it—this long, drawn-out dinner was for nothing? What will I put down for "Purpose" on my expense account—"Kissing Up to Author"?

"This was wonderful. We'll have to do it again soon," Dermot continued as he stuck out his arm to hail me a cab. Before I got in, he put his hands on my shoulders and looked into my eyes.

"I know we're going to be really good together," he murmured. I caught a waft of his cologne as he came closer. He just missed my lips, and for a split second I felt my knees go weak. Dermot helped me into the cab and shut the door. Through the window I watched him stroll down the street in the other direction; I knew from the rolodex card that he lived only a few blocks away.

The taxi flew downtown, easily catching a string of green lights since it was past ten. I gazed out the window, my thoughts flickering with the passing streetlamps. I pictured Dermot's strong hands turning his onyx ring; his smile flashing in his tanned face. *If I wasn't seeing Jack, I'd almost—*

The driver stomped the brakes for a cyclist, and I threw out my hands to avoid hitting the partition. I dug for the seatbelt, but it was buried too far down in the crack. *Listen, stupid,* I told myself as the cab zoomed forward. *What are you thinking? Even if you weren't with Jack, you can't dip your pen in the company ink. You could jeopardize your new job—and look like a fool. Dermot's flirting is probably just a knee-jerk reaction. He's the type of guy that comes on to any female under seventy.*

The taxi passed 23rd Street, and then 14th. *Sober up; you need to figure out what to tell Ted about the manuscript,* I thought. Maybe I should have pushed Dermot harder, but until the last minute I'd assumed he'd brought the pages with him. Hawtey was counting on this—and so was I. It was my first shot at editing a literary lion and a Book Award contender. Although I hadn't worked on the novel that was nominated, for a moment I let myself imagine Dermot's words of gratitude to his current editor in his acceptance speech; all eyes on me at the glittering ceremony. I'd have to do whatever it took to get him to hand it over.

The Floor's first concert had been the previous night, but I hadn't heard from Jack since he called to let me know he'd arrived. I knew the tour involved long, late hours, but I was still on-edge, particularly after what Suzanne had said about the seductresses who'd be circling.

Finally I got hold of him right before they left for the next city. With the bad connection, I could barely hear.

"How did it go in San Francisco?" I shouted into the phone.

"—whirlwind. So far, so good."

"What did you guys do last night?" I asked.

"We hit a few parties after the show. Hey, lemme say hi to Muddy."

I held out the phone and Jack called his name, eliciting frantic barks from our puppy. I put the receiver back to my ear. "He misses you too. How's the—"

"All right, I'm coming," he said to someone. "I've gotta go."

"I love you!" I called out, but he had already hung up.

"You must be so psyched," Vicky said as she took a bite of brown rice. The Life Café had opened a few months ago on Avenue B in the East Village. The tiny coffeehouse was already a happening place with its wildly collaged storefront, performance art, and poetry readings. Being into all things hip, Vicky had wanted to check it out.

"I can't wait. Only ten more days until my flight to St.

Louis," I said.

Vicky contemplated her tofu. "You lucky dog. Maybe I should have hung in there with Sammy, after all."

"He didn't deserve you." I tasted my chili. "This is delicious. I can't believe it's only fifty cents."

"They'll have to raise their prices if they want to stay in business. Although I imagine all the neighborhood junkies like the cheap eats." She was alluding to the heroin addicts who occupied the decrepit buildings around Tompkins Square. "Did you ever hear from Jack?"

"No, and I've stopped leaving messages. They're playing a different city every other day, so it's been chaotic." I supposed he had to be in his room sometime to shower and change clothes, but I hadn't figured out when exactly that was. He wasn't there at three in the afternoon, or six p.m., or even four in the morning. *Or else he was there, but too preoccupied to pick up,* a wicked inner voice suggested. "When I did get through to him last weekend, a bunch of other people were in the room talking at the same time. It's really frustrating."

"I guess that's to be expected." Vicky raised her finger to signal to the harried waitress. "You're getting me into the Madison Square Garden show, right?"

"I told Jack to put you on the list. You'll be right next to me in the front row."

Vicky smiled her catlike smile. "Maybe Sammy and I should have a reunion fuck."

"Vicky! Would you really?" But I already knew the answer to that.

"I kind of miss the whole rock star scene. None of the

guys I've been seeing really do it for me." She fluffed her blonde pixie cut.

"Are you still going out with that investment banker?" I asked.

"Once in a while. He's got an endless supply of toot, but he has trouble getting it up. I'm not sure it's worth the effort. And that guy from the Explorer's Club took me out to dinner. He wanted to come home with me, but I couldn't muster any interest."

"Maybe you're better off focusing on work for the time being. Until someone you really like comes along," I suggested.

"I don't know. This guy I deal with at a PR agency has been calling me. I may go out with him this weekend." She sighed. "Or I may just stay home and work. I have to come up with four press releases by next week. And we're getting ready to send Marcia Sitwell on a twelve-city tour for her new thriller. I really dread it; she's such a bitch."

"I took *my* big author out the other night." I filled her in on my dinner with Dermot.

Vicky narrowed her gold-flecked green eyes. "Sounds like he has the hots for you."

I finished the last dregs of my drink. "Oh, I'm sure he acts that way with all the girls. He made a big fuss over Elaine, and she has to be sixty if she's a day."

"I would string him along a little, at least until you get his manuscript." She waved again, and the server finally noticed us. "Then you can drop your sweet demeanor and snip off all his dangling participles."

"Having drunk my beer, the waitress brought the check," I said, riffing on Vicky's little grammar joke.

"Wearing a fabulous dress, the author admired his editor at the Book Awards," Vicky added as she put down some cash.

"Needing to keep her job, the taxi took the editor home so she could do some work." I left money for my half.

"Being a wet blanket, the publicist said goodnight to her spoilsport friend."

Laughing, we stepped outside and walked over to First Avenue, where we caught cabs going in separate directions.

Chapter 15

START ME UP

The third week Jack was gone, I started getting more and more excited about flying out to meet him in St. Louis. I imagined our passionate kiss; his hands on my body; making love over and over in a big hotel bed. I wanted to run my tongue over every inch of him, and I wanted to hear him say once again that he loved me. When I managed to get through on the phone the night before I left, I told him how sad I'd been dropping off Muddy at the kennel. Jack commiserated with me, and while our conversation was short, it was also sweet—somewhat assuaging the worries that had been building up over the weeks with hardly any contact.

I was so worked up on the plane that I couldn't even read my tattered copy of *Anna Karenina*. A driver held up a placard with my name in the baggage area, and I followed him to the car. The temperature in St. Louis was in the fifties; a nice break from the frigid weather back in New York. Jack couldn't meet me at the airport because he and Patrick had to do an interview, so I sat alone in the backseat on the way to the hotel, fairly vibrating with anticipation. I gave my name at the front desk and tapped my foot in the elevator on the way up. These lodgings weren't nearly as fancy as the Chateau Marmont, where we'd stayed for the concerts in L.A. last summer, but I couldn't care less. I would have been happy at a Motel Six.

I knocked a shave-and-a-haircut on the door of room 1009. It swung open, and Jack stood there with a tired smile on his face, deep smudges under his eyes. His unruly mane stood up in tufts, still damp from a recent shower. A five o'clock shadow darkened his cheeks. He was dressed the way I liked: no shirt and a pair of low-slung faded jeans, his lightning bolt necklace glinting on his bare chest.

"Hello, baby." He gestured me inside, and I dove into his arms. "Hey, I think you missed me," he said as I smooched his face.

"I couldn't *wait* to see you." Jack's embrace seemed to lack his usual energy, but even so, it sent flickers of desire zinging through me.

"C'mon in." He drew me back through the suite. It looked like a bomb had gone off in his luggage: belts and boots and guitars and rolling papers everywhere. I stopped short at the entrance to the bedroom and stared.

"Oh my god."

"What?" Jack said.

I pointed upward. A gigantic mirror covered the entire

ceiling, reflecting the messy bed, his clothes thrown over a chair, me standing there looking up. "What is *that*?"

Jack shrugged. "Came with the room. Okay with you if we lie down? I was just trying to get a little shut-eye; I've been up five nights running. We have to leave for the arena in a couple of hours."

This wasn't the reception I'd been anticipating. *Couldn't he have gotten some rest before I came?* I wondered.

I slipped under the covers and ran my fingers through the fine dark hair on his chest. Gazing down at his handsome face on the pillow, I saw how utterly wiped out he was; the lines at the sides of his mouth more deeply etched, traces of last night's makeup on his eyelids. I laid my head on his chest, feeling his heart thumping, breathing in his nice clean soap smell.

"Wanna order some food?" he mumbled.

"I'm fine. Maybe I'll just get some water." I dug my toothbrush out of my bag and went into the bathroom. As I brushed, I noticed that everything looked pristine; towels stacked neatly, toilet paper folded in a sharp V. A package of deodorants of an unfamiliar brand was sitting on the shelf next to a few unopened hotel soaps. I didn't see his toothbrush or razor. They'd been in St. Louis for over a day already, but there was no shampoo on the shelf. I touched the interior wall of the shower; it was dry as a bone. *Has Jack been staying in someone else's room?* The thought spasmed my gut. *But maybe he used Sammy's*, I told myself. I knew they sometimes passed out in the middle of partying.

Jack was already asleep, an arm flung over his eyes. I went to the living room and looked around. He'd definitely changed clothes in here; several times, by the looks of things. I noticed a few neat stacks of papers on a table. Recognizing Mary Jo's handiwork, I sat on the sofa and examined some piles of what looked like fan mail. Sure enough, loopy school-girls' love notes were mixed with women's monogrammed stationery, many sprayed with perfume.

I dropped the notes and picked up stapled sheets of The Floor's itinerary. It turned out they'd been here for *two* nights instead of one. I looked at the list of cities: Minneapolis, Los Angeles, Cleveland, Houston, Phoenix . . . They were criss-crossing the country, zig-zagging back and forth. I wondered why they didn't go in a direct route from West Coast to East, but there must be some method to the book-ings that escaped a straight-line logic.

I replaced the papers and went to the little fridge, getting out a lukewarm can of beer. Popping the tab, I sat on the couch and picked up the first of a stack of newspapers. The one on top was folded open to an interior column. A photo-graph caught my eye. Right in the middle of the page, there seemed to be a familiar face. Jack, appearing completely out of it, was squeezed up against a glamorous-looking blonde in a low-cut dress. She had her arm around his neck, and her mouth was open in a vicious laugh. *God, is she sitting in his lap?* It was hard to tell, but I could see that her hand was tucked inside his open shirt. The caption read: *Jack Kipling relaxes with actress Marissa Pfund after The Floor's sold-out L.A. concert.*

Snatching up the paper, I went into the bedroom. I started to shake Jack awake and demand to know what he'd been doing with this actress, whose name I recognized from a stray comment Patrick had once made. Jack was now lying on his stomach, his silky eyelashes brushing high cheekbones, thick hair draping his face. With the big concert just a few hours away, I decided to let him finish his nap.

I lay back on the pillow next to him and stared up at the ceiling. A long crack in one corner of the mirror slanted the room into separate refractions, making twins of our image and creating four people in the bed. Thinking about the neatly stacked papers, I realized that obviously Mary Jo had arranged them, knowing I was arriving today. Maybe this was some kind of setup on her part. Perhaps the thing to do was to play it cool and see what Jack said before I confronted him; I knew he reacted badly when cornered. Or maybe I should just pack my toothbrush and catch the next flight out.

I gazed up at the crazed halves of the mirror, each revealing a different angle of my wasted boyfriend. I wondered which account I would believe: his version, or that of the photograph. One of them had to be a complete illusion.

Jack didn't wake up until the phone began ringing insistently an hour later. He cracked one eye and said in a parched whisper, "Can you get it?"

I reached over him for the receiver. "The limo's leaving in forty-five minutes," came Mary Jo's tart voice. "Did you finally get some sleep?"

"This is Julia. Jack just woke up." I sat upright, the cord stretched across Jack's chest.

"Oh. He told me you were getting in today." Her flat tone

expressed a total lack of interest. I'd hoped we could put aside our unfriendly history and declare a truce during the tour, but that was being too optimistic.

"I got here a while ago. Do you want to talk to Jack?" I asked.

"Just make sure he's downstairs in half an hour. Has he picked his stage outfit yet?"

"I have no idea. I'll see to it that he's ready," I said.

"You do that."

She was about to hang up, but I wasn't going to let her off that easily. "I see the band's getting good coverage in the local papers," I said quickly.

I could practically hear her smirk. "They always do. The reporters got some nice shots, didn't they?"

Now that I was sure she'd planted it there, I wasn't about to give her the satisfaction of acting upset. "Yes, I like seeing all the press. Although the groupies seem so pathetic. I feel sorry for them, in a way."

"Why is that?" Mary Jo replied in a frigid tone.

I got up and walked around the bed, kicking aside a pair of his jeans. "Because they'll never get what they want, other than a passing fling. They should give up and focus on someone who'd find them interesting. As opposed to just a convenient way to get off."

"Some of them are very good at getting what they want," she said. "Maybe not the groupies, but I'm talking about the band's more prominent fans. Actresses and models, for instance."

I felt like wringing her pudgy neck. "Prominent in their

own minds, maybe. Anyway, I'll get Jack out of bed now. He was *so* happy to see me; we've just had a nice long . . . nap."

She hung up without saying goodbye.

"What was all that about?" Jack propped himself up on his elbow, and I handed him the newspaper clipping. "Oh. That." He rubbed his face wearily and dropped it onto the floor.

"Nice picture. I guess that was after the concert in L.A." I tried to strike a nonchalant tone.

"Must've been; I can't recall." Jack paused, but I didn't say anything. "Listen, Julia. They cram you into these things after the show. 'Oh, take my picture; now let's get a shot with this one, that one.' Half the time I don't even know who it is."

"Her name's kind of familiar. Isn't she the Marissa that Patrick mentioned last summer? The one that stripped in the hotel elevator?"

Jack looked at me. "How do you remember all this stuff?"

I met his gaze. "Certain things stick in my mind."

"Yeah, she is. But I didn't do anything with her." He scratched his chin. "She's just someone who likes the band. She always makes it to our shows when we're in town."

I guessed he could have been crammed into a photo op with this actress. *Or he could have hooked up with her for a quick one after the concert*, a green-eyed serpent whispered in my ear. But there wasn't time to pick a fight now. "Well, if you're going to make it to *this* show, you'd better get a move on."

Jack sat up. "We have a few minutes. I'm doing me own face, this tour. I don't like the new makeup girl; she lays it on too thick." He grabbed a dopp kit from the table and went into the bathroom. He unzipped the bag, laid out some little brushes and pots of color on the shelf, and peered into the mirror. "Hell, it's the morning after the night before," he muttered as I stood in the doorway. "Shades of the living dead. Guess I'll start by getting the red out." He dripped eye drops into each pupil, then dabbed a tissue at the excess running down his face.

"Why isn't Gary doing the makeup?" I mentioned the artist I knew he liked.

Jack frowned. "He's sick with this weird disease, wasting away to nothing. Mark, Suzanne and I went to see him in the hospital in San Francisco. They think he picked up some virus on a flight. I really hope he'll be okay."

"Me too." Gary had been nice to me when I'd met him backstage last year; I hoped he would recover quickly.

Peering in the mirror, Jack dabbed shadow on his lids with one long finger, then brushed color onto his cheeks. Expertly he added a streak of eyeliner. With his thick dark lashes, he never needed mascara. He turned to me with a campy swish of his hip. "Am I workin' it, girlfriend?"

I was flooded with lust for my don't-give-a-damn rock star, who wasn't afraid to act silly despite being the epitome of cool. "You're definitely workin' it. And then some."

"Here, let me do you." He flicked the brush over my cheekbones, then lightly ran his finger along the curve of my jaw, setting off sparklers in my abdomen. "Now hold still. I'll tart you up in no time." He dipped a finger into one of the pots. I closed my eyes as he spread a thin coat on my lids.

When I opened them, the blue of my irises flashed against the iridescent shade.

"Hey, you're good at this," I said.

"On our first few tours we didn't have enough bread to hire anyone, so we did our own faces. I've always been good at the artwork. Why don't you pick out a shirt for me?"

From a hanging wardrobe I chose a shimmery electric blue one, in keeping with the eye shadow. I put on a flouncy lavender skirt that I knew he liked.

Jack rummaged in my bag. "Why don't you wear these?" He withdrew a garter belt and pair of lacy black stockings in a floral pattern; one of his many Christmas gifts.

I sat back in the bed and pulled them on. *I guess we'll have our sexual reunion later,* I thought as I put on knee-high boots. Given the mild weather, we didn't need coats.

We were only a half-hour late to the lobby. Sammy ambled over, his shaggy brown hair brushing the top of his shoulders. "'Bout time you got here." His soul patch underscored his smile.

"Well, aren't you the dog's dinner." Jack fingered the lapels of Sammy's shiny green jacket. "Maybe a little flea-bit."

"Was that a compliment? Hard to tell with these Limeys." Sammy kissed my cheek. "I had to put on my struttin' gear."

"Watch out, ladies of St. Louis; he's going on the pull. But hang on." Jack went around behind him and lifted his coattail. "My god, are you wearing Jordache jeans? I thought you retired those."

"My Calvins are dirty." Sammy yanked his coat away. "How the hell are you, Julia?"

"I'm good. I just got in a little while ago."

"You're a sight for sore eyes. Where's Mark? He doesn't know whether to check his ass or scratch his watch," Sammy said.

"Here they come." Mark and Suzanne stepped out of the elevators in sunglasses. "*In*-cognito," Jack added with a laugh. Mark's roosterish spiky hair was dyed pink and green, and he wore tight stretchy pants with a chartreuse jacket and no shirt underneath. Suzanne towered over him in a yolk-yellow jumpsuit and see-through heels, her brilliant red hair in striking contrast to the bright eggy color.

Suzanne gave me a big kiss. "I'm so chuffed that you're here," she said, her posh pronunciation doing little to hide her Cockney accent. "I've been stuck with these barmpots for three bloomin' weeks. And Patrick's little twits are getting on me last nerve."

"It's great to see you too," I said as we walked outside. I took a deep breath of fresh air and looked up at the stars, which you never got to see in New York with all the bright lights. A gaggle of young girls rushed forward with autograph books. The guys quickly scribbled in them, then we hurried into the limo and the driver squealed out.

"Whew, who's wearing the musk?" Jack complained. "Did you douse yourself in it?" he leaned away from Sammy.

"It's that new deodorant they're promoting," Sammy said. "Didn't your bathroom come stocked with it? The concert tickets have the ad on them: *Clover Spray-on. Make her go crazy.*"

"'Make her gag like crazy' is more like it." Jack held his nose.

"Yeah, in spite of the great reviews, they're afraid we'll stink." Mark rolled his eyes. "Another one of Patrick's poxy ideas."

"If he ever got a good one, it would die of loneliness." Sammy drew a joint from his pocket and fired it up. "This'll get you higher'n a Georgia pine," he said, handing it to me. I passed it to Jack, wanting to retain my wits.

"You're right not to smoke that Rastafarian stuff," Suzanne said. "I have some that's a lot smoother."

"Weed lite," Mark commented.

Suzanne made a face. "Yours would knock an elephant for a loop."

"Julia doesn't do too well with the maryjane." Jack waved a cloud away from me.

The driver fiddled with the radio, and Elvis Costello's "Alison" came on. Mark said, "Hey man, switch stations, okay? Find us some blues."

"But I love that song," Suzanne complained.

"Show me one gal that don't," Sammy said. "Go figure, a tune about shootin' your old lady."

"It's a chick song, like 'Stand By Me'. Never met a woman that didn't love that." Jack took another hit and passed the joint to Mark.

"Yeah, like 'Killing Me Softly'." Mark's voice strained over his inheld breath. "Or 'It's Too Late.'"

"Those are great songs!" Suzanne said.

"Chick tunes." Sammy shook his head dismissively. "'Brass in Pocket.' 'Roxanne.' That song about the rollerskate key."

"Bang a Gong," Jack added with a smirk.

"I was crazy about that when I was thirteen," Suzanne said.

"See?" Sammy said. "I bet you liked 'How Deep Is Your Love.' And 'We Are Family.'"

"You hear that once, it gets lodged in your brain." Jack drilled his finger into his temples.

Sammy examined the tiny nub of joint that remained. "I got 'Dancing Queen' stuck in my head for a whole week in the mid-Seventies. 'Bout drove me around the bend." He put out his tongue, extinguished the roach, and swallowed it.

I laughed. "I guess it's no surprise you're all music snobs."

"I prefer to think of it as discriminating." Jack rolled up the window as we drove through the gates of the huge arena. The driver stopped at the backstage entrance, where a guard stood waiting to usher us inside. We rushed past other security and people with clipboards, into a large mirrored room. Their lead singer was in the makeup chair, surrounded by people. A young man was blow-drying the curlers on top of Patrick's head; a girl in a micro-mini was dabbing on foundation, and another was giving him a manicure. Mary Jo stood nearby, wearing a tailored pants suit that did nothing to disguise her solid shape. She was gesticulating at Patrick with a sheaf of papers in her hand.

"Oh, fuck." Jack rushed over, Mark and Sammy trailing behind. "Tell me you're not changing the set list again," Jack said. He took the drink from Patrick's hand and gulped it. Patrick's lips were momentarily stilled by the makeup girl applying gloss.

Mary Jo made eyes at Jack. "He's reversing the last two

numbers. And possibly the opening. I'll leave you to it." She handed him the papers and came over to me.

"You're forty minutes late," was her greeting. She tucked her shoulder-length brown hair behind her ears and fixed her piercing hazel gaze on me. "Jack's been having so much fun on tour, he's been late for every show. But I thought with *you* here, maybe he'd be on time for once."

I ignored her implying that now that I'd arrived, Jack wasn't enjoying himself. I also resisted the impulse to ask who he'd been having fun *with*. "He did his own makeup, so he's ready to go. Is Patrick changing the order of the songs?" Bait-and-switch was often the best way to deflect his manager's sharp tongue.

"His Royal Highness has decided his voice needs a break, so he's moving the numbers around. You're all dolled up." She scrutinized my outfit.

"Jack bought this for me," I said.

Mary Jo glared. "Yes, I saw the bills." I could never figure out if she hated me because she thought I was mooching off him, or if it was just generalized animosity toward anyone who took up too much of Jack's attention.

"What time do they go on?" I knew the tickets for the first show said "9 pm", but I also knew that time was fluid with these guys. They'd been known to start concerts over an hour late. However, Jack had told me Mary Jo was determined to keep them on schedule for this tour, since the contract stipulated that they had to pay a fine for every five minutes' delay. With a second show at eleven, and two shows per night for thirty cities, they needed to march to a strict drumbeat.

Mary Jo grimaced. "It's supposed to start at nine. The sponsor's about to shit a brick because they were a half-hour late in Minneapolis."

I was confused. "Why would a deodorant company care about that?"

"They like to sweat the details." Smiling at her little joke, Mary Jo stalked off to accost an official-looking guy in a suit. I went to find Suzanne, who was touching up Mark's face in the makeup chair. Jack and Patrick laughingly offered suggestions; it seemed they were over their tiff.

"I've done all I can," Suzanne said, putting a fluffy powder brush on the tray. "Let's go get our seats."

We kissed the guys' cheeks—all except Patrick, who didn't want his makeup mussed—and followed a guard down a long echoing corridor. He led us up some steps and we made our way to the middle of the front row, which seemed to be all-girl. The opening act had left the stage, and the crowd was getting rowdy. Mary Jo slipped into her reserved seat next to a group of young women wearing tee-shirts with the band's logo. I sat between her and Suzanne. The stomping and shouting grew to an unbearable pitch as the announcer's voice boomed over the loudspeaker.

"A-a-all right. Give it up for—FOUR TO THE FLOOR!"

The noise behind us was so thunderous, it was almost frightening. A piercing scream sounded as Mark and Sammy sauntered over to the drums and keyboard. Jack walked onstage, head down as he tuned his Telecaster. Women were sobbing behind me, screaming Jack's name. Then people started chanting, *Pa-trick! Pa-trick!* After a few minutes, he sprinted to the middle of the stage and took the microphone.

"Good to be back in St. Louis!" Patrick shouted, his voice almost drowned out by the frenzied roar.

Jack struck a razor-sharp note that singed my ears. The crowd went berserk as he ripped into the opening chords of one of their recent hits. As Mark came in with a driving downbeat, Patrick snarled the lyrics, underscoring his words with a funky bass line. Sammy banged out the melody, occasionally playing one-handed when he took a sip from a glass resting on top of the keyboard. The song wound up with a cymbal smash. Patrick bowed low as the others briefly ducked their heads.

The second number was one of their huge hits from the past. Jack was playing hard, eyes closed, muscled chest bare under his open shirt; the epitome of Sexy Rock Idol. I felt like pinching myself: *Am I really with him?* It was hard to reconcile the super-cool onstage image with the joke-loving, down-to-earth guy in torn jeans that I'd been living with for the past two months. The guy who liked dogs and bugs, and adored his little nephew. And who made love to me like we were the last two people on earth. *What does he see in me?* I thought with a pang as I watched the women around me practically having orgasms every time his fingers stroked the strings.

All of a sudden Jack stopped playing for a moment, staring at his hand. With a disgusted look he threw down the bent pick, grabbed another from his shirt pocket, and picked up mid-verse.

By the third number, Patrick had stripped off his shirt. He launched into one of their sexiest dance tunes, gyrating as he wailed the words. The sinuous melody made everyone leap out of their seats and shimmy in the rows, arms waving above their heads. Suzanne and I jumped up and boogied to the pulsing rhythm, occasionally bumping hips in the tight space. She looked so pretty with her wild red hair and blissful expression. *Mark's such an idiot not to appreciate her*, I thought as Jack and Patrick began belting out their anthem to partying; a foot-stomper that made your feet itch to be out on the floor. Then they launched into their infectious new hit that had been playing nonstop on the radio for several months. Patrick strutted across the stage as Jack hammered out the chords, dazzling the crowd with his smoking riffs.

Down the row, a mass motion caught my eye. The young women next to Mary Jo were lifting their Floor tee-shirts on every other downbeat, flashing their bare breasts. Patrick started laughing and fumbled the lyrics; Jack skipped a chord and made a comment to Mark. Sammy nodded encouragingly, and they all shrieked and lifted their shirts again.

Mary Jo screamed at the girl sitting next to her. "If you do that again, I'll have security drag you out of here!"

"You go right ahead!" the girl shouted, her frosty pink lips forming a pout. "My daddy's chief of police. He'll shut the whole place down!"

Mary Jo stared straight ahead, fuming. After a minute, she turned to her again. "If you'll stop, you can flash your tits backstage when it's over."

"Can you get us in?" the girl asked eagerly.

Mary Jo gave an evil smile. "Of course I can. I'm their manager."

After a whispered conversation, they all sat back in their seats. I could just imagine how Mary Jo planned to get revenge.

The rest of the show raced by, with the girls managing to keep their shirts on. The Floor did three encores, and then took a brief break to cool down. In the hiatus, Mary Jo gave a guard some whispered directions and motioned for the group of flashers to follow him in the opposite direction from where the men were. The crowd exited the arena, and a new audience filed in. Soon thereafter the band was re-announced and they clambered back onto the platform. By the end of the second show, their fans seemed ready to leap onstage and rip off their clothes.

When the last encore concluded, hundreds of lighters were extinguished and people stumbled down the aisles. We went backstage to find the men. Still buzzed, they were laughing and joking, toweling off their damp faces and guzzling beer. Patrick took Mary Jo into a corner for a few minutes, gesturing angrily. He stormed out and Mary Jo followed him, telling Jack they'd see us at the restaurant.

One of the roadies came over. "Need anything for tomorrow?"

"About eight packs of strings and a shitload of picks. C'mon, let's get out of here," Jack said to me.

Chapter 16

WHITE LINES

We piled into the limo and headed out to dinner. Jack was laughing with Mark and Sammy, slapping fives and stomping feet.

"That was fantastic. You guys were on fire," I commented as Jack tipped his head back to down a beer. In the opposite seats, Suzanne and Mark began arguing in an undertone.

"Yeah, the band was hot tonight. It's a real adrenaline rush to play for a great crowd," Jack said.

I'm sure it was more than adrenaline. "The coke probably had something to do with it, too," I said in a low voice.

Jack lifted an eyebrow. "What, are you keeping tabs?" He bolted the rest of his beer and grabbed the whiskey bottle.

Sammy turned to me. "Did you like my zebra ticklin'?"

I nodded. "Your solos were fantastic. I even heard some Mozart-type trills in there."

"We've gotta get her out more often," Sammy said. "I like the way this woman's mind works."

"What about *my* solos?" Jack asked, draping his arm around my shoulder.

"There you go, always fishing for a compliment," Sammy said.

"They were ethereal." I met Jack's eye. "I don't understand how you can keep all those notes going at the same time, and those choppy bursts of chords. It's like two different people are in your ten fingers."

"Thank you. I wanted to play my new song, but it still isn't ready. Hopefully it'll be done by the time we play the Garden."

Jack looked out the window. "Ah, here we are at something called 'Steak Emporium.'" He indicated the neon sign as the driver opened the door. We went into the restaurant and were ushered into a private room with a drooping Rotary Club banner. As we were ordering, Mary Jo came in with Patrick, followed by a curvy blonde in a tight red mini.

"You lot, meet Kim." Patrick plopped down across from us. "D'you have any sushi?" he asked the waiter hopefully, who said he'd check.

"I don't think you're going to get any of that here," Mary Jo said.

"Where I come from, we call that bait," Sammy commented. "Me, I'm jonesin' for some nice, juicy barbecue."

"Pass the plonk," Jack said. Mark handed him a bottle of red. Jack glanced around for a corkscrew, then took a closer look and unscrewed the top.

"And what do you do, Kim?" Suzanne held out her glass for Jack to fill.

"My family owns Bush Brewery." The woman adjusted her plunging neckline.

"How fascinating. Do you get free beer?" Mary Jo looked down her nose at the menu.

"Oh, we get free everything." Kim widened her eyes. "Jack, I really loved watching you play."

"Kim has great drugs," Patrick commented. He turned to the waiter, who said they were out of raw fish. "I'll just have some broccoli, if you can manage that."

"Which drugs, exactly?" Jack asked.

"Oh, you name it. Anything your heart desires," Kim cooed.

"Maybe Patrick can bring back a sampler." Jack nodded at their lead singer, who looked bored out of his mind. "If he's over his snit."

"I told you they'd screw up the costume changes," Patrick complained to Mary Jo. "That makeup girl you hired knows the square root of fuck-all."

"I think she's fantastic," Mark chimed in as Suzanne glowered.

"I'll replace her," Mary Jo said soothingly. "Soon as we get to Kansas City."

"Keep your knickers on," Jack said. "It's not the end of the world if you wear the pink blouse before the purple."

"And *you* fucked up the lead to 'Gone Away'." Patrick frowned at Jack.

"No, I didn't. I play it different every time." Jack sat back as the waiter placed an overdone steak in front of him.

Patrick lifted a limp piece of broccoli and dropped it. "We're out of here. See you on the plane." He got up and left without waiting for Kim. Quickly she reached into her purse and took out a large baggie of white powder. "This is for you, Jack," she said, putting it on the table and waggling off after Patrick.

"Built like a brick shithouse," Sammy commented as he watched her go. "Look here, she's left us her phone number." He held up a scrap of paper. "And a goodie bag. We can all get lacquered."

"We'd better not. Remember the bird that gave us the bad stuff in Memphis," Mark said, grabbing the paper.

"I'll take that." Suzanne confiscated the phone number and crumpled it.

Jack turned to Mary Jo. "Patrick threw a wobbler over a few shirts, huh? Is something else eating him?"

"You mean besides Miss Snatch? I mean Miss Bush." Sammy grinned. "He pitched a hissie-fit over the stage set, too, just before we went on. He was *extremely bothered* by the positioning of the mic."

"I told those guys to center it." Mary Jo looked exasperated.

"Have you ever known a bass player that wasn't an arsehole?" Mark asked.

"Nope," Jack said. "He's still in a funk over that woman in L.A.; the one that turned out to only like girls. Just forget it," he added to Mary Jo. "You know Patrice; always in a strop about something." He started to saw into his steak, then put down his knife. "D'you think room service has shut down yet?"

"Let's get out of here. Worst case, they have vending machines in the lobby." Mary Jo motioned for the check, and the five of us got back into the limo, as she had driven herself.

"I had an inchoate longing to return to the hotel," Mark said as the driver tore out of the gravel lot.

"I thought our dinner plans were fairly inchoate," Jack added.

"I still don't get what it means," Sammy said.

"Ask Julia, she's a walking dictionary." Jack gestured toward me.

"What are you talking about?" I asked as they chortled.

"Patrick's always wanting to toss these big words into the lyrics," Jack explained. "Yesterday it was 'inchoate'; he'd come across it somewhere and got fascinated. I told him *I* barely know what it means, much less our fans."

"Before that, it was 'lissome'." Suzanne snorted.

"Yeah, he had a line about a lissome young girl. I got him to change it to 'winsome'," Jack said scornfully.

"Then he got 'nubile' stuck in his noggin," Mark added.

"What a muppet. He was rhyming it with 'awhile'." Jack shook his head. "I told him he was being juvenile."

"Senile is more like it," Mark said.

"Honey chile, his lyrics are vile," Sammy said to me.

"Then again, they can be fantastic. Probably depends on what was in the medicine chest that morning," Jack commented.

I thought the others would retreat to their own rooms when we got to the hotel, but they accompanied us to Jack's suite and lit yet another joint.

"I've had enough for one night; I'm getting a contact high," Suzanne said. "Let's go in here." I followed her and we stretched out on either side of the bed. "I'd ask if you mind if I smoke, but since the place is one big pot cloud, it's beside the point." She reached around for the ashtray and lit a cigarette.

"Go right ahead." I lay back on the pillow, feeling dazed. I'd gotten up at five that morning in New York; with the time difference, to me it was 4 a.m.

"You and Jack seem to be getting along well." Suzanne blew a halo of white smoke. I watched it waft up to the ceiling mirror and dissipate.

"I don't know. When I got in, Mary Jo had left a picture of Jack being mauled by that actress, Marissa Pfund. Were they together in L.A.?" Normally I wouldn't ask Suzanne to tell tales, but I needed to know the truth.

"She's a real star fucker. Jack and Patrick both had her a few years ago." Suzanne grimaced. "This time she made a play for Mark."

Her comment wasn't all that reassuring, but I decided she would have told me if Jack had partaken of Marissa recently. "How's the tour going for you so far?" I asked, alluding to Mark's roving eye.

"Honestly, I'm thinking of leaving him. I can't take the cheating anymore. It's really in my face now; I can't even pretend it's not going on."

I reached over and touched her arm. "That's awful. I'm so sorry. Would it help for Jack to talk to him?"

Suzanne's face crumpled. "Nothing would help, I'm afraid.

And it's complicated; Jack's his best mate. Anyway, I haven't made up my mind yet. I'm going to see how the rest of the concerts go."

"You can talk to me anytime. I won't mention it to Jack."

"Thanks, Julia. I know you wouldn't. You're one of the few people I can trust."

Sammy came into the room with Mark. "Well, look what we have here. Two gorgeous gals in one bed." Sammy took off his boots and sprawled between me and Suzanne. "Now *this* is what I call a beautiful situation," he said, putting an arm around each of us. He gazed up at the ceiling. "Why does Jack always get the room with the mirror?"

Mark slipped in beside Suzanne and lay face-down on the pillow. "I could pass out right here."

Jack came in and looked at us, arms crossed. "Very funny. Okay, time to go back to your own rooms. Julia had a long flight."

"Aw, I was just gettin' comfortable," Sammy drawled, laying his head on Suzanne's shoulder. "Why don't you take my bed tonight, Jack? I don't think there's room enough for you."

"Oh really? I know how to make room." Jack sat at the foot of the bed and grasped one of Sammy's feet.

"No! Don't do it!" Sammy yelped. Jack started tickling as Sammy twisted and writhed. "Don't! I'll go!"

"D'you think he's had enough?" Jack asked, looking back at me.

I laughed. "I think you can let him go now."

Suzanne was trying to push Mark off the mattress. "Come on, get up. Julia needs her sleep."

Jack released Sammy's ankle and he sprang off the bed. "You're crazier'n a bessy bug," Sammy said as he picked up his boots.

Jack began unbuttoning his shirt. "I'm ready to be with my woman."

Suzanne managed to shove Mark off the bed as Jack started to pull down his jeans. "Stop! I've seen enough," she said. "See you later, Julia." She rushed out just as Jack bared his bottom.

"Ain't none of us need to see your tallywacker," Sammy commented.

"Your fault if you do." Jack climbed in next to me without getting under the sheets.

"C'mon, we can tell when we're not wanted." Mark went out the door.

"You ever get tired of that poor excuse for manhood, you know where to find a real man," Sammy said to me. He paused on his way out. "Don't let the bedbugs bite."

Jack started kissing my neck. "I couldn't wait to put my pin in yo' cushion," he said in his deep blues voice. "I'm going fishin', baby, with my long long pole. Gonna throw in my line and sink it deep." He kissed me on the lips, making my belly flip. "Lookit my pole jumpin' up and down."

His fingers began exploring me and I reached for him, craving him inside me. We wound up making leisurely love over the next few hours. At one point we both fell asleep, then woke up and started again.

"How d'you like it?" Jack asked some time later. We were splayed on our backs, legs tangled together.

I sighed. "That was great. I missed you so much."

"No, I mean . . ." He pointed up at the mirror.

"Oh, that. It was kind of weird, watching us. Like seeing a porn movie or something. Not that I'd know," I added.

"It's kind of a turn-on, though, isn't it?"

"I guess you've had these mirrors in your room before." *Obviously.*

"Maybe once or twice." Jack yawned and gave a feline stretch.

I gazed up at our reflection. "We look like two pieces of sushi on a big white plate."

"More like a couple of earthworms in the snow. Did you edit twenty manuscripts while I was away?" He traced the curve of my hip.

"Just about. But I didn't bring any work with me; just some pleasure reading." I pointed to my copy of *Anna Karenina* on the table. "I'm so excited about getting to see you play. You really burned up the stage tonight. Not to mention the show those girls put on in the front seats."

Jack grinned. "Yeah, that was kinda distracting."

"You'd think they'd have more self-respect," I said.

"I guess that's how they get their kicks." He shrugged.

"Speaking of kicks . . ." I hesitated. "You know, if you want to be a father eventually, you'd have to stop doing coke."

Jack's surprised expression told me he hadn't even considered this. Before he had time to reply, the phone rang. Jack mumbled into the receiver, then got up and pulled on his jeans.

"Sammy and Mark are in the lobby bar. I'm gonna go for

a while; I'm too wired to sleep." He pulled on a shirt, and I heard the door slam. I was so comatose, I had no idea when he got back.

Chapter 17

TRAIN IN VAIN

The phone woke me up at nine. I rolled over and grabbed it before it disturbed Jack.

"Can you send someone up to clean my room? The sheets are all sticky."

"Is this Patrick?" I was pretty sure the British voice belonged to him.

"Oh—Julia? Thought I dialed housekeeping. Sorry 'bout that." I heard him laughing as he hung up the phone. *Very funny, asshole.* I shoved the pillow over my face and tried to fall back asleep.

Checkout did not go smoothly. Bags were misplaced, voices were raised, and hangovers were hammering. Finally the woman at the front desk had had it. "Listen, we got twelve complaints about the noise last night. Don't you people know where to draw the line?"

Patrick pulled himself up to his full five-foot-eight and gave her a disdainful look. "Sure we do. We've been doing lines all week."

Mary Jo made a shooing motion. "I'll handle this. You guys take the limo; I'm driving with Patrick to go over some things."

En route to the airport, Sammy looked green. "I feel like nine miles of bad road," he complained.

"Elevenses." Mark held up a brimming shot glass and drained it. "At least that hotel was better than the last one."

Jack's face was pale beneath his sunglasses. "Yeah, it was the Hiatt of my experience."

When we reached the airport, the limo took us right onto the tarmac and over to The Floor's private jet. "I feel like a movie star," I said as I followed Jack up the narrow metal steps.

"You'll get used to it," he called over his shoulder.

We spoke to the pilot and took our seats, waiting for Patrick and Mary Jo to arrive. As soon as they stepped on board, the engine revved and the plane took off down the runway. Patrick went into the bathroom with his onboard bag.

"Scarfing down his coke so he doesn't have to share," Mark commented.

"What's the movie today?" Sammy asked. "That new one called E.T.'s supposed to be good."

"The flight's too short," Mary Jo said. "Only an hour and a half to Kansas City."

"I've always wondered why you can't just rent a film and watch it at home." Suzanne flicked her lighter at a cigarette. "Someone ought to start a business doing that."

"I think there's a guy in L.A. who does it on a small scale," Jack said.

"You mean those things Patrick had?" Sammy asked.

"Er, no. I mean regular movies."

Patrick emerged from the bathroom wearing a fluffy white robe over his tracksuit and sat next to Mary Jo. Jack reached across the aisle and fingered the edge of his sleeve. "Nice togs."

"Nicked it off the hotel; least they could do. Who's up for Scrabble?" Patrick asked.

Mark and Sammy groaned. "Not that again."

Jack sat up in his seat. "I'll bet Julia can beat you. Switch places with me."

"Oh no, I'm not that good." I didn't want to get into a competition with their cantankerous vocalist, but he got up and took Jack's spot next to me. Jack stood behind us, looking over the seatback as Patrick unfolded a travel board.

"Helps pass the time." He distributed the letters from a small velvet bag.

This is the last thing I feel like doing, I thought as I arranged my vowels.

"I'll give you the advantage. You can lead off," Patrick said, implying I'd need it.

"Okay … RETSINA. The Greek drink." I placed the letters on the board and held out my hand for seven more. I wound up with an X, making me wonder if he'd stacked the deck.

"Hmm." Patrick added H and E, making HER. I took the free H and made it into HEX, ridding myself of the difficult consonant.

Patrick surrounded the last A in RETSINA. "QAT. It's the African version of pot."

"I've had that," Jack said over my shoulder. "Rendered me legless, as I recall."

I appended a vertical TRAIN, and Patrick added PIZZA. I put down an O, forming a square with the N and Z.

"ZO's not a word." Patrick smirked.

"I believe it's a Himalayan cow," I said.

Patrick drew a little book out of his bag. "Let's just check." He thumbed to the page and frowned. "I guess you're right."

Suzanne snatched the dictionary. "No cheating. I'll hold onto this." She stood next to Jack as Mary Jo craned across the aisle to see.

Patrick sorted through his pieces. "I've got something." He placed TWAT on the board.

"I'm not sure that's in the dictionary, but I'll let you have it." I formed PEA as Patrick chose more letters.

"Here's a good one." Patrick put down the letters for PUSSY.

"That's not very sporting of you," Mark said as he joined the spectators.

"Oh, it's all right," I said. *If he can play dirty, then I can too.* I made TWAT into TWEE.

"Is that a word?" Sammy asked.

I looked at Patrick. "It means affected; sickeningly cute. Sort of prissy."

Patrick poked through his letters and wrote MERDE.

"Well, aren't you the head boy," Jack commented.

"We're using foreign languages? I'll keep that in mind." I appended MORON to his French word for shit.

"Why not?" Patrick made an OX out of HEX.

I added VAIN to MORON. "Fine with me," I said, drawing more letters. "I'm happy to bend the rules."

OI, Patrick wrote. "As in 'Oi, you're a pain in the arse.'"

"Yes, I get it." I used the R in MORON for CRETIN.

"Hmm." He formed the word BITCH.

"That bumps against the D in MERDE," Suzanne pointed out. "D-bitch isn't a word."

"Go ahead. I know you need the points," I said, enjoying Patrick's frustrated glare.

Suddenly the plane lurched and the letters slid across the board. "Game's over." Patrick scooped them up and stuffed them into the bag. *Mister World-Famous doesn't like losing to a lowly editor—or to a woman,* I thought.

"We've hit an air pocket." The pilot's voice came on as the plane made a sudden dip. "Everybody should sit down."

Mark held onto his armrest. "Blimey! Gives me the abdabs."

"This tin can's going up and down like a whore's drawers." Sammy's face was bilious. Jack held out a sick bag to him, but Mark snatched it and vomited into it as Suzanne rubbed his back.

"Now that was a tactical chunder," Patrick said. He seemed unaffected by the rollercoaster ride.

Holding onto the seatbacks, Sammy made his way to the

rear of the plane. The turbulence kept up until we landed in Kansas City.

As soon as we got to the hotel, Jack had to do a few interviews with Patrick. I hadn't eaten anything all day, so the cellophane-wrapped brownies in our room were a welcome sight. Grateful for the hospitality treat, I wolfed down two of them as I unpacked our things. Since the water in the tap was brown, I washed them down with a beer.

While I was hanging up some of Jack's shirts, I started to feel sort of weird. At first I wondered if it was a delayed reaction to the bumpy flight, but then the wooziness increased. I lay on the hotel bed—this time without a ceiling mirror— and tried to stabilize my whirling mind. Stray thoughts were rattling through my brain: *train . . . vain . . . moron . . . merde . . . Kim gives free . . . Marissa relaxes . . . Jack enjoys . . .*

Some time later, I felt a weight on the mattress. I opened my eyes and saw Jack gazing down at me.

"Hey. You all right?"

I heard a faint echo fading away: *ight–ight–ight . . .* I tried to tell him that I felt fine; in fact, I realized, I felt *amazing*. All the colors in the room were swirling together to form the most incredible dribs and drabs. Jack's chain sparkling in the lamplight became a waterfall rippling down his chest. I tried to reach for it, but the stream scattered and I fell back on the pillow.

"Julia." Jack cupped my face in his warm hand. His touch created an incredible rush, starting with a heat wave in my loins that surged upward through my abdomen. My nipples felt like tight peony buds ready to burst into bloom. I sat up and yanked my blouse over my head, getting stuck on my elbows until Jack helped me pull it off.

"Feeling lurgy?" he asked. "I can open a window."

"I'm good." I got up on my knees and then made it to my feet, the mattress rolling under my bare toes. Suddenly I had the urge to strip. "Can you sing something?" I asked, hearing my voice swoop around the room.

"Sure. Are you okay?" Jack got his guitar and sat in a chair. "What do you want to hear?"

"Something sssexy." The "s" sizzled off my tongue and set-tled around my ankles. I undid my top jeans button and did a belly-dancer hip-roll that I didn't know I had in me. *Where'd that come from?* I wondered abstractly.

Jack started strumming and crooning. "My woman's gone crazy, she's acting like a shady lady . . ." He looked at me. "What's got into you?"

"I have to get these clothes off!" Suddenly the fabric's weight was really bugging me. I undid another button of my jeans, then dipped my hand inside and touched myself through my panties—*wow*. I stood there with my mouth open, stunned by the buzzing sensation. I undid another button and pushed my jeans down to the top of my thighs. Jack was still strum-ming slow-hand chords, his dark gaze locked on me.

"*Ummmm.*" I shut my eyes and gave myself up to the dance, moving my hips to the rhythm; back, forth, back, forth . . . The denim created an unbearably pleasurable friction in my crotch. I slid the jeans down to my ankles and kicked them off. Then I turned around, my back to him, and swayed my hips in time to the music.

"I may have to join you up there in a minute," I heard Jack say.

"No! Keep playing." Turning to face him again, I gazed down at my breasts, which appeared to be bursting out of my bra. I stroked my nipples through the silky fabric and watched in amazement as they hardened into pink gumballs. *God, that feels incredible* . . . I undid the clasp and squeezed myself, sending a current of pleasure jolting through me. I glanced up at Jack. He had put down the guitar and was staring at me.

"If you're trying to turn me on, it's working," he said. "Can I get up now?"

"Jus' a minute." The only thing left was my pale blue bikini underwear. I slid one side down my hip, then back up. I slid down the other side, feeling the tightening in my folds, the bunched material becoming unbelievably wet.

Suddenly Jack was kneeling on the bed. He yanked down my panties and put his mouth on me. All he did was breathe one long hot breath, but it made my knees buckle.

"Want to lie down?" he asked, his face still at my crotch, the motion of his lips uncurling a spiral of heat from my core.

Jack put his strong arms around me and lowered me onto the sheets. Flicking my nipple lightly with his tongue, he reached down with one hand and undid his jeans. I felt him spring at me, nudging my thigh.

"Not yet," he said as I reached for him. He kissed his way down my chest, circling his tongue around my navel, lapping the softness of my belly. My hips were lifting of their own accord, my body overtaken by an uncontrollable craving. As his tongue approached I became one pulsing need, my whole being concentrated on his lips. I sang out when he put his mouth on me. After only three strokes I was coming, waves of sensation rippling out into a tidal pool spreading across my abdomen, surging up to my breasts.

"God, Julia," Jack murmured. He slipped his tongue inside me and then ran it slowly up the middle, making me gasp. I was still coming when he slid his full length into me. I cried out as he moved faster and faster. Then we were both chorusing, his climax ending in a long, melodic moan.

I woke up incredibly hungry. Jack opened his eyes as I shifted his arm out from under me.

"What're you doing?" he asked.

"I'm going to have another brownie."

Jack gave me an odd look. "You ate those?"

I shrugged. "I had two. I was starving."

"Julia. They're hash brownies from a groupie we know. I was gonna give them to Sammy."

"You're kidding. I thought the hotel left them for us." *No wonder I felt so strange.*

"Is that the first time you've had it?" Jack asked.

I nodded, feeling incredibly dumb.

"If you thought that was good, you'll have to try mescaline sometime," he said.

"It was amazing, but I don't think I'd do that again." I rubbed my pounding head and carefully lay back on the pillow. "Did I really put on a strip-tease?"

"You could earn a living in Vegas. Not that you'd want to. Listen, why don't you rest up a little? I'm gonna get my face on for the show. And I'll see if we can get some room service."

Chapter 18

I WANNA BE SEDATED

I awoke sometime later to Jack gently shaking my shoulder. "Knees up, mother brown. We've gotta get going. Do you want any of this?" He held up a wrapped sandwich, but I felt too logy to eat. I pulled on my jeans, washed my face and swallowed two aspirin, trying to avoid moving quickly so as not to set off the pounding in my head.

Sammy was waiting for us in the limo. He peered at me when I borrowed Jack's sunglasses for the ride. "What's up with you? You're usually fulla beans."

Jack put his arm around my shoulder. "Julia got hold of those brownies. She didn't know they were à la thai stick."

Sammy gave me a sympathetic smile. "Been there, done that. But I always say, if you can't run with the big dogs, stay under the porch. Here, have a little hair of the mutt." He cracked open a bottle of whiskey and handed it to me.

"I'll keep that in mind," I croaked as I took a big slug.

By the time we got to the backstage area, I was feeling somewhat better. On the wall next to the huge mirror was a peeling poster of Four to the Floor from their tour several years ago. I went closer to take a look. Jack was glaring at the camera, hair below his shoulders, a joint pasted to his lips. Mark and Sammy wore similar expressions; Patrick had a boa around his neck and was baring his teeth.

"That's a divine boa on Patrick," I said to Jack.

"Yeah, that was his Marlene Dietrich phase," Jack said. "We got along better back then."

"You won't be getting along at all if she keeps talking to the newspapers." Mary Jo stood next to us, hands on her hips.

"Excuse me?" I said.

"I guess you have a few contacts at the papers, too." She held out a copy of a national gossip rag. FLOOR FEUD! shouted the headline. BICKERING BASHES BRITISH BAND. The piece stated that the group's lead vocalist Patrick Bagley and guitarist Jack Kipling were arguing over the tour's sponsorship by a deodorant maker, and disagreeing about everything from the songs to hotels to costume changes.

"What do you mean? I didn't plant that!" I couldn't believe what she was implying.

"Oh really? Take a look at this." She indicated a quote with her fingernail.

A source close to the disgruntled guitarist stated, "Jack is sick of catering to Patrick's whims—in fact, he's sick of him altogether." She quoted Kipling as saying, "If Patrick would just focus on the music, he'd give better concert. As it is, his voice is weak and he's lost his groove. Instead of doing deals with deodorants, he should make sure his singing doesn't reek."

"No one but you and Suzanne knew about all that. The argument about the sponsor, the hotels, and so on." Mary Jo sized me up with her hazel glare. "That comment about Patrick sounds like it's straight from the horse's mouth."

"The Bush woman heard them bickering at dinner in St. Louis," I said defiantly. "Maybe it was her."

"Kim doesn't know Jack. She isn't capable of stringing together two words that sound like him." *Implying that of course, I did.*

"I would never—" I began as she sidled away.

"Read it to me." Jack was squinting at the tiny print.

I read it out loud. "I have no idea who did this, but it wasn't me."

Jack tossed the paper into a garbage can. "I'll talk to her." He went over to where Mary Jo was having a heated discussion with Patrick and spoke to them for a few minutes, gesturing toward me. *Surely Patrick doesn't think I ratted them out!* I told myself. But the dirty look he gave me made me feel like I'd grown a long, ropy tail.

Just then Suzanne and Mark rushed in, out of breath.

"Strike me pink!" Mark exclaimed, climbing into the chair. "Is it that late already?" As the makeup girl fussed over him, I motioned for Suzanne to step away from the others.

"Did you see that article Mary Jo's passing around? I had nothing to do with it!"

"You didn't by any chance talk to one of those reporters?"

she asked. "They can really twist what you say into something entirely different."

"I wouldn't talk to those people. I'm not that stupid," I said miserably.

Suzanne patted my arm. "These things happen. Try not to worry about it."

Patrick sauntered over as Mary Jo continued her conversation with Jack. "I didn't realize you'd take a little game of Scrabble so seriously. I guess you wanted to take me down a notch." His sneer made fine lines in the heavy stage makeup.

"That wasn't me!" I said, my face turning hot. "I'd never blab about Jack to anyone."

Patrick gave me a knowing look. "It's all right, sweetheart. Those papers aren't fit to line a birdcage. I'm sure you didn't mean any harm."

"But I didn't—" He turned on his heel and stalked off before I could finish. Suzanne placed her hand under my open jaw and gently closed it. "It'll blow over. Come on, let's grab our seats." Mary Jo still had Jack cornered when we left.

We got there just in time before the men came on. They launched into their first number to the same roaring acclaim as the night before, and then ran through a fantastic mix of past and present hits. Hearing so many great songs, one after the other, made you realize just how incredible the band was; most groups were lucky to have two or three at most.

Midway through, a roadie dragged out a stool and Jack tuned his acoustic guitar as people wistfully called out the names of their favorite songs. Jack began the haunting intro to one of their biggest ballads from a few years ago; a torchy melody that was unlike anything they had ever done. I loved the occasional squeak of his fingers on the Gibson's strings as he joined Patrick in crooning the lyrics. Even though I'd heard it a million times, the words still got to me:

I feel the echo of you in my mind, long after you left me for the last time . . .

They ran through the set list in an order similar to the previous show, with a few numbers reversed. It all sounded great, but I was distracted by the fact that I was now the black sheep of their in-crowd. Jack had once told me that Patrick didn't like him to be with any one woman, feeling that it took away from the band. I wondered if Patrick had had someone plant the article—I wouldn't put it past him. He'd always seemed to look down his nose at me; I guess because I wasn't a model, an heiress to a brewery, or one of his fancy hangers-on. But then I realized that the piece made Patrick look bad, too—and his whole deal was looking all good, all the time. I didn't believe he'd instigate negative press that could reflect badly on him.

I tried to snuff out my worries along with the hundreds of flickering lighters at the final encore. Sheepishly I followed Suzanne backstage, wishing I could just disappear into our hotel room without having to face the others. Luckily a big group of people talked their way past security and rushed in, so it was impossible for Mary Jo or Patrick to focus on me.

Jack started making his way through the crowd. Everyone he passed wanted to touch him, fawn over him, extract a piece of him. A pack of women approached him with a feral gleam in their eyes, as if they wanted to pounce on him and devour him whole. Two six-foot-tall ladies with suspiciously big Adams' apples swooped over and managed to kiss both Jack and Patrick full on the lips before Mary Jo had them escorted out.

Finally Jack made it to my side. "Do I have lipstick on me face?" he asked.

"A little." I wiped it off with my finger.

"I don't think I've ever been kissed by a man before," he mused.

"How was it?" I asked.

"Not half bad, except I got whisker burn."

He seemed to have forgotten the gossip rag for the time being, so I tried to do the same. "I loved the slow number in the middle," I said. "The emotion in it gave me the chills. You really sounded fantastic."

"Yeah, but Patrick's voice was a little weak, don't you think? And he definitely lacked groove." He laughed at my forlorn expression. "Just kidding. Forget about that dumb article. C'mon, let's get the others and head out. We aren't gonna bother trying to eat anywhere."

On the way back to the hotel, the limo got caught in a massive traffic pileup. "Sorry about this," the driver said as we sat stalled in an endless line of cars. "Looks like the stoplight's broken."

"Let's do 'what's your favorite'," Sammy suggested, breaking the seal on a bottle of whiskey from the car's side pocket. "We haven't done it with Julia yet."

Suzanne looked at me pityingly. "Julia may never come

back if she gets a taste of what you're like with a captive audience." I was relieved that the others didn't seem to be concerned about the supposed Judas in their midst—or perhaps they just figured Patrick had it coming.

"May as well, since we'll be stuck here for a while," Sammy said. He took a gulp and handed the bottle to Jack. "What's your favorite food?"

"Filet mignon." Jack swigged and passed the bottle to Mark.

They all looked at me. "Um, Jack's scrambled eggs."

"Aw, that's sweet, but you're bullshittin'. They're not that good." Sammy took another sip.

"I don't serve 'em to you with what I give Julia," Jack said. "A nice big sausage."

Sammy frowned. "Damn right you don't. I don't bat for the other team."

"Let's move this along. Mine is tuna nicoise." Suzanne shook out a cigarette from her pack.

"Bangers and mash," Mark said. The car ahead of us lurched forward, and again we were moving.

"All right," Sammy said. "Favorite sex position."

"Woman on top!" all three men shouted at once.

"Well, that was unanimous." Mark looked at me. "Julia?"

"You don't have to say," Suzanne added. "Really, you don't."

I thought about it. "I'm not sure if it fits in this category, or Jack's favorite things to eat."

For a moment there was silence, then they all burst into laughter. "She shoots, she scores!" Mark said.

"Nice one, sweetheart." Jack put his arm around me as I blushed.

Sammy gave me a thumbs-up. "Now there's a vote for your tuna nicoise. Julia, I wouldn't have thought you had it in you."

"You're rubbing off on her," Suzanne said to Jack. "Which is not necessarily a good thing."

"You haven't said yours," Jack commented.

"I'd have to go with Julia's choice," she said primly. "But with Mark, of course."

Jack smiled. "Don't knock what you haven't tried."

"You know the four types of orgasms, don't you?" Sammy asked.

I hesitated. "I'm not sure I do."

"There's the good ones: 'Oh yes, oh yes.' Then the bad ones: 'Oh no, oh no.' The religious ones scream, 'Oh God, oh God!'" Sammy leaned in toward me. "And the fake ones say, 'Oh Jack, oh Jack!'"

I laughed as the others groaned. Jack just shook his head.

"If you think this is bad, wait 'til you're cooped up with them in a hotel room for eight hours straight," Suzanne warned me. "Just prepare yourself. It isn't pretty."

Jack glanced out the window as we went by a 55 mph sign. "Hey, we just passed a double nickel."

Back in our suite, again it was a crowd of five. Jack got out his eight-track cassette player and inserted an Etta James tape.

"How 'bout a little poker?" Sammy grabbed a deck of cards from the table as Mark pulled up a chair.

"I'm not very good. I only played once or twice in college," I said as Etta growled the low notes.

"Always more interesting when someone loses big." Sammy shuffled the cards. "Down to underwear, or everything off?"

"No stripping." Jack flopped next to me on the sofa.

Sammy looked so disappointed, I had to laugh. "Aw, that's no fun," he said. "How about if just us guys strip? The girls can keep their stuff on. Or maybe take off their tops."

"Any excuse to remove his clothes," Jack commented.

"Can't blame me for trying," Sammy said. The guys felt in their pockets and dumped their change on the table.

Sammy dealt as Suzanne slid ten pennies over to each of us. "That's for your bets, Julia. Don't go too crazy," she said. They each pushed one cent into the middle.

Jack looked at my cards. "The person with the lowest card bets. That would be you, Sammy. Bring it."

The others played their hands, Jack showing me what to do.

"I'm out." Sammy started unbuttoning his shirt. "What?" he asked, looking at Jack. "I thought we were playin' down to our boxers."

"You don't have on any boxers," Suzanne said. "Just stop at your shirt. Julia doesn't want to see your birthday suit."

"Thank you, Suzanne. I'm gonna call." Jack slid two pennies over

"All right, down and dirty now." Sammy dealt a last card to each of us.

Suzanne flipped hers over. "Three of a kind." She slid the mound of pennies to her side of the table.

"Scoop it up. I've lost me shirt," Jack said, unbuttoning.

"I'm gonna get you next time," he added to Suzanne. I admired the flex of his bare arm as he lifted the bottle and took a drink. "My turn to deal."

"You've gotta watch him," Sammy said. "You should see how he cheats in Monopoly."

"I do not." Jack shuffled the deck.

"How come you always wind up with Boardwalk?" Sammy asked.

"Lucky, I guess." Jack grinned. He looked incredibly sexy sitting next to me with his shirt off, long legs crossed barefoot at the ankles and thick choppy hair going every which way. I put my hand on his thigh and felt his muscles tighten. As his fingers splayed around my waist, I fought a powerful urge to climb into his lap. The game ended with Jack winning the last hand.

"All right, time to split." Mark stood up and stretched. "I'm gonna hit the bar."

"Why don't you just come to bed?" Suzanne asked fretfully.

"I'll be back in a while." Mark hurried out, Sammy in tow.

Suzanne looked like she was about to cry. "I'm too zonked to follow him around anymore. Good night." She went out the door.

"I thought they'd never leave," Jack said as he reached for me.

Chapter 19

ANOTHER ONE
BITES THE DUST

A hunched old man with a scraggly beard leaned over a railroad track, hammering at an iron bar. He muttered to himself in French, paying no attention to me, but I could tell something horrible was about to happen. I awoke in a cold sweat and realized that someone was pounding on the door. Jack was conked out next to me. I looked at my watch. We weren't leaving for Orlando until the afternoon; who in hell could it be? Pulling on my jeans, I went to see.

Suzanne was standing there. Her face was smeary with tears, her beautiful red hair matted.

"What happened? Are you all right?" I asked, drawing her inside. "Is Mark okay?"

Suzanne shook her head. "I'm leaving. I wanted to tell you before I go. I can't take it anymore!" she wailed. I put my arms around her, feeling her tremble.

"Are you sure? Do you want to stay here with us?"

"He's been fucking the makeup girl!" she cried. "Right under my nose! I'm used to him picking up groupies; one-night stands with his little Floor Whores. But he's been screwing her the whole time!" She drooped onto my shoulder.

"You're right. You do need to leave him." I felt awful for her, and also realized how this would change everything.

Suzanne wiped her streaming eyes on her sleeve. "I hate to desert you in the middle of the cock-up about that newspaper article. Julia, listen to me. Mary Jo's trying to get you banned from the tour. Before the show last night, she and Patrick spent half an hour trying to convince Jack that you planted it."

My stomach sank. "Can they ban me if Jack doesn't agree to it?" *God, this is turning into a nightmare!*

"I don't think so, but don't underestimate Mary Jo. She's really devious; she's stirred up all kinds of trouble before. She's the one that hired that little makeup floozy in the first place." Suzanne's face crumpled. "This time I'm really going to leave him for good."

"I'm so sorry, Suzanne. But I think you're doing the right thing. Should I get Jack up?"

"No, let him sleep. He'd probably just try to talk me into staying." She reached in her bag for a tissue and blew her nose. "I'm going to stay with my Mum for a while in London. I'll call you when I'm back in New York. At least you and I can still be friends."

"Of course we can. We'll have dinner when you get back."

"I'm sorry to bail on you. Just keep your eyes open. Don't let Mary Jo pull any more of her stunts. I don't know what's wrong with that woman; she isn't satisfied unless she's making someone miserable."

We embraced again, and she left. Feeling abandoned, I got back into bed and looked at Jack's slumbering face on the pillow. He'd made a joke about the article, but what was he really thinking? He was smooth enough to act like he didn't believe I'd done it—but deep down, did he suspect me? And how would I convince him of my innocence without sounding like I was protesting too much? As Jack began to stir, I decided to just leave it for the time being. Instead, I told him about Suzanne's defection.

"She's left him before. She'll be back." Jack swiped his face tiredly.

His nonchalant tone pissed me off. "Don't you think it's awful the way Mark treats her? She's his wife. Doesn't that mean anything?"

Jack looked at me blearily. "Obviously it means something to *you*. Can we talk about this later? My head's killing me."

"You never want to discuss anything difficult. Or that you don't agree with." I crossed my arms.

"Last night I spent an hour defending you to Mary Jo and Patrick." His voice got louder. "*That* was pretty difficult."

"Are you implying I spoke to that reporter?" I raised my voice to match his.

"Give it a rest. I'm sick of the whole thing." Jack sat up, pulled on a shirt and jeans, and to my dismay, stomped out.

After several hours of tossing and turning, I finally drifted off while trying to read *Anna K.* Around two in the afternoon, I was awakened by the ringing phone.

"Can you come get Jack? He isn't feeling well," Patrick said in a low voice. "You'd better take him back to your room."

"What's going on?" I asked.

"I dunno, he seems kind of sick. You'd better hurry. Room 969."

"I'll be there in a minute." I hoped Jack wasn't coming down with something bad; I knew a few of the roadies were MIA with the flu. Although we'd just quarreled, I didn't wish that on him.

I took the elevator to the ninth floor, found the room and tapped on the door, which was cracked. "Come in," I heard Patrick say. Pushing it open, I stepped inside.

Patrick was standing behind a naked woman sprawled face-down on the bed. A purple sleep mask covered her eyes, and next to her was a mirror crosshatched with lines of cocaine. Mark was sprawled back in a chair, nude beneath his robe.

"Jack, it's your turn!" Patrick called out. He smiled at me. "Want to join us? We're playing Guess the Cock."

Before I could react, Jack came out of the bathroom. He stopped in his tracks. "What are—"

"You bastard!" I shrieked. I shoved out the door, flew across the hall and took the stairs. Racing down the flights,

I didn't bother stifling my screams. My hands were shaking so much, I could hardly get the key in the lock. I ran into the bedroom and started throwing my things into a suitcase. *You've got to get out of here before he comes back!* I told myself. As tears dripped down my face, the thought occurred to me: *I wonder if he'll even bother to come downstairs.*

The door slammed. "Julia!"

I turned to face him. "I'll be out of your hair in five minutes. You can go back to your sleazy friends!"

Jack came toward me, arms outstretched. "Calm down."

"*Calm down?* Don't tell me to calm down!" I shouted.

"I wasn't doing anything." He lifted his hands and dropped them to his sides. "Listen to me for a minute. I was just doing some blow. I figured I'd have one last binge before I go home."

"How can you expect me to believe that!" I felt like my brain was about to explode.

"I didn't do anything with her." Jack sat on the edge of the mattress. "We were hanging out in Patrick's room. She had on a robe the whole time; I was only there for the flake. I went to use the bathroom. When Patrick called out to me, I thought it was my turn to do a line. He must have set it up just to shock you."

"'Shock' doesn't really do it justice." My mind was working overtime. *How am I supposed to know what's the truth? God, is this just a slick lie?*

"I swear on my grandfather's grave. I wasn't doing anything." Still sitting, he gazed up at me. Looking into his deep brown eyes, I tried to gauge his sincerity.

"Listen, Julia. For whatever reason, Patrick sees you as a threat. He has, ever since he realized I was really into you." Jack sighed. "He likes me to hang out with him on tour. My hotel room's always been the party room, but now it's not. He isn't too happy about that."

"But *he's* always with different people. Why does he care who you're with?" I sniffled.

"That's just the point. He doesn't care if I'm with a different girl every night. It's *one* woman that makes him feel threatened."

Jack stood up and put his arms around me. "My band mate's a cunt. And I shouldn't have run out on you earlier. I was really hung over." He leaned in to kiss me, and I let him part my lips. His tongue met mine gently, and then passionately. I was only just starting to believe him, but my body was way ahead of my mind.

Jack pulled away and squeezed my waist. "I wouldn't be with someone else when I've got my own woman right here with me."

I managed a wan smile.

"Hot in here." He took off his shirt. "Let me get you something." He went to the fridge and opened a beer. I drank thirstily, my throat scraped raw from crying.

"That's my girl." He pulled me close, and I could feel his heart thumping. Again I looked into his dark eyes lowered to mine, jet-black lashes brushing his high cheekbones.

I guess I'm going to believe him. He said he wouldn't do that while I was here. But does that mean he would if I wasn't here?

Jack's lips brushed my neck. "Do you want to rest?" he

murmured. "I don't mean to jump you right after . . ."

I slid my arms around him. "I don't want to rest."

In a way, I was glad to get on the plane back to New York. Going to the concert in Orlando without Suzanne made me sad, and I was stuck sitting next to Mary Jo in all her huffy disapproval. I'd tried to explain again that I hadn't spoken to any reporters, but she turned her back on me, and I just sat there feeling dumb. I would miss Jack horribly for the next three weeks, and I wondered what he'd be up to when I wasn't around. But I'd had it with his self-righteous manager and vile band mate.

Chapter 20

JUST WHAT I NEEDED

Dermot Chase had promised me the entire first draft of his novel when I got back, so I was excited about meeting him for a drink that following Thursday. I was relieved that he was finally handing it in—especially since I'd fudged telling my boss that I hadn't even seen the first chapter yet.

I left the office at six and sprinted through the freezing March rain to the upscale bar that Dermot had suggested. I spotted him sitting at a table, looking suavely handsome in a dark suit and white shirt. His glossy brown hair fell in a wave over his forehead, giving him a boyish air despite his sophisticated duds. He got up as I approached, and extended his arms.

"Ju-li-i-a." He crooned my name to the tune of the John Lennon song. His voice wasn't bad, but of course it was nothing compared to Jack's. "Did you have a nice visit with your family?" He put his hands on my shoulders.

"I had a good week." Prepared for his Continental-style kiss this time around, I avoided bumping noses.

"You do look relaxed." His gaze swept up and down, making me flush. His flirting wasn't really appropriate, but what could it hurt? *Live a little*, I told myself.

"It was nice to have some time off. How was your week?" I asked. We took our seats at the small table, our knees touching. I started to move mine away, but then decided not to be so uptight.

Dermot gave me a smoldering look. "I missed you. But I made progress while you were gone."

The waiter stopped by. I asked for a glass of merlot, and Dermot ordered another scotch. "That's really great," I said to Dermot. "I'm looking forward to digging in. Quickly. With the tight deadline, Ted's a little anxious about it." Now that he was turning it in, I could acknowledge the pressure from my boss.

"Oh, not so fast. It's coming along . . ." Dermot looked at me, his irises dark pinpricks surrounded by crystalline blue. "But I'm not quite ready to hand it over yet. Actually I've been reworking the young female character. I told you about Penelope, right?"

I bit back my frustration. "Yes, you mentioned it."

"Since we met, I'm revising her to be more like you." Dermot gazed soulfully into my eyes. "Beautiful. Intelligent. Fascinating."

I choked on my wine. As I was spluttering, Dermot

offered his glass of water. "I'm not upsetting you, am I?" He flashed a big smile.

Rattled by his flattery, I tried to compose myself. "No, but I mean—we don't know each other very well. Maybe there's someone else you could base her on. Do you have a niece?" I floundered, trying to get the conversation back on a professional track.

"If it makes you uncomfortable, there are any number of young women who'd be thrilled to be my muse." He frowned, seeming a little insulted.

Oh god, I can't put him off. What if he has to go back and rewrite it? "I'm sure it'll be fine. When I go through the manuscript, I'll add in any . . ." *This is so weird. Am I supposed to edit it so she's like me?* "Any, um, characteristics that might be helpful."

"Great. And we'll need to spend more time together, so I can get her exactly right." He took my hand, his onyx ring cool against my skin.

"Sure, but could I have the first hundred pages? Just to get a sense of it." I extracted my hand, grabbed my wine glass and drained it.

"You'll have it all soon enough. But I *can* give you a copy of my acceptance speech for the Book Awards." He pulled an envelope from his inner coat pocket. "Everyone keeps telling me I'm going to win, so I've prepared a little statement. Maybe you could give it a once-over." He handed me the envelope, which I stuffed into my backpack.

"I'll let you know if I have any suggestions." I paid the bill with my corporate card, and Dermot helped me into my coat. "When do you think you'll have the first draft for me?" I asked in desperation.

"All in its own sweet time. Despite what those philistines in your contracts department think, a work of art can't be rushed."

I'd settle for a novel delivered on time, instead of a work of art six months late. "Okay, let me know how it's going."

"I will. And we'll be seeing each other soon at the Awards, right? They're coming up in a couple of weeks."

"I'll check with Ted to see who's going," I said vaguely. I hadn't focused on that in the least.

"Can I drop you anywhere? I'm going back to my solitary abode. For now, my only mistress is the book, and she's demanding." A lock of hair flopped over his eye, and he pushed it back.

"Thanks, but I'm heading downtown," I said.

Dermot did the double-cheek-kissing thing again and ducked into a town car that was waiting at the curb. I schlepped over to the subway in the sluicing rain and crammed myself into a crowded car. When I got back to the loft, Muddy greeted me with frenzied exuberance. After cleaning up his mess, I took him for an abbreviated walk in the foul weather. Then I waited until midnight for Jack's post-concert call, which never came.

"How's Dermot's manuscript coming along?" Ted stuck his head in my office door the next morning. "It is any good?"

"It, uh, promises to be good," I said. "By the way, he keeps asking about the Book Awards."

"Oh, we've bought our usual table." Ted pushed his glasses up his nose. "You're on the list, of course. Dermot will be seated between you and me, and you'll be flanked by Perry. If he doesn't steal your seat."

"Dermot seems pretty sure he's going to win. He even gave me a copy of his acceptance speech," I said.

"Could I take a look?" I handed Ted the pages, on which I'd made a few notes. Ted pointed to the opening paragraph. "Have him rearrange the order of the names here. I should be first, and then Perry."

"Should I run that by Dermot?" I was hesitant to be the one who removed the publisher from his first-place position.

"Here, I'll do it." Ted grabbed my red pencil and marked the page. "Just retype it so Dermot doesn't notice."

"All right." This seemed underhanded, but I guessed I had to. "When is the ceremony, anyway?"

"March 28th. It's black tie, so we'll all be in our monkey suits."

Something about the date rang a bell, but I couldn't place it. "Good to know. I'll get a fancy dress." I could borrow one from Vicky; she had a closet stuffed full of party outfits.

Ted saluted and left me retyping the speech. Just as I was licking the envelope to mail it to Dermot, Cathy came in looking frazzled. "Are you okay?" I asked.

She plopped down in my chair. "I just got out of the most awful meeting. I have these co-authors who are shrinks; they wrote *How to Speak So Your Husband Will Listen*."

I nodded, having seen the guide displayed in our lobby.

"They just had this huge brawl in the publicist's office.

Gillian got a booking on the *Morning Show*, but the producer only wants to have one of them on. They were arguing about who gets to do it. For a minute there, I thought we'd have fisticuffs."

"How'd you settle it?" I asked.

"Gillian made them draw straws. Then one accused the other of cheating, so they had to do it three more times. And supposedly *they're* the experts at sorting out people's problems." Cathy rolled her eyes. "Speaking of problems, how's Dermot coming along?"

I lowered my voice. "He hasn't even given me the first chapter. And Ted keeps asking me about it."

"Haven't you told him?" Cathy stared at me.

"I'm afraid if I do, he'll give it back to Erica, the in-house genius."

"That's true, but you'd better let Ted know soon. They'll blame you if it's late. Or la*ter*," she added.

My phone rang, and Cathy made a throat-cutting gesture on her way out.

Finally the day came when Jack was flying home. I had wanted to pick him up at the airport, but the best I could do was skip out at four after a never-ending production meeting. Midtown traffic wasn't clogged yet, so I splurged on a cab and flew downtown. I ran into the building and fidgeted in the elevator. When it opened at the penthouse, I could hear music pouring through the walls. I pushed through the door and saw him standing there: dark hair below his shoulders, a tired smile creating those sexy lines next to his mouth, sooty smudges beneath his eyes.

"Hey," he said as I flew into his arms. Then I was drowning in his lips, his ardent tongue exploring mine. Desire surged through me as his hands went to my breasts.

"I don't think we're gonna make it to the bedroom," he murmured, kissing my neck as he stripped off his shirt.

"God, you feel good." I ran my hands across his warm, muscled chest, feeling his nipples harden, then slid my fingers down his ridged abdomen. I squeezed his gorgeous butt as he slipped out of his jeans.

"Your turn." He tugged off my clothes and lowered me onto the couch. "Ahh, this is what I've been missing," he said, tonguing my nipples into ripe raspberries.

"I couldn't wait for you to get home," I gasped as he thrust into me.

Jack gazed at me and stopped his motion. "I'm gonna send you, baby." Bracing his body with one flexed arm, he reached down and began stroking me lightly with his fingers, ramrod-stiff inside me but holding still.

"That's all right, you can come," I said, mesmerized by what he was doing.

"Let's come together," Jack whispered in my ear. His abdomen brushing mine, he began moving his hips very slowly as he stroked me. I started to feel the heat spiraling. He increased the pressure slightly, and I drifted into that utterly still moment before breaking free. Just as I threw back my head and began to cry out, he rammed into me with four powerful thrusts, each setting off a fireburst of sensation. Utterly spent, we slept for a while in the afterglow before going back to the bed.

"How were the last couple of concerts? It's been hard to reach you." I turned to face Jack on the pillow.

"Yeah, we were moving around a lot. They went fine, except the filth arrested some fans in Atlanta for drunk and disorderly. It all went shambolic until Mary Jo paid off a city councilman."

The mention of his manager gave me an opening. "Did they ever figure out who blabbed to the press? She made me feel awful, accusing me of that."

"I forgot to tell you. Turns out, the makeup girl planted it. She was ticked off that I didn't use her to do my face. Also Mark was bonking her and blabbing to her about stuff."

After all I went through, he forgot to tell me? "Oh really? You could have called to let me know."

"I told you it didn't mean fuck-all. That woman was gagging to get back at me. She thought I had Mary Jo fire her, but in actual fact it was Patrick's doing."

"Patrick really likes pulling the strings, doesn't he?" I said hotly. "That was some scene I stumbled into, in his room." I hadn't been able to clear the image of the naked purple-masked woman from my brain; it popped up from time to time like an unwanted mental bookmark.

"I can't be responsible for what that wazzock does. Nor should you care—although I know it wasn't a pleasant sight." Jack put his hands on my waist, pulling me closer. "But now all the flake's out of my system. So we can get you pregnant." He bit his lower lip and ground his hips at me in an exaggerated motion.

"Jack, I'm not ready to have a baby. I've just started a new job, remember? And it's going great. Or at least it will be, if I can get Dermot Chase to hand over his book."

Jack scowled. "You seem obsessed with this guy. Any time I ask you about work, that's all you talk about."

"Dermot's my big project at the moment. Getting the book out of him, that is. But it's so good to have you home," I added, hoping to move the conversation in a different direction.

"Well, I don't see why *Dermot* needs to get in the way of our plans." Jack began kissing my breasts. "Don't you want to have my baby?"

I decided to be honest. "I think it would be great to have a child, eventually. But we need to be sure we're really solid. I wouldn't want to wind up raising it alone."

Jack turned to look at me, his head propped in his hand. "Who said you'd raise it alone? You have to get past this thing about your Dad leaving Dot. And guess what, the detective called Mary Jo two days ago. I didn't want to get into it over the phone, but he has a lead on your father. If he finds him, you've gotta go see him."

The thought sent ice water through my veins. "That's something else I'm not ready to deal with yet."

"But I *do* know I want a child." He exhaled forcefully. "It's the one thing I want more than anything else right now."

"What about what *I* want? Doesn't it take two?" I blurted

out. "I just think having a baby would be getting ahead of ourselves."

"What do you mean?" Jack seemed entirely clueless, but I decided to plunge ahead.

"I mean, I'd want to be married before I got pregnant."

Jack stared at me for a moment, looking like he'd seen a ghost. "Why would you need that? It's just a piece of paper," he finally said.

"Maybe I'm old-fashioned. I'm not like these women that follow you around, ready to rut at the crook of your finger." I couldn't keep the shrill tone out of my voice.

"A marriage license doesn't keep anyone together. It didn't keep either of our parents together." Jack sat up and crossed his arms.

"That's pretty cynical. Anyway, I know it's too soon to talk about it, but you're the one who keeps bringing up getting pregnant."

Jack looked off into the distance, visibly shaken. "I've never seen myself getting married. It's so uptight; all the formalities, the paperwork."

I took a deep breath. "I figured you felt that way. So now we understand each other: you never want to get married, and I don't want to have a baby with someone I'm not married to."

One week later, our icy patch still hadn't thawed. No matter what time I got home from work, Jack was still out doing whatever he was doing. He'd said they needed to practice a lot before their final big concert at Madison Square Garden, and that he was working hard to finish up his new song. So I assumed he was at the studio—at least some of the time. I started staying later at the office, figuring I may as well get more done.

Friday night I came home in yet another freezing rain to find several boxes on the living room floor. Mary Jo had dropped off more tee-shirts sent by Jack's doting fans. I pulled out a few: *We Shall Overcome Reagan*, and an ironic *Hugs Not Drugs. Ray-gun!* proclaimed another. As I was putting them into drawers in the bedroom, I heard the thunk of Jack's boots on the floor, then the gentler bump of his guitar case on a chair. Pasting on a smile, I went out to greet him. He was kneeling, letting Muddy lick his face.

"You're home early. Were you rehearsing?" I asked.

"Yeah, and then Mark and Sammy found a bar that has Pac-Man. It's this new game they got addicted to at the last hotel. Kind of like Donkey Kong, but this little yellow guy gobbles everything up."

"Sounds like fun. You got another shipment of tee-shirts. I was just putting them away." Jack stood up, and Muddy circled our legs frantically.

"Has he been out?"

"I took him when I got in." I glanced up at Jack, wanting him to kiss me. He looked so handsome with his long rain-damp hair, his nose slightly red at the tip. I cupped his cheeks. "Nippy out there, isn't it?"

Jack slipped his hands under my shirt. "Ooh, that's cold!" I cried out.

"I know how to warm 'em up." Grinning, he slid his icy

fingers further. I gasped at the contact points, my nipples becoming bullets. I stood on my toes and kissed his neck as I felt for his zipper. "C'mon back here. You can show me those tee-shirts," he said.

We went into the bedroom. Before I could count to three, Jack had stripped me and laid me out on the bed. As he slipped off his jeans, I was struck by his expertise in removing clothes. Specifically, women's clothes. The image of that purple-masked woman intruded yet again.

"What was really going on in Patrick's room?" I asked.

"I told you. I wasn't participating," Jack mumbled, his mouth on my breast.

"Why was she wearing a mask?" I asked.

Jack propped himself over me. "Are you curious about it?"

I flushed. "I don't know. I've never done anything like that."

"Want to try?" He lifted an eyebrow.

"Oh, no. I'd just feel ridiculous."

But Jack was already up and rifling through his drawers. "You might like it. Just lay back and relax." Before I knew it, he had slipped one of his silk scarves around my left ankle and another around my right, tying them tightly to the legs of the bed. He grabbed a couple more and kneeled over me, doing the same with my hands as I giggled helplessly.

"This is silly," I said.

"We'll see how you feel afterwards." Jack gave me a deep tongue-thrusting kiss, holding his body above me so he barely brushed my belly. Then he wrapped the last scarf around my eyes and tied it in back.

"*Now* you can't get loose," he growled.

I had to admit, I was starting to feel aroused. Not being able to see anything, my arms and legs spread-eagled on the bed, felt so open, so vulnerable. I tested the bindings around my wrists; the cool silk tightened, but held fast. So far, Jack hadn't touched me. I wondered if he had left the room.

"Jack? Are you there?"

Suddenly I felt warm breath on my body. A slithering sensation moved up the tender skin of my inner thigh, licking, giving gentle nips. The lips left me, and then they were at my nipples, flicking lightly, then sucking hard. Unable to see a thing but the dark blue pattern of the scarf, my sensations were unbearably heightened. I could only focus on the mouth that seemed to be everywhere at once; at my breasts, between my legs, at my lips. Whenever his mouth moved away, his fingers took up the slack.

My hips began keeping pace with his rhythm. His tongue played me with long, steady strokes, became light and flickering, then moved in tantalizing circles. His fingers slipped in and out of me, gently pinching my nipples, stroking me as his mesmerizing mouth cast its spell. His fingers became so slippery, it felt like three sets of lips were on me. Suddenly Jack moved upwards, and I opened my mouth to take him in. Just as I thought he was going to come, he pulled away and lapped me into an agonizing need. Right as I was about to take the plunge, he thrust inside and rode me to a shuddering finish.

Jack lay there for a few minutes, breathing deeply. Then he unwound the scarf from my eyes, untied my wrists and ankles, and dropped back next to me.

"That was amazing," I said, curling up against his chest. "Almost too intense."

Jack smiled. "No such thing as too intense. That felt good, huh? And the French think *they* invented this stuff."

"When do I get to tie you up?" I asked.

"Whenever you want, baby. I'll give you the ride of your life."

"You're pretty sure of yourself, aren't you?" I said.

He pulled me closer. "No comment. Let's not ever go another week without fucking. That was a ridiculous waste of time. And spunk."

I rested my chin on his chest. "You don't have to be gross."

"Nothing gross about it. It's all-natural, baby. Nature's finest." He twitched his hips as I laughed.

"That's true, I guess. What time do we have to be at the concert tomorrow? I want to go for a run before we leave." With all the rain, I hadn't been able to get as much exercise as I liked.

"Oh, it's not tomorrow. It's Sunday. We should probably get there around four."

I sat up straight. "But you always play on Saturdays!"

Jack stifled a yawn. "Patrick changed the date right before the tour started, so we had to take a Sunday. What does it matter?"

This can't be happening. Please tell me this isn't happening. "This Sunday is the Book Awards. Hawtey's bought a table, and I have to escort Dermot to it. He's up for best novel of the year. I'm sure I mentioned it."

Jack sat up next to me. "You aren't serious. You'd miss seeing us at the Garden?"

"I *have* to go to this awards thing. Dermot's one of our biggest authors—he'd be really upset if I didn't go. Ted and Perry would be furious at me!"

Jack got out of bed and crossed his arms. "Where do I fit in all this? You don't care that it's my final show? We won't be touring for two years, except some dates in Europe. This is our biggest concert in the States!" He glared at me suspiciously. "I can't believe you'd do that for some *writer.* Who is this guy, anyway?"

I jumped up and put my hand on his arm, but he shook me off. "Jack, it's really important to me. I've never been to the awards; it's a huge thing!"

"So is MSG!" Jack's face took on a hard look that I'd never seen before. "Don't fuck with me, Julia. You've got a thing for this guy, don't you? Mary Jo showed me his picture on one of his stupid books."

"I've had it with her! All she does is try to undermine me. I can't believe you'd suggest that. What, because I'm a woman, I can't be serious about my job? You think it has to be some sexual thing?"

"I guess you're impressed with his *literary* credentials," Jack snarled. "I thought you cared about me more than that."

"And I thought you cared enough about *me* to understand if I have to miss one concert!"

"It's not just any old concert; it's the culmination of the whole thing. Who knows when we'll be touring again!" Jack scowled. "I'm doing a song you've never heard. It's the world premiere of that new one I've been sweating blood over. *Nobody's* ever heard it before."

He did have a point. In the midst of my misery, I realized that maybe there was a way out. "What time does the concert begin?" I asked.

"Nine o'clock. You know the drill," he said in a sullen tone of voice.

"Okay. I should be able to make both. The Awards start at seven; I'm sure they'll be over by nine. I'll go there first and then catch a cab to the Garden. It's being held in a big hotel ballroom in Times Square, so it's only ten or so blocks away."

Jack's expression cleared. "I don't mind if you miss the first couple of numbers. I just want you to make the last half. My new song will be near the end."

"I'm sure I'll catch more than that. How long can a few acceptance speeches last?"

Wow, I thought as I leafed through the program at the Book Awards. *Who knew there were so many categories?* Children's books, pre-teen, young adult, history, mystery; first novel, middle novel, next-to-last novel, posthumously published novel. Memoir, inspiration, religion, politics. But at least the authors were limited to five minutes per speech; our publicity director had assured me of that. "They're really making an effort to cut down on the time this year," she whispered to me as the opening presentation began. "Last year it ran past midnight, and a lot of people complained."

Seated on my other side, Dermot touched my arm. "You're looking glamorous," he said. I'd borrowed a black velvet jacket and silver party dress from Vicky.

"Thanks. You're very debonair, yourself." Some people at the event seemed uncomfortable in their tuxes, but Dermot looked like he'd been born in his.

"So what do you think of my chances? I don't see Jeff Sharkey taking the prize. The *Times* tore his book apart." Dermot scrutinized the program's list of competitors for Novel of the Year.

"I think you'll definitely win." It was the third time he'd asked; I was getting a little tired of reassuring him. Luckily he turned to Ted to ask him the same question, so I could I sneak a glance at my watch. It was 8:05 now; I should be fine. The Floor wasn't due to start for an hour, and they usually opened a few minutes late.

My concert gear was in a small bag by my feet: leather pants and a tight leopard-print top. I planned to do a quick costume change in the MSG bathroom before I took my seat next to Vicky in the front row. I had given her the backstage pass earlier today when I'd stopped by her place to pick up the clothes. She had promised me to keep an eye on Jack, report on what went on before I got there, and also hold my seat.

The acceptance speech for Best Pre-teen Ghost Story concluded, and a new recipient stepped up to the microphone. As the winner of the Outstanding Novel about an Endangered Species droned on about his grandmother's love of groundhogs, I recalled how jittery Jack had seemed while we were getting ready at the loft. Since the concert was in New York, he was able to get dressed at home and then have

Rick drive him over to the arena. Normally Jack was incredibly blasé about performing, but tonight he'd seemed tense and on-edge. I could only surmise it was because of the new song, but when I asked him about it, he hadn't wanted to discuss it. I figured even jaded rock stars could have an occasional case of nerves.

I glanced at my watch again: 8:30. The Endangered Species guy finally walked off the podium, and now it was time for Memoir. An actor who'd been through rehab accepted his award with refreshing brevity. But that was made up for by a pompous academic who nattered on until 9:05. Dermot was holding his notes at table level, surreptitiously going over his speech. Perry looked like he'd fallen asleep sitting up. Based on how long this had been going on already, it would be another hour before it was time for Dermot's category.

I realized that I'd just have to take a taxi down to MSG, catch some of the show, race back up to Times Square to catch Dermot's speech, and then cab it back for the rest of the concert, which would end around 11:30. If I hustled, it should be no problem.

I told Dermot I was going to make a call from the lobby phone booth, and then leaned toward our publicity director. "I'll be back in a few minutes." She nodded, looking as if she could barely hold her eyes open. I grabbed my bag, took the elevator and raced out to the street.

Times Square was hopping on a Sunday night; panhandlers, prostitutes, and tourists vying for space on the packed sidewalks. I stood shivering on a street corner and tried to flag a cab, but they all seemed to be taken. I started walking downtown, turning around every half-block to scan the streets for a lit roof light. Finally one screeched to a stop. I leapt in and made the arena by 9:25.

The security guard took forever to look over my pass. At last he handed it back to me, and I ran into the bathroom to change. Yanking off the fluffy dress, I jammed my legs into the leather pants and pulled the tight top over my head. I hadn't bothered bringing an extra pair of shoes, since the silvery heels went okay with both outfits. I put the velvet jacket back on and did a quick touchup in the mirror, drawing cats-eye eyeliner and teasing my hair. *Now I look ready for The Floor*, I thought as I raced out, the dress stuffed into my bag.

I showed my pass to another guard and pushed through the heavy doors of the vast auditorium, filled with sweaty bodies gyrating to the driving beat. My spirits soared as I broke into a run, dodging around people cluttering the aisles. I tried to keep my eye on Jack as he moved around the stage, striking the gritty chords of one of their most popular songs. Finally I reached the front row and shouted "Excuse me! Sorry!" over and over as I made my way to the middle.

"About time!" Vicky said, grabbing my bag and stowing it under the seat. "Let's get up and dance! I was going to, but I was afraid the old bitch would bite my ear off." I glanced at Mary Jo, who was glaring at me. I gave her a little finger-wave.

"Why are you late?" she hissed.

"I had a professional commitment. But now I'm here!" I crowed.

Vicky pulled me up beside her. "It's amazing to be in the

front row!" she shouted as we shook our hips to the funky rhythm. Now I could see Jack in all his glory: shirt open, face lifted and eyes closed, sweat making his chest glisten, looking like a bronzed god. Patrick purred into the mic, whipping the crowd into a frenzy. Mark banged his drums and Sammy grooved on the keyboard, a simmering joint dangling from his lips.

"Are the awards all done?" Vicky said as the spotlights faded to blue and we took our seats. The Floor went into a moody ballad that was one of my all-time favorites. Even their so-called "lesser" songs were a thousand times better than other groups' biggest hits.

"They're still dragging on," I said. "I need to leave pretty soon to catch Dermot's speech. If he doesn't win, I'll run right back out."

Vicky's eyes widened. "Aren't you supposed to be here for the grand finale?"

"Definitely!" Jack seemed to look in my direction, but I knew it was just my imagination. He had told me that with the bright lights, it was impossible to see anything from the stage. "I should be fine," I shouted into Vicky's ear. "In fact, I'd better get going now," I said, realizing it was just after ten.

Vicky called out "Good luck!" as I grabbed my bag and crouch-walked across the justifiably annoyed front row. I raced up the aisle and out the main doors.

"Leaving so soon?" the security guard asked.

"I'll be back!" I shouted as I ran past him toward the bathroom. I rushed into a stall, withdrew the crumpled silver dress and draped it over the top of the door. Kicking off my heels, I struggled out of the leather pants, which were sticking to my sweaty thighs. I pulled off the clingy top, yanked the dress down over my head and jammed the concert clothes into the bag. Snatching it up along with my jacket, I hurried out of the stall and pushed through the bathroom door—right into a woman who was just coming in.

"Aagh!" we both screamed. I felt something cold on my chest. Backing away, I saw that she was holding a large crushed paper cup. The smell of beer rose in my nostrils as I glanced down the front of my dripping dress. *Damn!*

"Watch where you're going!" the woman said, barging past me. She went into a stall as I snatched some paper towels from the dispenser and tried to dab at the spreading wet patch. But it was no use; the dress was soaked. Frantically I shucked it off standing at the sink and blotted beer from my skin. *I'll just have to wear this!* I thought as I tugged the leather pants back on. *Maybe no one will notice. Anyway, the main thing is to catch Dermot's award.*

The taxi lane outside the Garden was usually jammed, but now of course it was empty. I ran the long block over to Seventh Avenue and luckily got a cab after only a few minutes.

"You okay, lady?" the driver asked as I panted in the backseat.

"I'm fine, but I'm late," I managed to gasp.

"Don't worry, gorgeous. I'll get you there." The driver ran the next three red lights and pulled up in front of the hotel. I stuffed a twenty into the receptacle and jumped out, not waiting for change.

"Thanks, doll!" the driver shouted as I slammed the door. I ran inside and tried to catch my breath going up to the ballroom. I hurried past a group of tuxedoed publishers and squeezed by the crowded tables as a woman announced the winner for First Novel. Quickly I slid into my seat next to Dermot. Empty wine bottles littered the table; everyone seemed totally looped. Perry glared at me as if to say, "Where the hell were you?", but I avoided his gaze.

"I like this new look," Dermot slurred, eyeing my tight leopard-print top. He leaned in closer and sniffed. "What's that smell?"

"It's beer." I fanned my neck. "Long story."

"Where've you been? I wanted to ask you about my speech," he demanded.

"I bumped into someone and got held up."

Dermot waved his hand impatiently. "Never mind. Should I put it this way: 'In all my years of toiling away at this book, I never thought I'd receive such an honor'— Or: 'In all *the* years . . .'"

I zoned out as he ran his alternatives by me. Ted seemed to be giving me an odd look.

"The second one sounds good," I whispered to Dermot. The First Novel winner was winding up his speech. I looked at my watch; it was 10:47. *Oh god, please don't win.*

The announcer stepped up to the mic. "And now, the winner for Best Novel of the Year is . . ."

Dermot grabbed my arm, banging my wrist against the edge of the table. *Please, don't be him*, I prayed.

"Dermot Chase!"

My heart sank as everyone at our table woke up. Beaming, Dermot rushed over to the podium as the audience stood for an ovation. Ted moved over next to me.

"Congratulations!" I said, although I felt like crying. Now I was stuck here for god knows how long.

Ted was looking at me curiously as he applauded. "Did you change clothes?"

"Oh!" I'd forgotten about my concert attire. "I've got a party right after this."

Ted just nodded as we all took our seats, and Dermot began talking. And talking. And talking. He seemed to have forgotten his carefully composed speech as he began thanking his great-aunt; his parents; his fourth grade teacher who'd encouraged him to write. I looked at my watch—10:50.

"I have to go to the bathroom," I whispered to Ted.

I bolted out of my seat. The elevator seemed to take ages. Finally I hit the lobby and ran out to the street: no cabs in sight. In desperation I started walking. Every few yards I turned around to see if anything was coming, but no such luck. I broke into a jog, but was hampered by the silvery heels. Finally I took off my shoes and ran the rest of the way in my shredded stockings.

"Back again?" the guard said as I whizzed by.

Just as I reached for the heavy arena doors, they flew open and a flood of jabbering people poured out.

I grabbed a guy's arm. "What's happened? Why are you leaving?" I shouted over the current of fans flooding past.

"Concert's over, man. It was outra-a-a-geous." The guy's bloodshot eyes focused on me.

"But it's only . . . 10:50?" I said, holding up my watch.

"Looks like it's stopped." The guy tapped the watch face and sauntered off.

Shit, shit, shit! I ran to the backstage entrance, where a bunch of teenage girls were arguing with the guards. Finally I got one of the men to look at my pass. He escorted me through the echoing hallway to where a crowd of people was milling around, laughing, chattering, pressing flesh. Frantically I scanned the room for Jack.

Mary Jo came up beside me. "Well, you missed a nice dedication. I guess your work obligations took precedence."

She smirked and went toward Sammy and Mark. I waved at them, but they just gave me a strange look. Vicky rushed over.

"I can't believe you missed it!" she said, drawing me away from the others.

Tears sprang to my eyes. "I can't either. Where is Jack? Was the song really good?"

Vicky's sympathetic gaze made me dread what she was going to say. "Julia, he dedicated it to you. He dragged out a stool and sat there with his acoustic guitar. He made this amazing speech about how his life had changed because of one particular person. He was looking in the direction of your seat the whole time; he couldn't see because of the stage lights. Then just as he finished, the whole place went dark and a spotlight shone down. Right onto your empty seat."

I gulped, and Vicky gripped my arm.

"Brace yourself. It was awful. The whole arena started laughing. They thought it was all a big joke. But you should have seen the look on his face when he saw that you weren't there. It was . . . I've never seen such an awful expression."

"Oh my god." My knees buckled and I slumped against the wall.

"Of course after that, he couldn't do his song. A roadie came out and removed the chair, and Patrick said, 'You'll have to excuse Jack; he's tripping.'" Then Mark and Sammy flew into the next number. Jack didn't get to do his song at all."

My heart was hammering in my chest; I felt like I couldn't breathe. "Oh god, this is a nightmare! I had to stay there for Dermot's stupid speech! What am I going to do?" I cringed at the thought of the audience's shrieks of laughter, picturing the look on Jack's face when he realized he'd been talking to no one.

Vicky grimaced. "If I were you, I'd try to find Jack. Want me to ask Sammy if he knows where he went?"

Wiping my eyes, I nodded. But when Vicky came back to me, she wasn't any the wiser.

"Why don't you go home and wait for him? Maybe he'll cool off; realize it wasn't your fault," she said as she escorted me out. We shared a cab, and she dropped me off with a hug.

By five a.m., Jack still wasn't home. Muddy followed at my heels as I paced around the loft. When the phone rang, I ran to it, dread twisting my guts. But instead of Jack, it was his manager.

"Hello Julia," Mary Jo said. "He's in pretty bad shape."

I started crying again. "Can I talk to him?" I sobbed, hat-ing that she had this power over me.

Mary Jo covered the receiver with her hand, and her muffled voice asked a question. She came back on the line. "I think you'd better just go."

I sat down hard. "What do you mean, 'go'?"

"It's best for everyone if you vacate the premises."

"But—" My mind was spinning. *He's breaking up with me over this? And he doesn't even have the nerve to tell me himself?* "Did he *say* that?"

Mary Jo sighed. "Just be out of the house by the time he gets back."

Knowing what I had to do, I went in the closet and did it. Once my things were packed, I put on my coat. Choking back great sucking sobs, I held Muddy for a long, long time, telling him I would miss him. Then I went out the door and caught a cab back to my cold, lonely apartment on Broome Street.

Chapter 21

SHATTERED

The next morning I dragged myself out to a deli to pick up some coffee and milk. Feeling like I could never eat again, I didn't bother with food for my bare fridge. As I stood in line, my eye fell upon the *Post* headline in the stack of newspapers:

KIPLING DEDICATES SONG TO PHANTOM GIRL

My stomach lurched as I read:

Was Jack Kipling so high that he hallucinated a girlfriend during The Floor's Madison Square Garden concert last night? But no matter—it turned out to be a prank. As usual the fans ate it up, along with the rest of the evening's incredible mix of current and past hits.

I threw down the paper, paid for my items, and stumbled back to my empty loft.

All day my chest had a hollow ache, as if my heart had been clawed out, chewed up, and discarded. I was in a state of shock; I couldn't believe that Jack had gone from saying he loved me and wanted to have a child with me, to having his manager evict me.

I tried putting myself in his place: sitting there onstage with thousands of fans laughing and pointing at the empty seat in the middle of the front row. Jack would have later realized they thought he was playing a joke, but at the time it must have been scalding. And although I'd never heard his new song, I knew how hard he'd been working on it. Suddenly I recalled Patrick's snide comment the day he'd been over our place. Having been so eager to put down Jack's solo efforts, he must have crowed about the fact that the acoustic piece didn't get its world premiere. And as if that wasn't bad enough, the song didn't get its commercial launch, either. Thousands of people who might have gone out and bought the single or requested it on the radio, now merely thought of it as a joke.

Then I recalled the piece in the *Post*. Any tidbits about The Floor usually got picked up in newspapers all over the country; over the years, the band's wild lifestyle had made them gossip magnets. The snippet about Jack's song was probably being reprinted all over—perhaps even internationally. I wondered if Jack had spoken to his mother and sister; I could just imagine their shock and dismay that I'd turned out to be such a traitor. I remembered Maggie's comment about my being a career girl. This would prove that her reservations about me had been right.

But even as the horror of what I'd done hit me over and over again, I still wanted Jack to love me enough to understand that I couldn't have missed seeing Dermot win. Ted and Perry would have had a fit if I hadn't made it back to the Awards; as it was, I dreaded their questions on Monday about why I'd vamoosed before his speech was over. I'd have to tell them I'd felt sick and had to leave. But instead of taking all that into consideration—that my job really was on the line—Jack had decided I wasn't worth it. Even with the crowd's laughter, the humiliating article, Patrick's crowing over his flop—I still would have expected him to forgive me. Or at the very least, to hear me out before he kicked me out.

All day, my mind whirled as I practiced speeches I wanted make to Jack, when I got up enough nerve to call him. I ran them through my mind as I alternated between crying on my couch and pacing my threadbare rug. My cold, narrow room seemed so bare and ugly to me now, after the vast expanse of Jack's penthouse. My pathetic milk-crate kitchen "table". The nails I'd driven into the walls to hang up my sparse second-hand wardrobe, since my bare-bones loft didn't come with a closet. My lumpy futon, contrasted with Jack's feathery king-sized bed. The wooden crates that held my books and records, which had once seemed so precious to me. I started to thumb through The Floor's albums that I kept in a special box of my favorites, but then covered it back with the scarf, realizing it would only make me feel worse.

Vicky came over to my apartment that night. We sat drinking beer as we played blues on my stereo. I lay on the couch and talked to her for hours, tears streaming down my face. Only now did I truly understand what the musicians were singing about.

Later that week Suzanne called me from London, where she'd been staying with her mother ever since she left Mark. "Mary Jo told me you and Jack broke up," she said after I'd asked how she was doing. "What happened?"

I described the MSG fiasco. Although she was sympathetic, I could also tell that she couldn't believe I'd missed the song's debut. "I'm so sorry," she said. "He's probably just feeling burned. It must have been a real blow when the crowd started laughing, even if they thought he was in on the joke. And not to have you there, when he'd set it all up in advance . . ."

"I know." My voice crumbled. "But I still can't believe he broke up with me like that."

"I know he really loves you, Julia. Just hold on; I imagine he'll come around. By the way, Mark's flying here next week. He wants to get back together."

"Are you going to?" I was surprised, given her speech to me at the hotel.

Suzanne paused. "It's complicated. I've missed him so much, and also I feel like, 'Who am I, if I'm not married to him?' I put my salon work aside to be the wife of one of The Floor. Who knows if my painting will ever take off? And—" She paused, and I heard the flick of her lighter. "I think he really needs me."

"Let me know how it goes. I'll be thinking of you too," I said.

"If Mark wants me back, he's going to have to work for it.

And you hang in there. I'm sure that deep down, Jack knows it wasn't your fault. He just has to get over himself."

For the next few weeks I cried myself to sleep on my futon every night, and lived on toast and tea when I managed to get anything down. Over and over I had picked up the phone to call Jack, but each time I stopped myself. The humiliation of being told to leave his apartment—as if I was some clingy hanger-on that he'd ejected—stung my pride like peroxide on an open wound. I kept trying to imagine what I would have done if I'd been in his situation. No matter how angry I'd been, I was sure I would have at least listened to his side of the story. But the fact that he didn't do me the justice of breaking up in person, made me think twice about calling him. I could just imagine the coldness in his voice when he heard it was me on the line. I could picture him cutting me off midway through my explanation about Dermot's speech. *I'm not going to beg*, I told myself yet again as I laid down the phone halfway through dialing his number.

I dove into work, trying to distract myself. My disappearance at the Awards didn't seem to have attracted much notice; everyone was so thrilled about Dermot's big win that my lame excuse about feeling sick went over fine.

But every single moment that I wasn't setting up dates with literary agents, sitting in meetings, or plowing through proposals, I was haunted by memories of Jack: his sexy British voice, his riotous head-thrown-back laughter, his sensual touch. At night in my lonely loft I spent hours recalling conversations, reliving intimate scenes. His ghost seduced me in my sleep, making every morning an awful new awakening to the fact that he was no longer part of my life. My third-floor walkup seemed so spartan after living in Jack's spacious loft, but it suited my dark mood. I had returned to a monastic lifestyle devoid of pleasure, existing only to work.

As a distraction, one Saturday Vicky suggested we go to the Pyramid Club, a nightspot we liked despite its threatening location. The East Village was one big crack den, which meant you were taking your life in your hands by venturing there. Yet nowhere else in town could you find such cutting-edge entertainment. And since the Pyramid's clientele was largely gay, I knew no one would hit on us—which justified the riskiness of entering Alphabet City after dark.

That night, I almost called Vicky to cancel. I hadn't washed my hair in two days, nor could I be bothered with putting on makeup. But after going back and forth, I decided that a change of scenery might do me good. I put on my tattered leather skirt that I'd scored for a few bucks at Trash and Vaudeville, and a ripped Ramones tee-shirt. I dug twenty black rubber bracelets out of the top drawer of my three-legged dresser, the missing leg propped up with a brick, and scooched them up my arms. Then I stepped into my scuffed low-cut boots.

I locked up and walked north to Eighth Street, where I was meeting Vicky. St. Mark's Place was heavy with the dusky scent of clove cigarettes, the street dealers hissing "sens, sensimilla" to passersby; everyone from drunken NYU students to punks in chains to leftover hippies roaming around in search of a good time. Slouching in his doorway, the owner of the Music Exchange said hello as I passed. I was hit with a huge pang of sadness, remembering the last time I'd been there with Jack, rummaging through the stacks of vintage 45s. *Don't think about it now,* I told myself. *Try to take your mind off him, for a change.*

Vicky was waiting on the corner in a short skirt and jean jacket. She threw her arms around me and gave me a big hug. "I was getting worried you'd flaked out on me. We'll have fun tonight; you'll see. Just like old times."

"Thanks, Vick. It's good to be out," I said half-heartedly.

We strolled arm-in-arm past the eclectic East Village shops; Electric Circus, Love Saves the Day, and Screaming Mimi's, where I'd bought some of my second-hand clothes. Glancing into the window, I almost tripped over a bong dealer who'd spread his wares on a soiled tablecloth on the sidewalk.

"Let's cut over on Third," Vicky said. We turned the corner and went past the Hell's Angels' headquarters with its row of gleaming hogs parked outside. We'd been told that it was a safer route to take because muggers were afraid of them. In the daytime I liked to walk across Second, which was empty but for one long wall of ever-changing graffiti.

We ran the last few blocks to the Pyramid's dented metal doors and ducked inside. It was too early for anything to be happening, but there was no cover charge if you got there before eleven. We took a seat, ordered three-dollar drafts, and spoke to Clarence for a few minutes. Despite his appearance—his right nostril was safety-pinned to his upper lip, giving him a permanent snarl—the bartender was a friendly guy who sometimes gave us a drink on the house.

Vicky's green eyes glowed in the low light of the votive candles. "Are you feeling any better? You look so thin. Have you been eating?"

"It's like all my senses have shut down. I feel pretty dead inside." Despite myself, I choked up.

"I know it's hard, sweetie." She gazed at me in concern. "This is worse than when you guys broke up last fall; at least back then, you hadn't been living together. Give it time, though. You'll meet someone new, and Jack will become a distant memory."

"It's hard to picture that. Right now I feel like I'll never get over him. I just can't believe he decided one screw-up was reason enough to ditch me."

"Well, it *was* a pretty big screw-up. Exacerbated by the fact that it happened in front of thousands of his fans." Vicky took a sip of her draft and crossed her skinny legs on the bar stool. "Why don't you call him? Maybe you can clear it up if you apologize."

"I did try calling, the other night. He wasn't there." Gloomily I stared into my glass.

"Maybe you should waylay him in his building," she suggested. "Have it out in the lobby."

"But it would be so embarrassing if he didn't want to see me. I'll just try calling him again." I aligned my beer on its cardboard coaster.

"At least Dermot won the award," Vicky said.

"Yeah, if I can ever get this new novel out of him, next year we can nominate it for Most Procrastinated." I managed a weak smile.

"Now, that's a good sign. You just made a joke." Vicky arched her eyebrows. "Keep it up, and soon you'll be back to washing your hair every night."

A couple of six-foot ladies came in, and we made room for them to clamber up on top of the bar. The music got louder and they started to dance. Sporting elaborate blonde beehives, faces shaven smooth under heavy foundation, they seemed much more feminine than any of the girls I knew. Vicky and I watched, in awe of the way they shimmied in their stilettos without knocking over the drinks. There seemed to be a haunted look in their eyes—or maybe in my bleak frame of mind, I was just imagining it. Perhaps they were perfectly content, waxing their chests and getting dolled up in their gowns. Maybe they were happier than most people I knew; at least they were free to express themselves.

Stella, one of the regulars, took a break and climbed down from the bar. Vicky and I pooled our dollars to buy her a Mai Tai. I always felt a little intimidated by her; she was exceedingly angular, and wore the most fantastic gear. Tonight she had on an evening gown in an eye-popping shade of puce, paired with dangly rhinestone earrings and six-inch heels. "How's it going?" I asked.

Stella lowered her eyes, her false lashes brushing against her powdered face. "I'm a little down tonight." She took a delicate sip of her drink. "I met the sweetest guy a few days ago, but he hasn't called. You know how that goes."

"We sure do," Vicky said. "That color's great on you."

"Thanks. I found it at my special little place. The owner always holds things in my size." Stella finished her drink, her Adam's apple bobbing. Then she unwound herself from the seat, hiked up her dress, and put one heel on the stool. I held it so it wouldn't spin, and with an agile bound, she was back on top of the bar. A guy with stiff green spikes gelled ten inches off his head took her place, his studded jacket clanking as he sat.

"Is it eleven yet?" I asked Vicky. I still hadn't gotten my watch fixed. As if on cue, the Meat Puppets started blasting from the back room.

Vicky drained her glass. "Close enough. Let's try to get Bruce to play something decent before midnight."

We went to the small dance floor and found an open spot next to a bald woman with striped stockings flashing above combat boots. For a while we moved around to some songs that were so off-the-wall, it made The Slits seem like bubble-gum. After that, we pogoed to the Fleshtones, Liquid Liquid, The Piranhas, and Swollen Monkeys. My love of dancing momentarily overcame my sadness, and I lost myself in the pounding rhythm.

Eventually Vicky and I left to refuel at Kiev, the all-night Polish diner on Second Avenue. It was crammed with people in dog collars and chains from CBGB, but we managed to nab a table and split an order of pierogis. Afterwards I took a cab home since it was four a.m., and I was utterly beat.

Several weeks later I was in a different cab, heading uptown. Ted had come into my office that morning with the news that Dermot was finally ready to turn in his first draft.

"He wants you to go to his apartment and pick it up." Ted

took off his glasses and gnawed the earpiece.

"Couldn't I send a messenger?" I had tons to do, and it seemed odd to have to go to his place.

"He's too superstitious to trust a messenger with his only copy. I know, he should have gone out and made a xerox, but we have to humor him. He said he'll leave it downstairs with the doorman. Just keep the cab waiting while you run in, and expense the trip. Thank god he's ready to let go of it."

I'd finally had to admit to my boss that I didn't have any of the book yet. Ted had been asking me daily for updates—so a lot depended on the outcome of this errand.

Zooming up Park Avenue, I looked at the yellow tulips that filled the median strip. April had arrived with warmer weather, but it had done nothing to thaw my frozen heart. I was still bitter over Jack's not understanding my inability to be two places at once. *He's just a spoiled rock star—used to getting what he wants, regardless of what anyone else needs*, I reminded myself.

Shaking off my gloomy thoughts, I got out at Dermot's imposing East 84th Street building. The doorman gave me a blank look when I said I was there to pick up a package. He buzzed upstairs, and after a brief conversation, told me go up to the eighth floor. I started to reach for the house phone to ask Dermot to bring it down, but the doorman had already hung up. *I'll tell him the cab's waiting and I have to make it quick,* I thought as I got in the elevator.

Dermot answered my knock, looking rumpled in a wrinkled button-down shirt and khakis. His furnishings were luxurious and formal: Persian carpets, gold-framed paintings, and polished antiques. A huge desk held piles of paper massed around a big black typewriter.

"Come into my humble abode. I've been revising non-stop." Dermot made as if to take my jacket, but I shook my head.

"The taxi's waiting with the meter on. I'm just here to fetch the manuscript and go back to the office. I have a meeting in half an hour," I lied.

Dermot frowned. "I thought we could discuss this one last issue with the plot. I'm not sure I've resolved it properly."

Desperately I looked around the room for signs of the manuscript. "I can't stay. I'll start reading tonight, and then we can talk. Ted's very anxious about it." I hoped the mention of my boss would add urgency to the long-put-off delivery. I *had* to get it now; with all the delays, we were dangerously close to missing our pub date.

"Don't worry. It's right here." Dermot moved aside to indicate a suspiciously thin manila envelope resting on the desk.

"Is that ... all of it?" *Please tell me it's not,* I thought. *Maybe he's divided it into two packages.*

Dermot crossed his arms. "It's a little less weighty than my last couple of novels, but I think that's the way of the world these days. I've noticed some very slim books hitting the bestseller list."

This looked more like a novella to me—but I'd take what I could get. "I'm dying to dive in," I said, reaching for it.

"Hold on. First, a little reward for all my hard work." Dermot took my outstretched hand and pulled me toward him. To my shock, he planted a big, wet kiss on my lips. He tried to force his tongue in my mouth as I struggled against him.

"Dermot!" I broke away. "I'm not—I'm your editor!" I fumbled for words that would flatter him. "You're our most important author. I would never do anything to compromise our working relationship."

He gazed at me, unperturbed. "It wouldn't compromise a thing. Erica had no problem with it."

God, this is a disaster! "Tell you what. Let me take the manuscript." I ducked around him and made a grab for it. "We'll get it into great shape, and then we'll see. First things first, I always say!" I gave a fake chuckle and edged away. Clutching the envelope, I backed toward the entrance. "I'm so excited! I'll call you!" I yanked the door open and got the hell out of there.

"So it's really that bad?" Vicky asked as I sat on my futon that night, surrounded by piles of paper. I shifted the phone to my other ear and shuffled through the pages.

"Just listen to this: *"I know you've wanted me from day one,"* Penelope proclaimed, her velvety lips parted in a teasing smile. "And I know how to prove it." She began unbuttoning her blouse, her nipples waving hello through the silken fabric.*

"*Waving* hello? Can a nipple do that?" Vicky snorted.

"That's not the worst of it. You'd think this was written by a horny tenth-grader. I don't know what's happened to him; his first novel won all kinds of awards. And the last one was Novel of the Year—unfortunately for me."

"Are you going to tell Ted it stinks?" she asked.

"No, because then he'd just hand it over to Erica. Who apparently slept with Dermot before Ted dumped him on me."

"Get out of here! Really?" Even Vicky was surprised—and nothing shocked her.

"According to Dermot." I stacked the pages next to me. "Anyway, I guess I'm going to have to really dig in and rewrite it."

"Maybe *you'll* win the Book Award next year," she said.

"Highly doubtful."

A little after midnight, I was just turning off my reading lamp when the phone rang. I figured it was Dot; she'd been calling more often lately, wanting to make sure I was okay.

"Hello," I said sleepily, settling back on the futon.

"Julia. It's Jack."

An electric current zipped through me at the sound of his voice. *What is he calling about? The selfish bastard!* Then the pathetic thought crept in: *Does he miss me?*

Jack cleared his throat. "That detective I hired. He's found your father."

Chapter 22

WAITING IN VAIN

For a minute, I just listened to the humming of the wires. "Are you there?" Jack said.

"I'm here." Suddenly I was freezing. With icy hands, I pulled the covers up to my chest.

"Listen, Julia. Regardless of what's gone on between us, you've got to go. You may never have a chance to see him again."

"I don't think it's any of your business anymore." My voice wavered.

"That may be true." Jack's tone was cool, as if he was talking to an acquaintance. "But I thought I should let you know."

I wanted to scream, *Why did you dump me over one stupid mistake?* But I controlled myself. "I'll think about it. Where is he?"

"He's in Richmond, Virginia. Paul Nash, 5748 Pine Street. He's been living there for a while."

I shut my eyes. *All this time, my Dad was only a few states away.* The hurt seemed just as fresh as when he'd first walked out. But maybe Jack was right; maybe it would do me good to confront him. *What is there to lose?* I thought. *Everything else has gone up in smoke.* "Okay, give me his number."

Jack cleared his throat. "The detective said it's best if he arranges the meeting. I'll come along too, just in case it falls apart. It's my fault this whole thing got started."

"The only way it could fall apart is if he doesn't want to see me in the first place. Which is entirely possible." Tears sprang to my eyes, not only due to thoughts of my father. I couldn't believe Jack and I were finally talking, but not saying anything about us. As if we were merely two people who had once known each other, but had happened to drift apart.

"Let's take it one step at a time," he said. "I'll have the guy arrange a place to meet him in Richmond."

What right does he have to get involved in my life, if he doesn't love me anymore? "I don't want you to come. I can do it alone."

"I'll stay out of your way. I should be there if you need anything, since I've been pushing you to do it."

So he just sees it as an obligation he has to fulfill. A dead weight to get off his back. The last reserves of resistance drained out of me. *I guess if he's so set on going, he can sit in a hotel room somewhere while I'm meeting my father,* I told myself. "All right. But there's really no reason for you to come."

"I'll let you know when it's arranged. You might keep the

next few weekends free."

I felt like saying, *As if all of my weekends haven't been free!* Despite Vicky's offer to fix me up with a blind date, I had no desire to meet anyone new. "I'll keep them open."

"Why on earth do you want to see your father?" Dot screeched into the phone. "That's a horrible idea. After everything you've been through lately, you want to set yourself up for another let-down?"

"That's what I told Jack, but he's insisting I go. Maybe I should call him back and tell him to forget it," I said miserably.

There was a pause, and I heard Dot light a cigarette. "I just think it's a bad idea to stir up all that stuff from the past. It's water under the bridge."

Something in her voice made me wary. "You've told me the whole story, right? Out of the blue, Dad accused you of sleeping with your manager at the hardware store. And he'd accused you of having affairs with other guys before?"

She took a puff and exhaled. "Paul was so jealous. Just because I liked to flirt a little with the guys at the store," she said in a wounded tone. "All I did was take a few rides home with Wayne after we'd closed up the place."

"Rides home? You never mentioned that." I gripped the receiver.

"Well, the other car was in the shop. You had the flu that week, and Paul was on the night shift so he could stay home with you during the day. He couldn't leave you alone, so I caught a ride with Wayne. We stopped for a beer once or twice; just a friendly thing. But your dad went crazy over it."

"You went out drinking with your boss?"

"It was no big deal, Julia. Your dad went out with his friends all the time, so why shouldn't I?" she asked defiantly.

This was sounding worse and worse. "But were his friends women?"

"They were guys. But that's very *sexist*, as you always like to say. Why couldn't I have a male friend, too? We were co-workers; Wayne was seeing someone else at the time. We weren't *doing* anything. I was so wiped out from being on my feet for nine hours straight. I just wanted one measly drink before I had to come home, get dinner on the table, and take care of a sick teenager. It was only twice, but Paul went nuts."

This put a slightly different spin on the matter. Sure, she had the right to go out for a beer with her boss, but it made a little more sense than my father's just making up everything from thin air. "Okay, Mom. I'm not accusing you of anything. I'm just trying to get the whole picture before I go down and see him. If he even agrees to meet with me."

"Are you going to let Jack come?" Dot asked.

"He keeps saying he is. Which really complicates things. It's going to be hard enough, without him there." Whenever I thought about seeing my former lover, my stomach knotted up.

"Maybe you can talk to Jack about what happened. Surely he'd understand why you couldn't make it back to the show," Dot said wistfully.

For the millionth time, I pictured him telling Mary Jo to ask me to leave. "I don't think he wants to understand."

Two weeks later, my nerves were shot. I'd squandered so much energy wondering whether it was a good idea to seek out my father—much less to have my ex-boyfriend accompany me—that my brain was fried. Jack had said he'd pick me up for the drive to the airport, and that afternoon I was pacing my scarred wooden floor, trying to imagine what we'd have to say to each other. Not to mention, what I would say to the man who had deserted me over a decade ago.

Hearing a horn toot twice, I looked out the window and saw the black car waiting at the curb. I shouldered my duffel bag, recalling the last time I'd packed it, fleeing Jack's loft. For a minute I stood in my doorway gazing down the steep flights of stairs, feeling like I was taking a leap into the unknown. Was my father being dragged into this against his will? Would it be horribly awkward, or even go horribly wrong? And what would it be like to spend two and a half days with Jack?

Grimly I locked up, thumped down the steps and went outside into the soft late-April breeze. The back door of the car opened, and Jack's long legs swung out. For a moment I was overcome by his sheer physical presence: his thick mane longer than I'd last seen it; his legs encased in tight jeans, stuffed into scuffed leather boots. His soulful brown eyes that seemed to soften when he saw me.

Jack held out his hand to shake. The impersonal gesture was so upsetting, I ignored it. He gave a wry smile, creating those handsome parentheses around his mouth. "Hello, baby. Good to see you, too." I gave my bag to Rick, who put it in the trunk.

I got in the backseat and slid over to the far side by the window. Jack climbed in, and Rick hit the gas. "Thanks for doing this. But I'm still not sure it's a good idea," I said stiffly.

Jack slid over to the middle of the seat. "Hey, you don't get many chances to reconnect with someone important from your life." The way he said *chahnces* got to me. Not having heard his voice in weeks, his British accent seemed even stronger.

"I guess." I looked out the window. It was so hard to sit next to him and not want to touch him. *Don't be an idiot*, I told myself. *That would really be asking for it.*

"So, what have you been up to?" The way he said *bean* created a twist of attraction that I tried to ignore.

"Just working hard." *It's going to be a long trip if I don't make a little effort*, I realized. "How about you?"

"I've been writing some new songs. Good stuff; I guess Patrick's theory proved right."

I didn't want to get into that, or anything related to our breakup. I wanted to leave all the hurt over our shattered relationship buried deep inside; at least for the next few days. I needed to focus on the fact that I was meeting my father for the first time in years. That was enough of an emotional overload, without the burden of my feelings about Jack— who, like my Dad, I had thought loved me.

"Sounds like you've been productive," I said. "Me, too. In fact, I have a manuscript I need to finish." I pulled a chunk of paper out of my backpack.

"Can't you leave it off for just one weekend?" Jack looked disgruntled, but that was too bad.

"I really have to work."

For the rest of the trip to the airport, I pretended to read. But it was impossible with his lithe body stretched out next to me.

Within three hours, we stepped off the plane into the humid Virginia air. I was surprised it was so warm, but the driver said they were having an early heat wave. Jack shrugged out of his light coat and asked the guy to whack up the AC. We hadn't spoken much during the flight; Jack had made one or two stabs at conversation, but when I responded curtly, he'd dropped it. *It's better this way*, I told myself, gazing out the window on the road to the hotel. We were passing some fields of early tobacco, the neat red-brown lines of earth divided by bright green growth.

"Looks like a strobe," Jack said as the rows flashed by. I merely nodded, not wanting to be drawn into casual chit-chat. *This is going to be hard enough without acting like he's my friend. He's just here out of some misguided sense of duty, to make sure I go through with the meeting.*

The meeting that I was really beginning to dread.

"There's only one room? But my manager reserved two suites." Jack frowned at the front desk clerk. When we'd arrived at the Jefferson Hotel in Richmond, our luggage—all except Jack's guitar, which he carried himself—was whisked out of the limo and spirited away by a friendly bellhop who didn't seem to recognize Jack behind his sunglasses. Jack still had them on inside, which seemed like an instant tip-off, especially with the guitar slung over his shoulder—but who was I to comment? I was stunned by the opulence of the Jefferson's crowded lobby, with its *Gone with the Wind*-style double marble staircase, gigantic Corinthian columns, and gleaming grand piano. But I was even more stunned by the incorrect booking.

"I'm sorry, Mr. . . . Ripper." The clerk looked at the alias on the reservation card. "But we only have one suite available. In fact, it's the only room we've got a'tall," he drawled, his voice like dripping molasses. He gestured at the lobby, teeming with people. "We're smack-dab in the middle of the peanut convention."

Jack slid his shades down his nose and took in the throng of conventioneers, loudly glad-handing each other. "I see. So there's nothing to be done?"

"Wait a minute," I said. "Where are you going to sleep?" I stared at Jack, then at the clerk. "We *have* to have two rooms. If not, you need to book me a different hotel."

The clerk smiled apologetically. "Honey, you were lucky to get this one. The convention's took up everything until next weekend. You won't find an extra room from here to Goochland."

"*Gooch*land?" Jack muttered. "All right, let's see where you've put us." The clerk handed him a key with a maroon tassel, and I followed him to the elevators.

"Jack, I can't stay here. There has to be somewhere else," I said as we exited the creaky elevator and padded down the thickly carpeted hallway. Jack unlocked the door, and we stepped into the suite. It was huge and airy, with antique furniture, real paintings on the walls, and French doors opening onto a marble balcony overlooking the street below.

"I'll call Mary Jo; maybe she can find another place. But look," Jack said as he tipped the bellhop for bringing up our luggage. "I could sleep out here on the sofa."

There did seem to be several rooms; I guess that was why they called it the Presidential Suite. But I didn't want to be in such close physical proximity. "Could you call her? There has to be somewhere else." I was sure Mary Jo would be happy to arrange separate quarters for us; she was probably still rubbing her hands in glee over our breakup.

"I will. But if she finds one, I'll take it and you can stay here." Jack propped his guitar on an armchair and poked around in the fridge. A huge glass jar of unshelled peanuts sat on a table, a big green bow tied to the lid.

"No, I'll move. I don't need such a fancy place." I took the beer he held out to me.

"We'll see about that. I imagine you're uptight about meeting your Dad tomorrow. Want to hear some of the stuff I've been working on? That might relax you." He unzipped the case and pulled out his Gibson.

"I'm going to lie down. I'm pretty beat." I took my bag into the bedroom and locked the door behind me. As I drew the plush curtains and pulled down the covers, I heard Jack strumming quietly out front.

I must have fallen asleep because I was awakened by tapping on the door. The room was totally dark. "Yes?" I called out as

I flipped on the bedside lamp.

"I'm going down to the bar. D'you want to come along?" Jack's voice came through the door.

A drink sounded really, really good, but then I'd have to face him. *Don't be such a coward*, I told myself. *He doesn't care a thing about you anymore.*

"Okay," I said. "Give me a minute." I dug in my bag and pulled on a pair of dressy pants and a crumpled silk blouse that I should have hung up as soon as I arrived. Glancing in the tall gilt mirror, I noticed how pale I looked. Usually I had a little color from all the running I did, but that had faded over the brutal winter. I applied some blush and eye liner, dabbed on lip gloss, and brushed my too-long brown layers. Then, annoyed at myself for primping, I took a tissue and rubbed off the blush. *Who am I trying to impress?* I asked myself as I stared at my image in the dusky gloom. *I'm sure Jack has moved on to his blonde model types. Just like my father moved on long ago.*

Suddenly I realized this whole trip was a mistake. I unlocked the door and went to the living room. Jack had changed clothes; he was now wearing a dark blue jacket, the frilly white sleeves of his shirt showing beneath the cuffs. He'd brushed his hair, which fell beneath his shoulders in a way that begged to be touched. I felt an instantaneous kick of attraction—which on second thought, revolted me.

"Very nice, Miss Nash," he said in a low voice.

"Jack, I don't think I can do this. Can you call the detective and cancel?"

"Why not? We've come all this way; we're in the middle

of the *peanut* convention." He took my arm. "Let's talk it over. No need for a hasty decision."

Before I could protest, he had ushered me out into the hallway.

"I don't need to talk it over," I whispered as an older couple got into the elevator.

We got out on the ground floor and Jack looked around for the bar. The lobby was still jammed with people. Someone dressed up as a huge peanut with a tall top hat was posing for pictures with the conventioneers. Jack took my arm and led me along the edges of the crowd, his head ducked to avoid recognition. We came to an echoing rotunda, where a marble statue of Thomas J. stood beneath a stained glass dome. Something crunched beneath my heel. Lifting my foot, I flicked off a crushed peanut shell.

"This way." Hand on my elbow, Jack ferried me into the mirrored bar. We slid onto the last stools at the end, and he ordered a bottle of Wild Turkey with beer chasers. The bartender either didn't recognize my date or didn't get worked up over musicians, because he set the drinks in front of us without comment.

Jack lifted his shot glass. "Another day, another bender. No retreat and no surrender." He clinked our glasses and belted his down. I tipped mine to my lips and let the smoky liquor sear my throat. Jack poured us each another. "Your turn." He held his drink, waiting.

"To forgiveness." I looked him in the eye, thinking he'd flinch, but he met my gaze steadily.

"That's a good one." He touched his glass to mine. We

drank our shots, and Jack poured again. "All right, top this."
He lifted his glass. "I'd rather have a bottle in front of me,
than a frontal lobotomy."

Jack downed the amber liquid in one gulp. It never seemed
to affect him, but I was starting to feel tipsy. "Drink up, or we
can't do another toast." The way he said *cahnt* tickled my ears.
I swallowed mine and chased it with a sip of beer.

Jack turned on the barstool to face me. I pushed my knees
together so his leg wouldn't be between mine. But now his
spread thighs enclosed me, taut muscles straining his tight
black pants. Even from a foot away, I could feel his heat. Or
maybe it was the heat of the whiskey, spreading up my chest,
making me flush. I picked up a bar coaster and fanned my
face with it.

"Feeling warm?" Jack asked.

I put down the coaster. "It's so muggy here."

"It is rather hot." *Rahther* hot. Why did his accent do those
things to me? I met his intense brown gaze, then immediately dropped my eyes. But that didn't help because now I
was staring at his tawny chest beneath the snowy white shirt.
As usual, he'd left the top three buttons undone, and I could
see the fine dark hair on his skin. A picture of the rest of him
slithered into my mind; his ridged abdomen, the line of hair
leading below his navel like the trail of a powder keg . . .

"D'you feel all right?" Jack was touching my arm, staring
at me intently. "We could go up to the room, catch a breeze
on the balcony."

"Think I've had 'nuff." Unsteadily I slid off the stool. Jack
grabbed my hand and led me out of the crowded bar, into the

much-cooler rotunda.

A young man was leaning against the statue's pedestal, wearing a rumpled brown costume. The huge peanut head with its top hat was collapsed on the floor beside him. "Have they gone to the buffet yet?" the guy asked, peering at us through wire-rimmed glasses.

Jack stopped suddenly and I ran into him. When he put his arm around me, I felt like dissolving into his body. Woozily I regained my balance.

"It's still pretty packed in there." Jack made as if to keep going.

The guy scratched his shaggy head. "Man, those peanut growers are in*tense*. I only get paid for eight hours, but they've kept me way past that. You aren't part of the convention, are you?"

"Er, no," Jack said.

The guy looked at Jack more closely, screwing up his eyes behind his wire-rims. "Hey, I know you. You're with The Floor! What're you doing here?"

"We're on private business. Have a good night," Jack said, and started to walk away.

"Hey, wait a minute. I'm a musician, too—I play the banjo. That's why I have to do this goober gig; it helps with the rent. I haven't played a bar for tips in a month of Sundays."

I was so tired, I was tottering on my heels. Jack paused and drew me closer, his arm around my waist. "A banjo picker, huh? What kind of stuff do you do?" His fingers splayed on my hip, and a tsunami of lust surged through me. *God, I'd love to be with him tonight,* my witless body whispered. *Not on your life, you slut!* my wasted brain replied.

"Oh, country, rock, blues. I even do covers of some of your songs." The guy smiled eagerly. "Maybe we could go up to your room and jam for a while. I've got my banjo in the car."

To my relief, Jack said, "Maybe later." His arm still wrapped around me, we continued down the hall.

Peanut Man grabbed the top half of his outfit and walked alongside us. "You know why banjos are better than guitars? They burn longer."

"Uh-huh," Jack said. "I've heard that one before."

"How do you like the Jefferson? Pretty cool hotel, right?" the guy said as he fitted the costume over his head. "I'll get fired if I don't keep this on," he added, his voice now muffled.

Jack kept walking. "Yeah, I dig the digs."

"You know the King stayed here, back in the Fifties."

"Was that George VI?" Jack asked.

"No, I mean the one and *only* King." The guy lifted the bottom edge of the peanut head and gazed at Jack meaningfully.

"Ah," Jack said. "You mean Elvis. Yeah, he put out some great stuff." We reached the elevator bank. "I guess this is where we part ways."

"See you around." Peanut Man nodded, his top hat wobbling with the motion, and sauntered back to the lobby.

Dizzily I leaned against the wall as we rode up to our floor. Jack helped me down the hall and into the room. *I should have eaten something before I drank all that whiskey,* I told myself. The carpet's ornate pattern began to swirl, and I lurched forward.

"You okay?" Jack grabbed me, his hands gripping my waist.

I looked up into his eyes. *It would feel so good to . . .*

"Gotta get—to bed," I managed to gasp as my knees gave way.

Suddenly I was swooped up off the floor, into Jack's strong arms. Taking long strides, he carried me into the bedroom. I closed my eyes, feeling his heart thumping, cradled against his chest. I began to struggle, but Jack held me close. "Relax, baby. I'll put you down," he said.

With one hand he yanked back the sheet and laid me in the bed. High above me, the molded plaster ceiling was spinning. I squinched my eyes shut and heard him rummaging in my bag.

"I'll help you off with your things," he said.

I tried to protest, but my tongue was thick and numb, my eyelids weighted. Nimble fingers plucked at my blouse, undoing the buttons. Cool air chilled my arms as the sleeves were withdrawn. I heard the snick of a zipper, and my pants came off. A soft cotton something was pulled over my head.

"I'd undo your bra, but then I'd never be able to leave," Jack murmured as he pulled my limp arms through the holes of the tee-shirt. Warm lips brushed my forehead. I tried to lift my eyelids, but they refused to budge. As I turned my face into the pillow, the light went out and the door sighed shut.

Chapter 23

SEVEN YEAR ACHE

I sat up far too quickly the next morning. A wisp of light drifted in through the curtain's crack as I pressed my hands to my pounding head. Two thoughts hit me simultaneously: *God, I feel horrible . . . I'm meeting my father today!*

Moving slowly, I got out of bed and put on the dress I'd chosen for the occasion. It was a deep periwinkle shade that brought out the color of my eyes—which were the exact same blue of *his* eyes, as I recalled. I started to pull on pantyhose, but then gave up, realizing they'd be too hot. I didn't want to be a sweaty mess when I saw my father for the first time in years. *And this could be the last time*, I told myself as I left the bedroom.

Jack was sprawled asleep on the couch, wearing jeans but no shirt. I crept over to take a peek at him. His sensuous mouth was slightly parted, eyelashes jet-black against his cheekbones, his hair flared over the sofa cushion. Even though I'd heard him shaving last night, his face had a five o'clock shadow. The silver lightning bolt on its thin chain rose and fell with his even breathing. I leaned in to get one last good look before he woke up.

Jack's eyes popped open.

"Oh!" I jerked upright. "I was just . . . I was seeing if you were awake."

"I am now." He raised his arms above his head, stretching his body with a catlike motion. "How did *you* sleep?" He scratched his chin, the stubble making a raspy sound.

"Like the dead. But now my head feels dead." I rubbed my temples.

Jack sat up and pulled on his tee-shirt. "I guess that makes you a Deadhead. Let's call for room service, then we'll get the show on the road."

The phone rang as we were finishing our toast and coffee. Jack grunted into the receiver and hung up. "That was the detective. Your father wants to come here instead of the diner. There's a spare room off the lobby where you can have some privacy. That all right?"

My hands went ice-cold. "Okay," I said faintly. I felt like a piece of straw being dragged along by a swift current, without the will to stop my downward plunge.

"He'll be here in fifteen minutes. I'll go with you." Jack stood up and swept crumbs from his jeans.

I fled to the bathroom, brushed my teeth and hair, and with shaking fingers tried to apply some color to my lips. I felt trembly, like little earthquakes were going off inside me. I gulped a few breaths and went back out front.

"All set?" Jack had put on a nice shirt. He looked a little apprehensive himself.

I said yes, and we went down to the main floor. One of the desk clerks ushered us into a carpeted sitting room with mahogany-paneled walls, but I was too anxious to take in my surroundings. I fidgeted, sat in an armchair, and then stood up again. Jack was waiting by the door. There was a knock, and a tall, slim man stepped into the room, wearing a light work shirt and slacks. His hair had a little gray and he had a few wrinkles, but otherwise he looked the same. Our eyes met, and I caught a flash of blue.

"Julia," my father said as he came toward me, a tentative smile on his face. "You're all grown up." His deep voice with its slight Southern twang unearthed a memory of the two of us sitting on our old front porch, listening to 45s on my record player.

"Hello," I said, determined not to call him "Dad". I went past him and sat down.

Jack nodded at my father. "Jack Kipling."

They shook hands. "Paul Nash. Thank you for bringing her here."

"I'll let you two talk." Jack darted out, and Paul sat in a chair next to me.

"I don't know where to start." His eyes met mine again. "I've thought about you so much. I should have tried harder to find you."

A flush of anger seared my cheeks. "Hard*er*? How about,

you should have tried to find me, period? It's not like Dot and I didn't stay put. It was *you* that moved away, and never called or wrote." I blurted out the words, dangerously close to tears.

Paul sat forward in his seat, hands on his knees. I noticed the callouses, one thumb encased in a band-aid. "I did write to you."

I glared at him. "Why didn't I get any letters then?"

"They all came back 'Addressee Unknown'." Paul sighed. "I called a buddy of mine from the factory, and he said you were moving around a lot. I should have driven up there that fall, but I didn't want to run into your mother. She threatened to have my wages garnished wherever I wound up working. I needed to get myself set up, and I couldn't do that on half-pay. And I didn't feel like she deserved me supporting her, after what she'd done."

Instead of appeasing me, this just added fuel to the fire. "But what about *me*? We were barely scraping by after you left. The reason we kept having to move was because she was so broke! We kept getting kicked out of places for being behind on the rent. I had to take a job bagging groceries after school."

Paul gave me a guilty look. "I didn't know all that. She made good money at the hardware store."

My anger boiled over. "That's because you didn't bother to find out. She wound up having to quit her job at the store because after you left, she *did* start seeing her boss. Then when that ended, she had to leave. She bounced around from job to job after that. And she—" I hesitated; I didn't want to give him more ammunition against Dot. "She really wanted to settle down again, but that didn't happen. She was drinking a lot, and she went out with a bunch of different guys. And all that was really hard on me."

Paul's lips were pressed into a thin line. "So what I heard was true. She *was* sleeping around all over town."

"Only after you left!" I cried. "Mom told me the whole story. She wasn't having an affair with her boss—she just caught a ride home with him because I had the flu!"

"I don't think she *did* tell you the whole story," Paul said quietly.

A cold spurt of fear trickled down my spine. I really did not want to hear that my mother had slept with other men while she was married. I couldn't stand it if my only family relationship was based on a lie.

But it looked like I wasn't going to have a choice.

"Did she tell you she went out with my best friend?" Paul asked, eyes blazing.

His words punched me in the gut. With the heat of the room and the residue of last night's drinking, I felt like I might throw up. I hunched over, clutching my stomach.

"Well, she did. We'd been dating for six months. I had already told her that I loved her, wanted to marry her. She went out on me behind my back."

I straightened up slowly. "But you weren't married then?"

"I was planning to ask her. I'd even gone to look at rings. Then she started seeing Rafe. They didn't even have the decency to tell me; I had to find out from other people."

"But then, why did you two get married?" I asked.

Paul gave me a pitying look, and suddenly I knew what was coming. "I guess she really kept you in the dark about a lot of stuff," he said.

I repressed the impulse to plug my ears.

"She was pregnant, Julia. She didn't know it when she started seeing Rafe. But soon after that, she came to me and told me," he continued. "I wasn't about to leave her in the lurch. I still loved her, even after what she'd done. So I swallowed my pride and took her back, and we went to the J.P. to get a license. You were born six months later. Everybody was whispering about it, but things died down when the next scandal came along."

I felt like the walls were caving in on me. "So I was just a huge mistake."

"No, not at all. I was in seventh heaven, having a little girl. Don't you remember all the things we did together?" He spread his hands. "I'd sit you up on my shoulders at the county fair. We'd listen to records together; you liked all the same singers I did. Every day when I got off work, I couldn't wait to come home and see my gal."

Tears were streaming down my face. "Then how could you have left me like that? I kept thinking you were coming back to get me. All those years, I felt so rejected."

My father frowned. "Dot and I had a lot of problems. I never felt like I could trust her, after what she did with Rafe. I wanted her to stay home, not go out to work. We could have made it on my pay. But no, she hated being in the house all day. Then when she started moonlighting as a cocktail waitress, I was sure she was running around on me. She'd come in late with this look on her face, like she'd been having the time of her life."

He handed me a tissue from a box on the table, and I blew my nose. "I don't think she was doing anything with anyone," I said. "She swore to me that she wasn't."

"Maybe not. I know I wasn't the easiest person to live with. I couldn't get it out of my head that she was going to run out on me again. I'd accuse her, then she'd convince me she was toeing the line, and then I'd get suspicious again." He looked down at the floor. "Your mother was really beautiful back then; I knew any man would jump at the chance to be with her. So some of it might have been my problem."

"So that's the reason you left her. But why did you leave me?" My voice wobbled.

Paul gripped the armrest of his chair. "I messed up, Julia. I thought everybody in town was laughing at me, thinking I was a fool. That she was sleeping with her boss right under my nose—just like she'd done with Rafe. I didn't have any proof, and she always had an alibi for where she'd been. But I let that one thing from the past make up my mind for me."

My thoughts were racing as Paul handed me another tissue. "I did come up there once," he said. "I met Dot at the bar, to ask if I could see you. But all she did was scream at me about money, and how she was going to hire a lawyer to get my pay. She said she'd see me in the poorhouse. And she said it would be a cold day in June before I got to see you. I should have tried to find you anyway, but she wouldn't tell me where you were living. And I was so mad; I had to get away from her before I did something I'd regret."

I looked at him in shock. Dot had never told me he'd come to Pikesville. "When was this?" I asked.

"That December after I moved out. I should have come on a school day, waited for you at the high school gates. But I'd just started a new job and they wouldn't give me a weekday off." Paul's eyes glistened.

My own tears had finally run their course. "She never told me that. But I could have met you down here in Virginia. I could have easily taken the train."

"That last time I saw her, she said she'd never let me see you. And I believed her; I'd heard that she was still bad-mouthing me all over the place. I was a coward, Julia. I didn't want to deal with her, so I let that convince me to let go of my own daughter."

We gazed at each other for a moment. I felt emptied out; like a tide had surged on the shore of my self, leaving behind only shattered bits and shards when it receded.

"But now that I've found you again—or you've found me—will you tell me about yourself? If you don't mind," he added.

I almost got up and left the room, but something held me back. I wanted him to know that I'd managed without him. "A lot has happened. Like I said, my high school years in Pikesville were pretty awful. I went to college in-state, then I moved to New York for grad school. I got a Master's in English Lit, but realized I didn't want to stay in academia, so I took a job in book publishing. Now I'm an editor at Hawtey House."

"I believe I've seen the name." Paul nodded. "That sounds

great. I always knew you were bound for big things."

This only rekindled my anger. "It *is* good now, but it was really tough going for a long time. It would have helped me so much if I could have seen you once in a while. Even once a year, at Christmas."

"Julia, I'm sorry. I should have come back for you."

"Yes, you should have!" I cried.

"Please forgive me. I've missed you something awful."

Should I just walk out now—leave while I'm ahead? To collect my thoughts, I went to stand by the window. Conventioneers were pouring into the hotel, holding burlap bags of peanuts. I took a few breaths and went back to my seat. "What have you been doing all this time?" I asked.

"Well . . ." He hesitated. "I've remarried."

Hearing him say this felt like another betrayal. I clenched my hands together so he wouldn't see them shaking. "I thought you might have."

"And we have two kids," he added.

The words hit me like a kick in the gut. "You have other children?" *Of course he wasn't interested in me*, I thought. *He had his own kids to raise.*

Paul gave me an uneasy glance. "They're five and seven. Both boys."

Maybe if I'd been a boy, he would have stayed in touch. "How nice for you," I said coldly.

"I've been working at a factory outside of Richmond. I've just been made line manager," he said.

"Good for you." I faked a smile, my cheeks stiff with dried tears.

"Please don't be that way, sweetheart." Paul got out of his chair and stood in front of me. "Now that you've found me, I want to be part of your life again, if you'll have me. If you can ever forgive me." He took my hands in his, but I pulled them away. "Or not even forgive me, but at least let me see you. I know that's a lot to ask, but please think about it."

He reached in his pocket and put a slip of paper on the table. "You don't have to say anything now. Here's my address and phone number." He cleared his throat. "Call me if you're ever ready to see me again. You can come back here to visit, or I can come up to New York; whatever you want. Your boyfriend can come too."

"He's not my boyfriend," I choked out. "We used to be together, but now we're just friends."

Paul gazed at me. "I don't know how you feel about him, but I can tell from the way he looks at you. That's not friendship in his eyes."

He went over to the door. "I know I don't deserve to be forgiven. But I'm still asking you to." He shut the door gently behind him.

I sat there for a few minutes until I was sure he'd gone. Then I went upstairs, trying to hold it together until I got back to the room.

Jack rose from the couch as I came in. "How did it go?" he asked, but then he got a good look at me. He came over quickly and put his arms around me. I clung to him, crying, the fabric of his shirt becoming damp.

"Want some water? A drink?" Jack asked.

"Please just hold me," I sobbed into his chest.

Jack took me to my room, and we lay on the made-up bed. He held me tightly as I cried out the hurt; the utter misery of being unwanted, feeling unworthy of anyone's love. The pain of my own father not giving a damn.

After what seemed like hours, I'd run out of tears. I lay shuddering on Jack's chest as he rubbed my back. When I was finally still, he wiped my face with his shirttail.

"You're going to ruin your nice shirt," I said, sniffling. I moved away and lay on the pillow.

"Want to tell me about it?" He turned toward me, head in his hand.

"It's even worse than I thought." I reached for a tissue and blew my nose. "He and Dot had to get married. They were pregnant with me. And she went out with his best friend when they were dating. I don't think she ever did anything while they were married, but Paul said he could never trust her again. Then he got so suspicious about her boss that he just left us high and dry."

Jack touched my arm. "I'm sorry, Julia. That's a lot of heavy stuff."

"He did come to Pikesville once, but he had a huge fight with Dot and left without seeing me. I can't believe Dot didn't tell me that when we had our little heart-to-heart last fall. Or about her going out with his friend. She lied to me about being totally innocent."

Jack gazed at me. "So your Mum's not blameless either. Most people aren't."

I thought about saying that since he was so understanding about other people, he might reconsider why I had to miss the rest of the concert. But I was so upset already; I couldn't handle it if this veered into our breakup. "Paul said he's remarried. And he has two kids. He didn't even have a good excuse for not getting in touch with me." I had to wait a moment for the lump in my throat to subside. "He said he wrote me a couple of letters, but they all came back; I guess since we moved around a lot. Some flimsy excuse."

"So he did try to contact you. Although he didn't pursue it," Jack said.

"He says he wants to be part of my life again. He told me to call him when I'm ready, but what would be the point?"

"Your father made a huge mistake, never coming to find you. But it seems like you'll lose out as much as he will if you never see him again. Unless he's just a total bastard." Jack gave me a questioning look.

"I don't think he's like that. Actually, I don't know what to think. But I do know," I said with sudden conviction, "that if I ever *did* have a child, no force on earth could keep me apart from her."

"I feel the same way," Jack said softly. He reached over and moved a wisp of hair from my face. His hand grazed my cheek, and I met his eyes. Suddenly his mouth was on mine, parting my lips, tentatively and then more demanding as I responded. I put my hands around his neck and pressed myself against him. I wanted to lose myself in physical sensation; to obliviate all the pain of today, of the past ten years. I gasped as Jack pushed up my dress and kissed my breasts. He moved on top of me, his hard body melding into mine. The sensation was ecstasy; his mouth moving from my neck, to my breasts, to my lips.

Jack stopped and looked into my eyes. "Julia, if this is a one-time thing—"

Mentally I finished the sentence for him: *If this is a one-time thing, that's fine, but we aren't getting back together.*

I put my finger to his lips. "No talking."

"Are you sure this is what you want?"

In answer, I pulled him toward me.

I didn't wake up until late the next morning. Jack was still asleep beside me. I looked at his dark tangle on the pillow, muscled shoulders tapering to his long, lean waist. Sickened by what I'd allowed myself to do, I quickly got dressed and threw my stuff in the bag. I found my plane ticket and went downstairs to get a cab.

As I was leaving the hotel, the peanut man was coming in. "Oh, hey," he said, reaching into his pocket. "Jack gave me this while you were in your meeting, but I felt bad about taking it. Can you give it back to him?" He held out a big wad of cash.

"I'm sure he'd want you to keep it. He has plenty more."

"All right." He gave me a curious glance. "Looks like you're leaving. Have a good trip." He continued toward the lobby, and I got into a taxi. I assumed there'd be no problem changing the flight to an earlier one, and I was right.

Chapter 24

STOP YOUR SOBBING

"So you slept with him." Vicky poked her chopstick into the small green mound and swirled it in her soy sauce. "I hate to say it, but that was probably a mistake." She dipped a piece of sushi and bit into it, then quickly reached for her beer, eyes watering.

"Of course it was a mistake," I said. "Are you okay?"

"Wasabi bomb." She coughed and took a few more gulps. "Are you going to call him?"

"So I can have him politely explain that he's moved on, but best of luck? No thanks."

"And you're really sure that's what he'd say?" she asked.

"He started to warn me that he'd sleep with me the one time, but not to expect anything to come of it. I can't believe I still went ahead with it. I was just so done in by seeing my father." I put my face in my hands.

"*I* can't believe all that stuff your dad told you. Way to lay it on a person," Vicky said. "Have you talked to Dot yet?"

"I'm gearing up for it," I said. "She hasn't called *me*, which means she's probably guessed that I know she slept with his best friend."

"Gosh, my family's so boring. All they ever do is argue over whose turn it is to do the dishes."

"You're lucky." I belted the rest of my sake.

"I'm just kidding." Vicky patted my hand. "I thought last fall was intense, but you've had it even intenser lately. If that's a word."

I smiled. "It's not, but you can use it."

She speared a piece of ginger with her chopsticks. "I'm probably taking the train to Long Island this Friday. Want to come with me? You could spend the weekend with my parents and kid sister. Have a few exciting rounds of Parcheesi."

"Thanks, but I think I'll stay in town. I have loads to catch up on."

Goaded by my conversation with Vicky, I decided to call Dot that night and get it over with. I put down my mug of coffee and dialed the number.

"How did it go in Richmond?" she asked cautiously.

"Well, it was very interesting," I said. "There were a number of surprises. Such as the fact that you and Paul had to get married because you were pregnant with me."

Dot exhaled into the phone. "I hoped you'd never find that out. I didn't want you to think you weren't wanted, Julia. The timing wasn't perfect, but we really were happy about having you."

"I can just imagine. Having to go to a J.P., and everybody knowing it was a shotgun wedding. Must have been a barrel of laughs." I twisted the coiled phone cord around my finger.

"It wasn't easy at the time, but everything settled down after a while. Pikesville can be judgmental, but we weren't the first ones to have a baby in less than nine months. People got over it."

"But it sounds like Paul never got over *you* sleeping with his best friend. What was *that* about, Mom? You left out that little detail."

Dot was quiet for a minute. "First of all, I didn't sleep with him. We just went out a few times. And I was really young. Paul was older than me, and right from the start he was so serious. But I wasn't at all ready to settle down."

"Until I came along, you mean."

"Well, yes. Of course that changed everything. Then once I had you, I was glad I did."

"But you never would have married him if you weren't pregnant." To my mind, it wasn't even a question.

She hesitated. "I felt like I had a lot more living to do before I got tied down. So no, probably not."

I pictured my mother at twenty; young, fresh, her dreams still intact. "I really ruined your life, didn't I?"

"No, you didn't. It was just different from what I'd planned. But you also made my life better in so many ways. And if Paul ever could have trusted me again, I'd still be with him." She waited for a beat. "Has he remarried?"

"Yes. He's living outside Richmond, working in a factory.

And he has two boys, five and seven years old. Which really hurts. All that time he was raising his children down South, he never bothered about me. Except that one time that you *didn't tell me about*, when he came up to see me. How could you have not let me know about that?"

"I guess I should have. And he did write a few letters. I had the postman send them back."

My coffee mug shook in my hand. "You did? *Why?* You knew I was dying to hear from him. I can't believe you kept that from me!"

"I was so angry at him for leaving us. I didn't think he deserved to be part of your life," she said defiantly.

Fresh hurt scraped my scabbed-over wounds. "But why didn't you tell me when I was older? Or all those times I asked if you knew where he was?"

She sighed. "After a while his letters stopped coming. I didn't keep his address."

"But it would have meant so much to me!" I cried. "I could have forgiven him a little bit, if I knew he'd at least tried to reach me."

When she spoke, she sounded utterly defeated. "I guess there are some things you'll have to forgive me for, too."

There was a small crowd by the water cooler. Approaching with my cup, I saw Brenda from accounting in the middle of a clutch of women. She had dark circles under her eyes, but she was smiling beatifically. "Take a look at this gorgeous little one," Cathy said to me.

Brenda passed me the picture. The baby had two wisps of

auburn hair and an adorable button nose. "Congratulations!" I said, handing it back. "She's beautiful. I'm so happy for you."

"We're having her baptism this Sunday. I've got her the prettiest crocheted Easter dress," Brenda cooed as the others returned to their offices.

"How are you feeling now?" I asked in a low voice. Brenda looked confused. "I mean the water retention," I said. "Have your feet gone back to normal size? And the acid reflux; I assume that's all better."

"Oh, that. I don't even really remember. Anyway, it was all worth it. I mean, look at her!" She beamed.

"It definitely was. Well, congrats again!"

I filled my cup and went back to my desk. Stuart, the head writer for the late-night show, was dropping off the first chapters of the humor book today. Since he was such a live wire over the phone, I was looking forward to meeting him in person.

But when the receptionist buzzed me, her voice sounded strange. "Stuart is in the lobby. You'd better get out here right away," she said.

"What is it?" I asked, but she had hung up. I hurried down the hall toward the lobby. At first I didn't understand what was happening; a skinny guy in a tee-shirt was running around, darting at what looked like whizzing cotton balls. He picked one up and approached me, cradling a large spotted rabbit in a football hold.

"Hi, I'm Stuart. I guess my little joke didn't go over too well," he said.

I gasped at the rabbits bounding around the room. "What did you do?"

"I thought it would be funny to bring you an Easter gift. We're big on gags at my office. Here, you hold Thomas. Come back here, Peter!" He made a snatch for a big black bunny with tufted ears. The receptionist had put one on her desk, and was trying to keep it from gnawing her pencils.

Ted came running into the lobby. "Julia! What is this?"

I made a grab for a flop-ear and just managed to get hold of its hind legs, which were surprisingly strong. I hefted it up and held it against me as it struggled. "Ted, meet Stuart. Stuart wanted to play a little Easter prank. He says they do this all the time at their office," I added as the rabbit kicked maniacally in my arms.

"Matthew, come back here!" Stuart shouted as he darted after a gray ball of fluff. "They're named after the apostles. Why don't you catch him, I'll try to nab Judas," he added to Ted.

"Okay," Ted said as he took off down the hall. "I was on the track team at Harvard!"

An hour later, we'd rounded up all the rabbits and sent them packing with Stuart. I was still catching my breath at my desk when my line lit up.

"Ms. Nash. I hear we had a rodent infestation on your floor." Perry sounded apoplectic.

"I'm so sorry! I had no idea he was going to do that," I said.

"I hope you realize that if word got out, we could lose our lease. The landlord's been trying to get rid of us for the past four years."

I gulped. "I don't think anyone will tell. It was just me, Ted, Stuart, and the receptionist. And the bunnies." I stifled a nervous snicker.

"Hmph. See that it doesn't happen again." Perry slammed down the phone.

The one good thing I did that week—other than not get fired—was to send Dermot's novella back to him. It was covered in so many red marks, it looked like it had been drawn and quartered. I was a little anxious about his reaction to the heavy editing, since I knew people tended to tiptoe around him. But I had to get it into the best shape possible in the little time we had left. I figured if he didn't like my comments, he could always have another go with Erica.

I was sitting in my open window in a tank top and cutoffs, trying to catch a late afternoon breeze, watching the lights change from red to green further down Broome Street. Now that it was mid-May, New York was experiencing its own early heat wave. In an attempt to keep my electric bill down, I'd been trying not to run my window unit. Feeling too lethargic to move, I almost didn't answer the phone. Finally I grabbed it on the fourth ring.

"Somebody wants to say hello." There was a rustling sound, and I heard heavy panting. Jack's voice came back on the line. "Muddy really misses you. Why don't you come over and see him? We can share custody."

I was hit by a longing to hold my dog. I'd missed his excitement at going out for a run; the way he listened as if he understood every word. "Could I take him for a walk?"

"I'll have him leashed and ready. Want to meet me here?" Jack asked.

I didn't want to go up to his apartment. "I'll wait outside your building."

"Can you come now? He's going crazy, now that he's heard your voice."

"Sure, I'm not doing anything. I'd like a little fresh air; it's stifling." I lifted a corner of my tank and wiped my sweaty face.

"What do you have on?" Jack's voice deepened.

"Um, a tank top and cutoffs. Why?"

"Leave that on, okay? Don't change a thing. I'm wearing cutoffs too," he added.

"All right, I won't change. I'll be there in fifteen minutes."

"Good boy! Good Muddy!" I knelt on the sidewalk and hugged our puppy, who'd gotten even bigger in the weeks since I'd last seen him. Muddy put his paws on my shoulders and licked my face ecstatically. I was laughing and crying at the same time. "Hey, boy. It's so good to see you," I murmured into his furry neck.

Jack extended his hand and pulled me up as Muddy ran circles around us, trailing the leash behind him. Jack held onto my hand for a moment longer, and my smile faded as our eyes locked. He broke away first, bent down and picked up the leash. He stood up slowly, taking in my short cutoffs, my thin white tank. "You didn't change your outfit." His face had a glazed look that I knew well. *It doesn't mean anything,*

I reminded myself. *He's probably thinking we can run upstairs for a quick one-off, like that time in Richmond.*

"I told you I wouldn't," I said lightly. "You didn't either." His own shorts came to mid-knee, and he wore one of his favorite tee-shirts, tie-dyed Rastafarian red, yellow and green.

"I'm gonna come along with you. He almost got away from me the other night." Jack wrapped the leather strap around his wrist a few times, and we headed east. "He likes to run around Tompkins Square. We just have to make sure no used needles are lying about."

We reached the small park on Avenue A, and Jack and I scoured the area for junkie debris. The enclosure was clear, so he shut the gate and unhooked the leash. Muddy ran around frenetically barking, nosing up clods of dirt. Jack drew a toy from his pocket and threw it for him over and over. I watched the flex of muscle in his forearm; the outline of his shoulders in the worn tee. I would have thought my attraction to him would have faded with the passage of time, but apparently that wasn't the case. *Don't be ridiculous*, I told myself. *You're only here to see your dog.*

Muddy came trotting over, tongue lolling. "Let's take a break," Jack said. We went over to a shaded bench and Muddy lay at our feet. Jack put his arm on the back of the bench. "Why'd you vanish on me in Richmond?" His dark brows furrowed.

For a moment I listened to a bird insistently chirping in a tree. *Why are they always so happy?* I wondered. "I needed time to think. About my father," I clarified.

"Are you going to call him?" Jack leaned closer, and I could feel the light touch of his hand on my back.

I looked down at my lap. "I haven't decided yet. Dot admitted some things that made a little more sense of his disappearing act."

"I think you should give the guy a second chance," Jack said.

I almost blurted out, *You're one to talk about giving second chances!* But I maintained my cool. Suzanne had called me just last week; she was back in New York, and living with Mark again. She'd also said that Jack was going out on the town every night. I was sure he was back to his old ways, screwing around with various flavors of the week. He had definitely moved on; I didn't want to make a pathetic play for him when obviously it was hopeless.

"I have a confession to make," Jack said. "I had Mary Jo book only one room at the hotel. I figured if you really pitched a fit, I could go somewhere else." He gave me a guilty smile.

So he had his little seduction scene all planned out. He manipulated things for his own benefit, just so he wouldn't have to go without sex for a few days. Even with everything that was going on with me, he put his own selfish needs first.

I jumped up off the bench. "I'm heading back. Muddy should stay and rest some more." I started toward the gate.

"What are you doing? Here, I'll walk you home." Jack caught up with me, Muddy in tow.

"I'm going to pick up some groceries. You can't bring him in the store." I was striding briskly, but Jack stayed by my side.

"We can wait outside while you shop. Slow down; where's the fire?" he added as he yanked Muddy away from a piece of garbage on the sidewalk. Jack put his hand on my arm, and I stopped. "Why don't you come up and say hello to the mantises? They won't be around much longer. I'm gonna release them in the Botanical Gardens soon. Now that they're grown, I need to set them free."

He thinks I'm so desperate that I'll sleep with him with no strings attached—the way I did in Richmond. I took one last long look at his dark arching eyebrows, his luxuriously thick hair, those sexy lines around his mouth. For the last time, I met his warm brown eyes.

"I'm sorry, Jack. I don't ever want to see you again."

Chapter 25

LET'S DANCE

"All right, time to begin." Ted polished his glasses on his shirt sleeve. "Anything good on submission this week?"

Erica picked up a sheaf of papers. "I have in a very strong proposal about . . ." Her voice died away.

Perry strode into the room, putting a stop to the conversation. "I have an announcement to make. For the first time in two years, we have a title debuting at number one."

All eyes turned to Erica, who had a memoir by a controversial senator that was expected to hit the list at any minute. She tilted her face expectantly.

"*Little Things Can Be Big* has the top spot in this Sunday's *New York Times*," Perry said.

A jolt zipped through me as a gasp went around the room.

"Congratulations, Julia!" Ted exclaimed. Cathy started to clap, and the others joined in.

"Senator Mallard's at number five, so congrats to Erica too," Perry added.

Erica stood up and bowed, as if she'd won an Oscar.

"Is it okay if I go call the author?" I asked.

Perry nodded. "Sure. Where's he from, Ohio? Tell him we want to bring him to New York. We need to start making some publicity plans."

"Actually he's from Omaha," I said.

Perry waved his hand as if there was no difference. "The *Times* is calling me today to interview me about it. I always knew that little book had potential."

Ted caught my eye and winked as I went out the door. I had memorized my author's number from our frequent phone calls, so I didn't have to pull the rolodex card.

"Are you sitting down?" I said when he picked up.

"Yes, I am. Is everything okay?" came his chipper Midwestern voice.

"It's more than okay—your book is number one on the *New York Times*!" I screamed.

"Woo-hoo! That's great! Hold on a second, let me tell my wife." He put his hand over the phone and gave her the news. I heard her whooping in the background. "Well, that is just dandy," he continued.

"Better than dandy! Our publisher wants to bring you here. I think he might want you to do a tour."

"Well, I'm at your service, all except this weekend. It's our twentieth anniversary, and I want to take Marjorie somewhere special," he replied.

"I'm sure we can work around it," I said. "Congratulations

on your anniversary—and your number one book! I had a feeling something good would happen!"

"Thank you so much, Julia. It wouldn't have, without you. And never forget, little things . . ." He paused.

"Can be BIG!" I shouted.

As I hung up the phone, Erica stepped into my office. "Well, you're quite the cheerleader."

I was so elated that her dig didn't bother me. "He's such a nice guy. I'm so happy for him."

"Doesn't reflect badly on you, either, does it? Unlike Dermot's book. I hear it's very short, and not all that good." Erica smirked. "Which could apply to a certain body part of his, now that I think of it."

I shrugged. "I wouldn't know."

She surveyed me coolly. "I came down to make a lunch date. Are you free next Thursday?"

I guess now that I have a bestseller, she has time in her busy schedule. "Sure. I don't make plans that far ahead."

"Pencil me in. We'll have a lot to talk about."

I was getting dressed to go for a run the following Sunday afternoon when my phone rang. Reluctantly I reached for it; I didn't feel like getting into another long conversation with Dot right now. She'd been trying to justify not telling me about Paul's visit, and while I'd told her to forget it, I was tired of rehashing it with her.

"Hello," I said.

"Julia. It's me." Jack's voice made the hair on my arms stand up.

"Oh . . . hi."

"I just heard about the bestseller list. Your book's number one, huh?" he said.

I sat on my futon. "Yes, I'm really happy about it."

"Sammy noticed it in the paper. So . . . why don't I take you out for a drink to celebrate?"

My heart was pounding so hard, for a minute I couldn't breathe. This wasn't about our dog, or my father—or his wanting a quick roll in the hay. This meant he wanted to see *me*. "Sure, that would be great."

"Pick you up around five?" he asked.

Oh god, oh god. I'm going to see him! "Perfect." I hesitated. "I can't wait to see you, Jack."

"Me neither."

In a tailspin, I put on my favorite Floor album and tried on four different things before I decided on a short summer skirt and sleeveless top that I knew he liked. *Maybe he's just being nice about my book,* I tried to tell myself. But something in his voice made me hopeful. When Jack called up to me from the street, I stuck my head out the window and said I'd be right there.

I flew down the three flights barefoot and put on my strappy heels at the bottom. Jack was leaning against the brick wall in a crisp white shirt and jeans.

"Hello, Miss Nash. Long time no see." His accent always slayed me—not to mention his expressive eyebrows that now seemed to be raised in appreciation of my outfit.

"Nice to see you." I was feeling too emotional to say much.

Jack waved his hand toward the car in an "after you" gesture, and I went to get inside. Purposely I sat in the middle rather than sliding to the far window.

Rick drove a few blocks and came to a stop in front of Fanelli's, where we'd had our very first date last summer. We went to the back of the bar, which wasn't very busy on an early Sunday evening. We ordered beers and sat facing each other on the stools. "To your success," Jack said, tapping his bottle against mine.

"And to yours." I took a sip of beer. "I keep hearing songs from the album on the radio."

"It's done pretty well," Jack said. "I'm happy for you though. I know your writers are like your babies. You must be really proud of this one."

"Not so much the writers, but the books are my babies, in a way. I want them to do well, once they're out in the world. And I'm thrilled for the author. It was such a great feeling to sign up his book, and then have it work."

Jack nodded. "Like having a number one hit in the Top 40."

"Maybe a little like that." Sitting so close to him, taking in his handsome face and deep brown eyes, was almost unbearably sad. "Jack." I touched his arm. "I want to apologize for missing your song. And your dedicating it to me."

Jack started to say something, but I put up my hand. "Let me finish. I never got a chance to say how sorry I was. It was a huge thing, and I missed it for a stupid speech. I probably should have just told Ted I had a prior commitment and skipped the awards."

Jack gazed at me from beneath his silky lashes. "No, you shouldn't have. I knew it was a big deal for you. And I admit, I was a little jealous of your author with his literary reputation. There I was, struggling along with *Henry and Beezus.*"

I sat back in surprise; that never would have occurred to me. "But I should have been more understanding," Jack added.

I took a deep breath. "What *I* didn't understand was why you kicked me out. I just wish we'd had a chance to talk it over at some point."

Jack's brows furrowed. "Kicked you out?"

"Told me to move out. Of your apartment," I said.

Jack leaned forward on the barstool and put his hands on my shoulders. His dark brown gaze met mine. "Baby, I didn't tell you to move out. *You* walked out on *me.*"

I went back to that horrible night; the conversation with Mary Jo. Her covering the phone, asking him the question. "You told Mary Jo I should leave. *Didn't you?*"

Jack narrowed his eyes. "Who said that?"

Suddenly the room began to tilt. I grabbed the sides of my stool. "Mary Jo. Or she implied it. She called me when I got back to the loft that night."

"Wait a minute. You talked to her?"

I felt like I was occupying some alternate version of reality. "She called me at your place. I asked her if I could speak to you, and she covered the receiver like she was talking to you. Then she told me I'd better go. I asked her what she meant by that, and she told me to be out of the house before you got back."

So many expressions were flitting across Jack's face; disbelief, then anger, then outrage. His furious glare would have been terrifying if it had been directed at me.

"Julia. I had no idea. You thought I'd told you to *move out*?" he asked.

Tears were streaming down my face. "Yes! That's the only reason I left! I was waiting for you to come home that night, so I could apologize!"

"I would never have done that. I was ticked off, sure. But I was expecting you to be there when I got in." He took my hand. "When I saw you'd packed up and moved out, I figured you'd decided you wanted to be with Derrick."

"Dermot. I never had any interest in him. I just wanted to extract his *book* from him. Which turned out not to be very good—"

My words were stopped by his kiss. It was amazing to feel his lips on mine again; his warm hands, his sensuous tongue. I was so weepy and happy, I felt delirious.

Jack got up off the stool and pulled me up next to him. "C'mon, baby. Let's go home."

Jack's head was resting on my bare stomach, the sheets twisted around us, Muddy sprawled at our feet. Every once in a while our dog pricked his ears and looked at us, as if to say, *About time you two worked things out.*

Jack turned toward me. "Listen, Julia. If anything like that ever comes up again, we have to talk it over. Don't take anyone else's word for what I may say, or think. Same for me." He moved up next to me on the pillow. "And I won't walk out on you in the middle of a fight. I know I've been guilty of that."

I traced the lines at the corner of his mouth. "And I won't try to be two places at once. Or listen to your manager. Or your band mates. Or anyone else who's trying to come between us."

"I'm gonna have to deal with her." His fierce expression almost made me feel sorry for Mary Jo.

Jack moved on top of me, his hair falling into his eyes. "You can never leave me again. I've been absolutely gutted."

I wrapped my arms around his neck. "I won't. Ever again. I promise."

Chapter 26

BODY AND SOUL

"Take a look at this," Jack said, opening the flaps of the large box that a delivery man had just brought to the door. With a flourish, he removed a gleaming new guitar from the packaging. "Dan Armstrong made this for me. Isn't she a beauty?"

"What is that wood?" I asked, admiring its reddish tint.

"Honduras mahogany. See, I had him make the pickup a bit higher. And the tailpiece wraps around."

"It's really gorgeous." *We'll have to keep Muddy away from it*, I thought.

"I know a tailpiece that's even better." He gave my butt a pinch.

"Thank you. Now let me get this thing together in the kitchen. I think you're going to love it."

"You really don't have to. Don't you have editing to do?" he asked.

Still haunted by the ghost of Robin's lasagna and his mother's bangers, I was determined to give it one more stab. "No, I really want to make it."

This hot June night was the one-year anniversary of when Jack and I had first met. Dot had sent me a recipe that she swore by, and I had a foggy memory of the delicious dessert that she'd baked when I was a child. In fact, I remembered my father asking for seconds; something I'd reminded him of on the phone a few days ago.

I had spoken to Paul twice so far, and he was planning to visit me in New York soon. After Jack forgave me for missing his song, calling my dad seemed like the right thing to do. Lately I'd felt more whole than I had in years, knowing where my father was, and that I could talk to him any time I wanted to. It was like my favorite scene in Virginia Woolf's novel, *To the Lighthouse*, when Lily at last finishes her painting; something that had been missing for so long in my life, had finally clicked into place.

And in terms of things clicking, Jack and I had been getting along great since I'd moved back in. In fact, in the flood of good feeling, I'd talked Jack out of firing Mary Jo. I knew he'd be lost without her to manage all the details of his career, and I certainly didn't want to step into that role. Nor did I particularly want to risk his hiring a younger, sexier replacement that he'd be spending loads of time with. Sure, I trusted him—but why stir up trouble? And since Jack had told Mary Jo she would have been fired if it weren't for me, I was pretty sure I'd earned her grudging respect.

My thoughts returned to the task at hand. I lined up the

ingredients on the counter, along with the egg beater that I'd picked up at the Canal Street flea market for fifty cents. As Jack sat out front and tuned his new toy, I opened my mother's note.

"Apple Brown Betty," she had scrawled in her chicken scratch. "1 stick butter, 1 c. oatmeal, 1 c. flour, 1 c. brown sugar, ½ tsp. cinnamon, 2 cans apple sauce."

I poked through Jack's cabinets in search of a measuring cup. I couldn't find one, so I used a shot glass, figuring that two shots probably equaled one cup. I did locate a cake pan, or at least a pan that was square. I dumped the ingredients in the pan and stirred—why dirty a bowl? Then I set the oven to 375.

Now for the hard sauce, which I recalled as amazing. It only had three ingredients: a package of confectionary sugar, 3 T. cornstarch, and 6 T. of water. I looked at my mother's scribbles more closely. Was that 3 t., or 3 T.? I couldn't tell, but how much difference could it make? I got a larger spoon out of the drawer. The cake was putting out a wonderful cinnamony aroma. *It'll be nice to have something homemade*, I thought, *after all the takeout.*

I stirred the icing ingredients together in a small dish, then went to get the eggbeater out of my backpack. Noticing a rust spot on the handle, I ran it under the tap. Now I was all set. As I tried to push the mixer into the frosting, I was astonished that it had stiffened so quickly; it took a big effort just to get the beater submerged. The handle was so hard to crank that I thought it had rusted together. But when I lifted it out, it turned easily. I thrust the beater back into the bowl and by really putting some elbow grease into it, I got it to go around. *Boy, they aren't kidding when they call this hard sauce,* I thought.

The cake was now an appealing golden brown. I took it out of the oven and spackled the icing on it. *There,* I thought, admiring my handiwork. *This will prove I'm not a total loss in the kitchen.*

As I was washing up, the mixer fell apart in my hands. I picked up the pieces and saw that the two little bolts on either side of the handle were missing. *Wonder where they could've gotten to? Did they fall off while I was making the icing?* Pained, I looked at my beautiful cake, which was emitting a tantalizing aroma. *No big deal,* I decided.

Jack came into the kitchen. "What's that great smell? Did you buy a candle?"

"It's Dot's recipe for Apple Brown Betty," I said proudly, moving aside to reveal the cake.

Jack had a wary look in his eyes. "You didn't have to do that."

"Oh, it was a cinch. Come on, let's try it."

I cut a piece for each of us and put two glasses of milk on the table. Jack forked a big bite and put it into his mouth. "Mmm. This is good."

"Oh, just one thing," I added, recalling the mixer. "There may be bolts."

Jack stopped mid-swallow. "Bolts?"

"I think one or two fell off the mixer while I was making the frosting."

Jack took a big gulp of milk. "*Bolts* from a mixer?" he asked with a strange expression.

"Just a couple little ones. Don't worry, you should be able to feel them."

Jack's eyes were wide. "All right, I'll go slowly." He took his fork, cut a small bite and mashed it several times on the plate before putting it into his mouth. Then he worked the cake around with his tongue, and washed it down with milk.

"It's good, isn't it?" I said, taking another bite. If you felt through the icing with your tongue, you could easily tell if there was a bolt in there, or not. So far, so good, on my end.

"Fantastic." Jack gave me an odd look. "Nice of you to go to the trouble."

Suddenly I realized what a disaster this was. I jumped up, grabbed both our plates, dumped the cake into the trash and then started scraping the contents of the pan into the garbage. Jack came up behind me.

"What are you doing? That was good." He put his arms around my waist.

"No, it wasn't! You could have choked. I can just see the headline: BOTCHED BETTY BUMPS OFF BAD-BOY BRIT!" I dumped the pan in the sink and turned to face him. "I'm never going to be a domestic goddess. I know your mother's a great cook, but I just can't seem to get the hang of it. And I know you hated it that she had to work, but I love my job. I'm no good at this other stuff."

Jack smiled down at me. "Baby, I don't care. You edit a mean manuscript. What's more, you cream my corn. Make my eyelashes curl and you blow my top. So don't worry about the cooking, all right? We can always go out to eat." He cocked an eyebrow. "And you know how I like to eat in."

After we cleaned up the mess, Jack wanted to try out his new guitar. A few days ago he'd mentioned that he planned to take me somewhere nice for our anniversary, and I was excited about getting dressed up in the outfit he'd bought me last weekend. It was a short, silky number that we'd found in a SoHo boutique, along with a pair of high heels that made my legs look almost as long as Vicky's. I couldn't wait to wear my new dress, but Jack didn't seem to be in any rush to get ready. *Maybe he forgot about going out,* I thought. *Or maybe he forgot that tonight's the night.* I swallowed a little lump of disappointment and sat next to him on the couch, watching his long fingers strumming.

"I never got to play you my song. Wanna hear it now?" he asked.

"I'd love to." I felt a rill of anticipation. I'd been too guilty about my blunder at MSG to dare ask him to sing it for me.

Jack began in a husky voice as he stroked the strings:

Nothing takes me by surprise; seen too many crooked smiles
Lying hands and dirty minds, cringing whinging parasites
Snitches thieving, whores deceiving, 'til at last like a bolt from the blue
Feeling numb, used up and dumb—I was stunned by the jolt of you.

The realization of what I'd done to him hit me again hard, as he continued:

Never lost my heart, didn't think I could
Didn't want to, never thought I would
But your lovin' arms and smile
Make me wanna stay . . . for a long long while—"

Jack stopped abruptly and threw down the pick. "Ahh, it's bent. D'you mind bringing me the new bag of picks? They're on top of the dresser."

I was bowled over by the song. "That was beautiful, Jack. Those lyrics . . . I'm just so honored."

He smiled. "Fetch me the picks, and you can hear the rest."

That was even more amazing than I'd imagined, I thought as I went back to our room. *Hearing his song is better than any dinner date; we can always go out tomorrow night.* I looked on the dresser and found the plastic bag of picks tossed on a pile of change. I brought the bag back to the couch and held it out to Jack.

"Could you get one out for me?" he said, his eyes on the guitar neck, adjusting the pegs.

"Okay." I couldn't wait for the rest of the song. Quickly I poked around in the bag and handed him a purple pick.

Jack shook his head. "Not that one."

I had no idea what he wanted. "Which one then?"

"Keep looking. You'll see it."

I poked around in the bag. Something glimmered among the dark picks. I plucked it out and stared at a white-gold band lined with sapphires encircling a large, antique-cut diamond.

"What is this?" I asked.

Jack put down the guitar. "It was Mum's. She made me take it when we left England." He took the ring and fitted it onto my finger. Of my left hand.

I was in shock. "Does this mean . . ."

Jack got down on his knees and took my hands in his. "It means what you think. If you'll have me."

"Jack, I love you!" Tears sprang to my eyes.

He smiled. "So you'll marry me?"

"Yes!"

"That's good," Jack said, getting back on the couch. "My knees were killing me."

After we'd kissed and kissed, Jack stopped for a minute. "Let's set a date quickly, all right? Like maybe next month."

"That's really soon, but I'm sure it can be done," I said through my happy tears. "Dot's going to be ecstatic. Maybe she can help with some of the arrangements."

"Which I hope we can keep to a minimum. And then once we're hitched," Jack raised an eyebrow. "The next thing on the agenda is getting you pregnant. That is, when you feel the time is right. I know you're going to keep working, so we'll just have to find a good sitter. Or two."

I thought about my huge new self-help hit, and the humor book coming out next spring, which was sure to do well. The raise that I'd just been promised. The pile of manuscripts from agents who seemed to be beating down my door, now that I'd had a number one bestseller. Then I pictured Brenda from accounting, joyously flashing her pictures—carrying on.

I jumped up and pulled Jack off the couch. Still holding his hand, I started walking toward the bedroom. "No time like the present," I said.

The End

Come Dancing, the first novel about Jack and Julia, is available at online retailers in ebook and paperback editions.

Dear Reader,

If you enjoyed *Keep Dancing*, it would mean so much to me if you'd post a review. Reviews are tough to come by these days, and you, the reader, have the power to make or break a book. Thanks so much again for taking the time to read *Keep Dancing*!

In gratitude,
Leslie

Sign up to receive an email when
Leslie's next book is ready:

www.lesliewellsbooks.com

ABOUT THE AUTHOR

Leslie Wells is the author of *Come Dancing*, the first novel about Jack and Julia. Leslie left her small Southern town in 1979 for graduate school in New York City. After receiving her Master's in English Literature, she got her first job in book publishing. She has edited forty-eight *New York Times* bestsellers in her over thirty-year career, including thirteen number one *New York Times* bestsellers. Leslie has worked with numerous internationally known authors, musicians, actors, actresses, television and radio personalities, athletes, and coaches. She lives on Long Island, New York.

www.lesliewellsbooks.com

ACKNOWLEDGMENTS

The minute I finished writing *Come Dancing*, I knew I wasn't done with Jack and Julia yet. The response from readers and reviewers was so rewarding, and I felt I had another novel in me. From that impulse came *Keep Dancing*.

The following people were very helpful in providing early reads and suggestions: Jessica Hatch, who is an amazingly astute editor; and also my friends Sheri Betuel and Amy Turza. Thanks to Hilary Malecki, Sue Nicoletti, Charles Salzberg, and Jill Sansone for being so supportive of my writing efforts.

The gorgeous cover for this book, as well as for *Come Dancing* and *Dancing with Mistletoe*, were provided by the wonderfully talented designer Laura Klynstra. Laura also did the interior design for the paperback editions of *Come Dancing* and *Keep Dancing*. Thanks again to Kassiah Faul for my fabulous website. Lucinda Campbell did a great job with the ebook formatting. Amy Bruno of Book Junkie Promotions, a real pro who's as enthusiastic as she is organized, set up my blog tour.

My children put up with their mom working her day job as an editor, and then writing in the wee hours of the morning and late at night. My husband, Peter, listened to me read the whole book to him several times, providing insightful suggestions and being incredibly supportive. *Ciao, bella!*